PAUL TEMPLE AND THE LAWRENCE AFFAIR

Francis Durbridge

WILLIAMS & WHITING

Cover design by Timo Schroeder

9781915887085

Williams & Whiting (Publishers)
15 Chestnut Grove, Hurstpierpoint,
West Sussex, BN6 9SS

Titles by Francis Durbridge published by Williams & Whiting

1   The Scarf – tv serial
2   Paul Temple and the Curzon Case – radio serial
3   La Boutique – radio serial
4   The Broken Horseshoe – tv serial
5   Three Plays for Radio Volume 1
6   Send for Paul Temple – radio serial
7   A Time of Day – tv serial
8   Death Comes to The Hibiscus – stage play
    The Essential Heart – radio play
    (writing as Nicholas Vane)
9   Send for Paul Temple – stage play
10 The Teckman Biography – tv serial
11 Paul Temple and Steve – radio serial
12 Twenty Minutes From Rome – a teleplay
13 Portrait of Alison – tv serial
14 Paul Temple: Two Plays for Radio Volume 1
15 Three Plays for Radio Volume 2
16 The Other Man – tv serial
17 Paul Temple and the Spencer Affair – radio serial
18 Step In The Dark – film script
19 My Friend Charles – tv serial
20 A Case For Paul Temple – radio serial
21 Murder In The Media – more rediscovered serials and
    stories
22 The Desperate People – tv serial
23 Paul Temple: Two Plays for Television
24 And Anthony Sherwood Laughed – radio series
25 The World of Tim Frazer – tv serial
26 Paul Temple Intervenes – radio serial
27 Passport To Danger! – radio serial
28 Bat Out of Hell – tv serial
29 Send For Paul Temple Again – radio serial

Murder At The Weekend – the rediscovered newspaper serials and short stories

Also published by Williams & Whiting:
Francis Durbridge : The Complete Guide
By Melvyn Barnes

Titles by Francis Durbridge to be published by Williams & Whiting

Murder On The Continent (Further re-discovered serials and stories)
News of Paul Temple
One Man To Another – a novel
Operation Diplomat
Paul Temple and the Alex Affair
Paul Temple and the Canterbury Case (film script)
Paul Temple and the Conrad Case
Paul Temple and the Geneva Mystery
Paul Temple and the Margo Mystery
Paul Temple: Two Plays For Radio Vol 2 (Send For Paul Temple and News of Paul Temple)
The Passenger
Tim Frazer and the Melynfforrest Mystery

INTRODUCTION

Francis Durbridge (1912-98) began his career in 1933 as a prolific writer of sketches, stories and plays for BBC radio, mostly light entertainments including libretti for musical comedies, but a talent for crime fiction became evident in his early radio plays *Murder in the Midlands* (1934) and *Murder in the Embassy* (1937). The *Radio Times* (11 February 1938) mentioned that Durbridge had by then written some one hundred radio pieces, and Charles Hatton commented in *Radio Pictorial* (28 October 1938) that "He is one of the very few people in this country who have succeeded in making a living by writing for the BBC."

So Durbridge continued to write plays and serials for BBC radio for many years, using his own name and occasionally the pseudonyms Frank Cromwell, Nicholas Vane and Lewis Middleton Harvey, while capitalising on a particular brainwave. In 1938 he created the dream team of novelist/detective Paul Temple and his wife Steve, and the success of his serial *Send for Paul Temple* led to sequels over several decades that built an impressive UK and European fanbase. Following the receipt by the BBC of more than 7,000 listeners' requests for more of Paul Temple, Durbridge responded later in 1938 with *Paul Temple and the Front Page Men* and from 1939 to 1968 there were another twenty-six Paul Temple mysteries of which seven were new productions of earlier cases.

In the mid-twentieth century radio detectives were extremely popular, with Paul Temple's rivals including Dick Barton (by Edward J. Mason), Philip Odell (by Lester Powell), Dr. Morelle (by Ernest Dudley), P.C. 49 (by Alan Stranks) and Ambrose West (by Philip Levene). In fact in the 1940s, in addition to the Temples, Durbridge wrote radio dramas featuring investigators called Anthony Sherwood,

Johnny Cordell, Amanda Smith, Gail Carlton, Michael Starr, André d'Arnell and Johnny Washington, and he even wrote a radio serial in 1940 featuring the legendary Sexton Blake.

Paul Temple and the Lawrence Affair was broadcast on the BBC Light Programme in eight thirty-minute episodes from 11 April to 30 May 1956 and repeated from 29 April to 17 June 1956. Peter Coke (1913-2008) appeared as Temple for the third time, having taken over the role for *Paul Temple and the Gilbert Case* in 1954, and he remained for every other serial until the concluding *Paul Temple and the Alex Affair* in 1968. Indeed Coke and his co-star Marjorie Westbury (1905-89) are regarded as the definitive pairing of Paul and Steve Temple with their eleven serials, although Westbury excelled numerically as Steve with her twenty-two appearances overall. Before Coke, Marjorie Westbury had partnered Barry Morse in *Send for Paul Temple Again* (1945), Howard Marion-Crawford in *A Case for Paul Temple* (1946) and Kim Peacock on nine separate occasions. But mention must also be made of the veteran radio actor Lester Mudditt, who appeared as Sir Graham Forbes of Scotland Yard in nineteen productions from the original *Send for Paul Temple* in 1938 until *Paul Temple and the Spencer Affair* in 1957/58.

As well as their appeal at home the Temples acquired an enormous European following, with translated versions broadcast in the Netherlands from 1939, Germany from 1949, Italy from 1953 and Denmark from 1954. *Paul Temple and the Lawrence Affair* was broadcast in the Netherlands as *Paul Vlaanderen en het Lawrence mysterie* (30 September - 18 November 1956, eight episodes), translated by Johan Bennik (pseudonym of Jan van Ees) and produced by Kommer Kleijn, with Jan van Ees as Vlaanderen and Eva Janssen as Ina; in Germany as *Paul Temple und der Fall Lawrence* (12 September – 31 October 1958, eight episodes), translated by Dagmar Schnorr-Nick and produced by Eduard Hermann, with René Deltgen as Temple and Annemarie Cordes as Steve; and in Italy as *Paul Temple e l'uomo di Zermatt* (17 July – 4 September 1961, eight episodes), translated by Pietro Robespi and produced by Umberto Benedetto, with Adolfo Geri as Temple and Renata Negri as Steve.

In an interview published in the *Radio Times* (21 October 1971) Durbridge said: "Twenty years ago in the United States, a producer told me that I was wasting my time by not going into television. So that's what I did – I tried to build up a reputation with serials, since I'd vowed never to write a Paul Temple episode for television." So in 1952, while continuing to write for radio, Durbridge embarked on a long sequence of BBC television serials that achieved enormous viewing figures until 1980. While his reputation from 1938 onwards had rested largely upon the regular radio exploits of the Temples, it was his parallel television career in the 1950s that firmly established his name in popular culture – with gripping serials including *Portrait of Alison*, *My Friend Charles* and *The Scarf*. And later, as his radio productions became fewer, his television career blossomed with serials such as *The World of Tim Frazer, Melissa, A Man Called Harry Brent* and *Bat out of Hell*. His popularity on the small screen was phenomenal, with the result that for all his serials from 1960 (beginning with *The World of Tim Frazer*) the BBC gave him the unprecedented accolade of the "Francis Durbridge Presents" screen credit before the title sequence of each episode.

Durbridge became a multi-media writer, with his name going even further than radio and television. His radio career lasted until 1968, overlapped by his television serials from 1952 to 1980, and overlapped again by his career as a stage dramatist from 1971 in the UK and even earlier in Germany. The latter saw him change his style from the "whodunit" form, and he became known for intriguing twist-after-twist plots in such stage plays as *Suddenly at Home, Murder with Love* and *House Guest*.

Unlike many of the Paul Temple serials, *Paul Temple and the Lawrence Affair* has never been novelised. A recording of the original broadcast serial was, however, marketed on audiocassettes and CDs (BBC Audio, 2003) and later included in the CD box set *Paul Temple: The Complete Radio Collection: The Fifties 1954-1959* (BBC, 2016).

Melvyn Barnes
Author of *Francis Durbridge: The Complete Guide* (Williams & Whiting, 2018)

This book reproduces Francis Durbridge's original script together with the list of characters and actors of the BBC programme on the dates mentioned, but the eventual broadcast might have edited Durbridge's script in respect of scenes, dialogue and character names.

PAUL TEMPLE
AND THE
LAWRENCE AFFAIR

A serial in eight episodes
By FRANCIS DURBRIDGE
Broadcast on BBC Radio
11 April – 30 May 1956
CAST:

Paul Temple . . . . Peter Coke
Steve Temple . . . . .Marjorie Westbury
Mary Gardner . . . . Dorothy Holmes-Gore
Freeman . . . . Allan McClelland
Bob Gardner . . . . Leonard Trolley
Det. Insp. Ivor . . . . Manning Wilson
Charlie . . . . James Beattie
Sir Graham Forbes . . . . . .Lester Mudditt
Brian Dexter . . . . .Simon Lack
Johnny Teako . . . . Brian Haines
Linda Teako . . . . .Belle Chrystall
A Commissionaire . . . . James Thomason
Max Burford . . . . Allan McClelland
Mills . . . . .Geoffrey Hodson
Det. Insp.Vosper . . . . Arthur Ridley
Ernest de Silva . . . . .John Gabriel
Mrs Purdie . . . . .Molly Rankin
Stan Walters . . . . .Denis Goacher
Salty West . . . . Brewster Mason
George Wadford . . . . . . Leonard Trolley
Sir Carlton Ross . . . . . Richard Williams

Sylvia Ross . . . . .Annette Kelly
Arthur Main . . . . Geoffrey Hodson
Julie de Silva . . . . .Marjorie Mars
Tom Chepstow . . . . .George Merritt
Doris . . . . Dorothy Holmes-Gore
Bell . . . . Hamilton Dyce
Luigi . . . . Manning Wilson
Barker . . . . Hamilton Dyce
Sergeant Thomas . . . . . . Gordon Davies
Foster . . . . Geoffrey Hodson
Other parts played by Cecile Chevreau,
Gretta Gouriet, Jeffrey Segal
and Michael Turner

EPISODE ONE

THE LITTLE THINGS …

OPEN TO: The Sound of the Sea and Seagulls.
FADE these sounds to the background.
FADE IN the sound of a door bell ringing and the door closing.

STEVE: Good morning!

MARY: Oh, good morning, Mrs Temple! I didn't recognise you at first.

STEVE: (*Laughing*) I expect it's the scarf! My word, it's windy this morning!

MARY: Have you been for a walk?

STEVE: Yes, I've been down to the quay and almost as far as the lighthouse.

MARY: You must have felt energetic!

STEVE: Yes! I'd like a packet of postcards, please, Mary, and some envelopes.

MARY: Yes, certainly.

STEVE: I saw your brother Bob – down at the quay. He's taking us out in the bay this afternoon.

MARY: Oh, good! Bob will be pleased; he's been wanting to meet Mr Temple ever since you've been down here.

STEVE: He's quite a salesman, that brother of yours!

MARY: (*Laughing*) Oh, Bob's no fool!

STEVE: The hotel told us to make arrangements with an old boy called Salty something-or-other but your brother …

MARY: Salty West! It's a good job you didn't. He's a dear old soul, but he's never sober.

STEVE: That's exactly what your brother said!

MARY: You'll be all right with Bob, Mrs Temple. He's got a very nice boat; he'll look after you. It should be very pleasant this afternoon if the wind drops.

STEVE: Does the wind ever drop in Downburgh?

3

MARY: Occasionally – then it rains.
STEVE: Well, it's a heavenly spot anyway. I adore the harbour.
MARY: It's all right out of season, but don't come here in August.

MARY hands STEVE the postcards and envelopes.

MARY: That'll be one and seven, Mrs Temple, please.
STEVE: Thank you.
MARY: What made you choose Downburgh? We don't get many visitors this time of the year.
STEVE: My husband's writing a book and he wanted somewhere quiet, away from the telephone.
MARY: Oh, yes, of course! There was a piece about it in the local rag. (*Brightly*) I once read a book by Mr Temple.
STEVE: (*Politely*) Did you?
MARY: Yes, I got it from a library.

The door opens. The door bell rings.

MARY: Very good it was too, it was all about a man who decided … (*She stops; quietly*) Excuse me.
FREEMAN: (*We must feel that he is looking at STEVE, but addressing his remarks to MARY*) I'd like some cigarettes, please.
MARY: I'm sorry, we don't sell cigarettes.
FREEMAN: (*Hesitantly*) Oh, well –
MARY: You can get them, across the street, opposite the Plough and Anchor.
FREEMAN: Oh, thank you. Do you sell matches?
MARY: No, I'm sorry.
FREEMAN: Across the street you said?
MARY: Yes, there's a shop on the corner, opposite the hotel. You can't miss it.
FREEMAN: Thank you. Sorry to have bothered you.
MARY: That's all right.

FREEMAN goes out.

The bell rings as the door opens.

MARY: Well! He'll certainly know you again, Mrs Temple!

STEVE: Yes, he certainly will! Have you seen him before, Mary?

MARY: No, never. But you know, it's surprising the number of people who come in here for cigarettes.

START FADE.

MARY: I said to Bob, only the other week, if we could get a tobacco licence and extend the back parlour …

COMPLETE FADE.

FADE UP the noise of a typewriter.

A door opens and closes.

The typewriter stops and a sheet of paper is taken from it.

STEVE: Hello, darling!

TEMPLE: Oh, hello, Steve! You're back early! I thought you were going for a walk?

STEVE: I've been for a walk – ages ago. Do you know what time it is?

TEMPLE: No?

STEVE: It's a quarter to one.

TEMPLE: What? By Timothy, so it is!

STEVE: Have you had a good morning?

TEMPLE: (*Rising from the table*) Wonderful! I've done over two thousand words.

STEVE: Two thousand words! Clifton Webb wrote twenty thousand – in one night.

TEMPLE: Twenty thousand?

STEVE: Yes.

TEMPLE: Impossible!

5

STEVE: You saw him, darling. (*Singing*) Three coins in a fountain …

TEMPLE: Oh, that was Cinemascope, it doesn't count. Come along, Steve – let's go down and have some lunch.

STEVE: Paul …

TEMPLE: Yes, dear?

STEVE: You remember, the other day – I think it was Thursday – I went for a walk and I noticed a man sitting on the bench at the top of the cliff, the place they call Fisherman's View.

TEMPLE: Yes, I remember.

STEVE: I saw him again this morning.

TEMPLE: Well?

STEVE: I was buying some postcards and he came into the shop.

TEMPLE: Well?

STEVE: Paul, I still think I was right the other day; I know you think it was just my imagination, but …

TEMPLE: I don't think it was just imagination! You said he was watching you; well, he probably was. Why not?

STEVE: Yes, but – I'm sure that's why he came into the shop this morning.

TEMPLE: What do you mean?

STEVE: He wanted to have another look at me.

TEMPLE: What was he like – this man?

STEVE: Oh, he was about your height. Dark. Wore glasses; those rimless ones – what do you call them, bi-focal?

TEMPLE: Yes. How old?

STEVE: Oh – forty-seven or eight, perhaps fifty.

TEMPLE: Had he an accent?

STEVE: Yes, I should say he had a slight accent.

TEMPLE: What kind?

STEVE: Irish.

TEMPLE: Irish? Did he carry a walking stick?

STEVE: He did the first time I saw him, but not this morning.

TEMPLE: Well – what did he say when he came into the shop? Did he speak to you?

STEVE: No, he asked Mary if they sold cigarettes, but –

TEMPLE: But what?

STEVE: But he was looking at me most of the time.

TEMPLE: Well, for heaven's sake, why not? You're a very attractive woman, Steve. You must expect men to look at you!

STEVE: Come off it! I wasn't looking very attractive this morning, my hair was all over the place and I was trying to cope with this wretched scarf.

TEMPLE: Well, what do you want me to do – have him arrested?

STEVE: Don't be silly!

TEMPLE: Come on, let's go down. I've a lot of work to do this afternoon.

STEVE: Yes, but you're not doing it.

TEMPLE: What do you mean – I'm not doing it?

STEVE: You're taking the afternoon off! You've had your nose glued to that typewriter ever since you came down here. You're beginning to look like a piece of carbon paper!

TEMPLE: Darling, I've got another chapter to write and if I don't start it this afternoon …

STEVE: You'll start it tomorrow morning!

TEMPLE: Well, we'll see.

STEVE: We'll see, Mr Temple!

FADE SCENE.

7

FADE UP the sound of the sea and seagulls and the noise of a small motor launch.

BOB: (*A pleasant young man who is in charge of the launch*) That's Pinford Point over there, Mr Temple.

TEMPLE: Pinford Point?

BOB: Yes. (*Amused*) You remember Pinford Point …

STEVE: Isn't that where Lord Nelson went out to meet …

BOB: No, no, it's got nothing to do with Lord Nelson …

TEMPLE: (*Thoughtfully*) Pinford Point …

BOB: Yes. Don't you remember, Mr Temple?

TEMPLE: It strikes a chord, but –

BOB: You mentioned it in one of your books.

TEMPLE: By Timothy, so I did!

BOB laughs.

TEMPLE: What's the joke?

BOB: You said there was a path right down to the sea.

TEMPLE: Well, isn't there?

BOB: I'm afraid not, Mr Temple – it's a sheer drop; about a hundred feet.

TEMPLE: Oh dear!

STEVE: You'll have to change your reference library, Paul!

TEMPLE: It looks very much like it!

STEVE: Do you read very much, Bob?

BOB: Mostly crime stuff; detective novels an' that sort of thing. (*A pause*) Mr Temple, what do you usually look for when you're investigating a crime?

TEMPLE: I don't know that I look for anything; I just hope to goodness I'm going to be lucky.

BOB: Yes, but it isn't just a question of luck, surely?

8

TEMPLE: Luck plays a very important part – you'd be surprised.

BOB: But in your last book the principal character – the detective chap – said that …

TEMPLE: Look, Bob, you can't believe everything you read …

STEVE: Especially if my husband's written it!

They all laugh.

STEVE: What did this detective chap say, Bob?

BOB: He said, in the final analysis it was always the little things that became important. The sound of a voice … finding a name in a diary … remembering a face at the right moment …

TEMPLE: Did I write that?

BOB: Yes.

TEMPLE: It's jolly good! Now, would you mind changing the subject?

STEVE: What would you like to talk about – fish?

TEMPLE: And why not? By Timothy, there's a whopper!

STEVE: I'll bet he's the one that got away!

Again they all laugh.

A pause.

BOB: What time do you want to be back at the hotel, sir?

TEMPLE: Oh, we're in no hurry – six o'clock.

BOB: We'll go as far as the headland then.

STEVE: Paul, is that someone waving to us?

TEMPLE: Where?

STEVE: On the cliff …

A pause.

TEMPLE: I can't see anyone …

A slight pause.

BOB: I can't see anyone either, Mrs Temple.

STEVE: There was a man on the cliff. I could see him quite distinctly a moment ago.

BOB: He's probably crossed over to the other side, we'll see him again when he gets round to …

BOB is interrupted by the sound of a shot from the cliff.

BOB: (*Quickly*) What was that?

There is a second shot and the sound of a bullet ricocheting off the boat on to the water.

TEMPLE: There's someone firing at us … (*Quickly*) Keep down!

There is the sound of another shot and the noise of the bullet hitting the water.

BOB: What the devil is he playing at? (*Shouting*) Hi, you! What the hell do you think you're doing?

TEMPLE: He can't hear you, Bob! Get down!

There is the sound of another shot.

BOB gives out a cry of pain.

STEVE: He's been hit!

TEMPLE: Stay where you are, Steve! Bob, are you all right?

BOB: (*In pain*) It's my … arm … It's nothing, it's just … just …

TEMPLE: Keep down, Bob – don't move …

STEVE: Is he all right?

TEMPLE tears the shirt sleeve on BOB's arm.

TEMPLE: Yes, it's nothing serious … Don't come over here, Steve. I don't want our sharp-shooting friend to take another pot at us.

STEVE: It must have been the man I saw on the cliff. He was obviously watching the boat, Paul.

TEMPLE: Yes. (*To BOB*) Is it hurting you, Bob?

BOB: No, it's not too bad, Mr Temple.

TEMPLE: Lie still for a while. I can handle the boat.

STEVE: I think he's gone, Paul. I can't see him.

BOB: I'd like to get my hands on him …
TEMPLE: Take it easy, Bob. I'll try and turn the launch round …
BOB: Push that lever over, Mr Temple – the one on the left.

TEMPLE pushes the lever.

TEMPLE: Is that it?

FADE UP the noise of the motor.

BOB: (*With a little laugh*) Yes, that's it!

FADE UP the noise of the sea and the motor launch, then slowly FADE DOWN.

FADE UP.

MARY: … Now it's no good being silly about this, Bob. You'll have to stay in bed for two or three days, if you don't …
BOB: (*Irritated*) I've never heard such nonsense! Bed! What the devil do I want to stay in bed for?
TEMPLE: (*Amused*) You do what your sister tells you to do, young man, or there'll be trouble!
BOB: All right, Mr Temple, if you say so.
TEMPLE: I do say so! I'll send you some books over from the hotel.
BOB: (*Grinning*) Thanks.
IVOR: Can I have another word with you, sir?
TEMPLE: Yes, of course, Inspector.
IVOR: Good night, Bob – take care of yourself.
BOB: Good night, Inspector!
TEMPLE: Good night, Bob.
BOB: Good night, Mr Temple!

A door opens and closes.

IVOR: (*A faintly patronising manner*) Mr Temple, this mysterious stranger your wife was telling us

about, the gentleman with the slight Irish accent
…

TEMPLE: Yes?

IVOR: Do you think he's the man who fired at you?

TEMPLE: My dear Inspector, your guess is as good as mine. Steve – my wife – was the only person who saw the man on the cliff. She's already told you that she couldn't identify him.

IVOR: Yes. Mr Temple, forgive my saying this, but – during the course of a not entirely uneventful career you must have made quite a lot of enemies.

TEMPLE: Yes, I suppose I have. And a few friends, I hope.

IVOR: Yes, I know Sir Graham's a friend of yours, sir.

TEMPLE: (*Faintly irritated*) What's at the back of your mind, Inspector?

IVOR: (*Bluntly*) Mr Temple, have you any idea who fired those shots?

TEMPLE: No, I haven't. If I had, I should tell you.

IVOR: (*Drily*) I hope you would, sir. How long are you staying in Downburgh?

TEMPLE: Oh, another four or five days, perhaps a week.

IVOR: Rather a curious time of the year to come down here, sir.

TEMPLE: I wanted to be quiet, away from the telephone. I'm writing a book.

IVOR: I see. Where are you staying, Mr Temple?

TEMPLE: At the Crescent Hotel. (*A suspicion of sarcasm in his voice*) Room 32 …

IVOR: (*Unperturbed*) Thank you, sir. Well, I'll be making a move. If anything develops I'll let you know.

TEMPLE: Thank you, Inspector. I'll do the same for you.

The door opens and closes.

FADE UP some incidental music.

FADE DOWN of music.
FADE UP.
STEVE is packing a suitcase; TEMPLE is lying on the bed.

STEVE: What did you do with that cream shirt, Paul?
TEMPLE: Which cream shirt?
STEVE: The one with the collar attached.
TEMPLE: I'm still wearing it.
STEVE: Oh!
TEMPLE: By Timothy, just look at that suitcase! You'll never get that dressing gown in.
STEVE: Yes, I will, you leave it to me.
TEMPLE: Steve, when it comes to packing you're a genius, an absolute …
STEVE: Yes, well would you mind getting off the bed and making yourself useful for a change!
TEMPLE: Well, I like that, I must say! A moment ago you told me to do nothing – you said I was in the way.
STEVE: Well, you are in the way! Look, if you really want to help put those books in your valise.
TEMPLE: Hello, where did they come from? They're the books I lent Bob Gardner nearly a week ago.
STEVE: Yes, I know. I saw him this morning and told him we were going back to Town.
TEMPLE: Where did you see him – down at the quay?
STEVE: Yes.
TEMPLE: How was he?
STEVE: Oh, he was full of beans. He started work on Tuesday. Paul, pass me that dress.

There is a knock on the door.

TEMPLE: You're not going to try and get that in the suitcase!

13

STEVE: Would you like to put it in your valise?

TEMPLE: Don't be silly!

STEVE: Then it's got to go in the suitcase!

There's another knock on the door.

TEMPLE: (*Calling*) Come in!

The door opens.

IVOR: Mr Temple …

TEMPLE: Oh, hello, Inspector! Come in!

IVOR: (*Quietly; no trace of his previous manner*) I'm sorry to disturb you, sir, but I heard you were going back to London this afternoon …

TEMPLE: Yes, we're catching the five-ten.

STEVE: Is anything wrong, Inspector?

IVOR: Yes, Mrs Temple.

TEMPLE: What is it?

IVOR: Bob Gardner's had an accident …

TEMPLE: What kind of an accident?

IVOR: Apparently Bob and a man called Salty West tried to rescue a dog. It was trapped on what we call Lighthouse Cliff, that's near Pinford Point.

TEMPLE: Yes, I know –

IVOR: Bob tried to get down the cliff, it was a damn fool thing to do with a bad arm and only Salty holding on to him … Suddenly the dog started to bark and the old boy slipped …

TEMPLE: Was Bob – ?

IVOR: Yes; we found his body on the beach, he must have been killed instantaneously.

STEVE: Oh, poor Bob.

TEMPLE: What about old Salty West?

IVOR: He was pretty badly shaken of course, but he's all right now. He managed to scramble back on to the top of the cliff.

STEVE: What a terrible thing to have happened …

TEMPLE: Inspector, you're quite sure this was an accident?
IVOR: Oh, yes, sir – there's no doubt about it. We've got a complete statement from Salty and we found the dog.
TEMPLE: I see.
IVOR: Is there a doubt in your mind, sir?
TEMPLE: Is there a doubt in _your_ mind, Inspector – that's the point.
IVOR: No, sir, there isn't.
TEMPLE: Good.
IVOR: But …
TEMPLE: Well?
IVOR: It seems a curious coincidence after what happened the other day.
TEMPLE: But you took it for granted that the shots were meant for me, Inspector – or my wife.
IVOR: Why, yes, sir – naturally. But I suppose they could have been meant for Bob Gardner.
TEMPLE: The thought did cross my mind, Inspector.

FADE SCENE.
FADE IN incidental music.

FADE DOWN incidental music.
We hear the noise of a front door of a house which opens and closes.
CHARLIE: Hello, Mrs Temple! Welcome home!
STEVE: Thank you, Charlie.
TEMPLE: Here you are, Charlie – take this suitcase. No, the heavy one!
CHARLIE: Oh, beg pardon, sir.
The door closes.
STEVE: Oh, Paul, just look at these letters!
TEMPLE: Mostly bills, I'll bet!
STEVE: Never mind, it's nice to be home.

CHARLIE: I hope you had a pleasant journey, sir?
TEMPLE: (*Shivering*) Cold, Charlie. Very cold.
CHARLIE: Well, there's a very nice fire in the drawing room, sir – (*Almost an afterthought*) and Sir Graham Forbes.
TEMPLE: You mean Sir Graham's here?
CHARLIE: Yes. He telephoned this morning: I said I thought you'd be home about eight o'clock.
TEMPLE: How long has he been here?
CHARLIE: About a quarter of an hour, I should say.
TEMPLE: Right. We'd best see what he wants.

A door opens.

FORBES: (*His manner is pleasant, yet obviously worried*) Ah, here you are, Temple.
TEMPLE: Well, this is a pleasant surprise, Sir Graham!
FORBES: Let's just say it's a surprise. You look very fit, Steve.
STEVE: And you look very worried, Sir Graham.
TEMPLE: What's happened this time? Don't tell me all the bright little boys at Scotland Yard …
STEVE: Paul!
TEMPLE: (*Seriously*) What is it, Sir Graham?
FORBES: Temple, do you think I could have a drink?
TEMPLE: Good heavens, yes! You should have helped yourself.
FORBES: I did. I'd – like another one.
TEMPLE: Of course.
STEVE: What is wrong, Sir Graham?

We hear the sound of a drink being poured and a soda syphon.

TEMPLE: Here's your drink, Sir Graham. Just a minute, Steve.

FORBES:	Thanks. Good health. I haven't been to bed for thirty-six hours; I dashed up to Liverpool last night but it was a wild goose chase.
TEMPLE:	Why Liverpool?
FORBES:	There was a report that she'd been seen in Lime Street, but unfortunately …
TEMPLE:	Sir Graham, don't you think you'd better start your story at the beginning?

A pause.

FORBES:	Sylvia Ross has disappeared.
TEMPLE:	Sylvia Ross?
FORBES:	Yes.
TEMPLE:	When? When did this happen?
FORBES:	Three days ago. A young man called Brian Dexter took her to a concert at the Festival Hall. That was on Tuesday night; after the concert …
STEVE:	Who is Sylvia Ross?
TEMPLE:	Steve, please! Go on, Sir Graham.
FORBES:	Well, there's not much to tell. After the concert they had supper at a restaurant in Maiden Lane. They left about eleven-fifteen and Dexter dropped her in Berkeley Square – you know the house, Temple? – at about a quarter to twelve.
TEMPLE:	Was Carlton there?
FORBES:	No, he was in Geneva. He flew back yesterday morning.
TEMPLE:	Dexter … Brian Dexter …
FORBES:	His father's the managing director of Anglo-Chemicals. He seems a very agreeable young man; good background. Eton, Oxford.
TEMPLE:	Who introduced him to Sylvia?
FORBES:	Carlton did; he's a friend of the boy's father.
STEVE:	Look – would you mind telling me – who is Sylvia Ross?

FORBES: She's Sir Carlton Ross's daughter.
TEMPLE: He's the head of M.I. 5.
FADE IN incidental music.

FADE DOWN the music.
A door opens and closes.
DEXTER: I'm awfully sorry to have kept you waiting, sir.
TEMPLE: That's all right, Mr Dexter. It's very nice of you
          to see me.
DEXTER: Can I offer you a glass of sherry?
TEMPLE: Not just at the moment, thank you.
DEXTER: Do sit down. Sir Graham telephoned and said
          that you wanted to have a word with me.
TEMPLE: Yes.
DEXTER: I presume it's about Sylvia.
TEMPLE: Yes.
DEXTER: Is there any news?
TEMPLE: No, I'm afraid not.
DEXTER: It's extraordinary. Quite extraordinary. I just
          don't believe it.
TEMPLE: Dexter, I've heard your story, second-hand, from
          Sir Graham. Would you mind repeating it for me,
          in your own words?
DEXTER: Not at all. If it'll help, I'll repeat it a hundred
          times.
TEMPLE: When did you first meet Sylvia Ross?
DEXTER: I went to Switzerland for the winter sports and
          Sylvia and her parents happened to be staying in
          the same hotel.
TEMPLE: I see. Go on …
DEXTER: Well, where do you want me to go on from,
          exactly?
TEMPLE: Tell me about your relationship with Miss Ross.
          Did you see a great deal of each other?

DEXTER: I saw her three times in twelve months. Once at a garden fete, once at the theatre, and last Tuesday night.

TEMPLE: What happened last Tuesday?

DEXTER: Well, she telephoned me at about half-past four and asked me if I'd care to go to a concert with her. Quite frankly, I wasn't very keen on the idea but I was at a loose end so I decided to go. I picked her up about seven o'clock; we left the Festival Hall at half-past ten, had supper at Shorts in Maiden Lane, and got back to Berkeley Square about eleven-forty.

TEMPLE: I understand you took a taxi from Maiden Lane?

DEXTER: Yes; I'd been having a spot of trouble with my car so I left it in the Strand and took Sylvia home in a cab; the cab took me straight back to where my car was parked. I didn't even get out of the cab – in Berkeley Square, I mean.

TEMPLE: Why was that?

DEXTER: It was raining slightly and Sylvia seemed to be in rather a hurry; she simply jumped out of the taxi, waved her hand, and disappeared.

TEMPLE: So you didn't actually see her go into the house?

DEXTER: No, I'm afraid I didn't.

TEMPLE: And that was the last time you saw her?

DEXTER: That was the last time.

TEMPLE: You say you left the Festival Hall at half-past ten?

DEXTER: (*Hesitantly*) Yes.

TEMPLE: Was that when the concert finished?

DEXTER: Why – yes.

TEMPLE: You don't seem very certain. What was the concert?

DEXTER: What do you mean – what was it?

TEMPLE: Well, what did the pianist play? Chopin? Beethoven? Debussy?

DEXTER: I'm afraid I can't remember. I'm frightfully vague about that sort of thing.

TEMPLE: You are indeed, Mr Dexter. There wasn't a pianist. It was the Birmingham Symphony Orchestra.

DEXTER: Oh. Oh dear.

TEMPLE: You didn't go to the concert, did you?

DEXTER: No.

TEMPLE: Then why on earth did you tell Sir Graham …

DEXTER: Look, surely the important thing is the fact that I took Sylvia home and left her there at about twenty-to-twelve. If you don't believe me …

TEMPLE: It isn't a question of not believing you; as a matter of fact the taxi driver confirms your story.

DEXTER: Well, there you are then!

TEMPLE: If you didn't go to the concert, where did you go?

DEXTER: It's not important.

TEMPLE: On the contrary, it might be very important.

DEXTER: (*Reluctantly*) We went to the Strand Palais de Danse.

TEMPLE: (*Surprised*) The Strand Palais de Danse?

DEXTER: Yes.

TEMPLE: What on earth made you go there?

DEXTER: Look, Mr Temple, if I tell you what happened – what really happened – will you make me a promise?

TEMPLE: That depends – on the promise.

DEXTER: Will you promise not to tell Sylvia's mother, Lady Ross, about this?

TEMPLE: I see no reason why I should tell Lady Ross anything.

DEXTER: Well, after I picked up Sylvia we drove down the Strand towards the Embankment. Suddenly, on the corner, near the Aldwych, Sylvia spotted a large neon sign advertising the Palais de Danse. Well, to cut a long story short, I suggested – more as a joke than anything else – that it would be much more fun to go to the Palais de Danse than the Festival Hall. To my surprise she jumped at the idea.

TEMPLE: Are you sure it wasn't her idea in the first place?

DEXTER: No, it was my idea because … (*He stops*)

TEMPLE: Because what?

DEXTER: (*Quietly*) Wait a minute! It was my idea, but I'm not so jolly sure that she didn't put it into my head.

TEMPLE: Why do you say that?

DEXTER: Well, it's just occurred to me. I didn't want to go down the Strand in the first place. It was Sylvia's idea.

TEMPLE: Which way did you want to go?

DEXTER: Down Whitehall and across Westminster Bridge.

TEMPLE: But Sylvia suggested that you went down the Strand?

DEXTER: (*Thoughtfully*) Yes.

TEMPLE: How long did you stay at the dance hall?

DEXTER: Until half-past ten; then we went to the restaurant. The story I told Sir Graham was perfectly true except for the visit to the Festival Hall.

TEMPLE: Why didn't you tell Sir Graham the complete truth?

DEXTER: Because what we did earlier in the evening – or rather what we didn't do – didn't seem to me to be very important.

21

TEMPLE: And you didn't want him to tell Lady Ross?

DEXTER: Yes.

TEMPLE: Why not?

DEXTER: Well, they're pretty important people; Sir Carlton's a friend of my father's and – well – in spite of what I've said I suppose the dance hall was really my suggestion.

TEMPLE: I see. Now tell me what happened at the Palais de Danse? Did Sylvia speak to anyone?

DEXTER: (*Laughing*) Good Lord, no! We sat in a corner most of the night drinking lemonade and laughing our heads off.

TEMPLE: What were you laughing at?

DEXTER: A character called Johnny Teako. He's a sort of compere-cum-danceband-leader-cum-pianist-cum-the whole bag of tricks.

TEMPLE: I think I've heard him on the radio.

DEXTER: It's possible. He's a pseudo-American – straight from Battersea. Still, he's got a very good band. Sylvia was crazy about it, she made him play her favourite number.

TEMPLE: I thought you said she didn't speak to anyone?

DEXTER: She didn't.

TEMPLE: Well, how did she …?

DEXTER: She sent him a note.

TEMPLE: Did you see it?

DEXTER: The note?

TEMPLE: Yes.

DEXTER: No, but I know what was on it.

TEMPLE: What was on it?

DEXTER: I've told you; it was a request.

TEMPLE: For what?

DEXTER: For a number; a song.

TEMPLE: What was the song?

DEXTER: Good heavens above! Is that important?
TEMPLE: It might be.
DEXTER: Well, the number was called Goodbye, My Baby, My Baby Doll. It doesn't sound very important, does it?

A slight pause.

TEMPLE: Dexter, have you any idea what's happened to Miss Ross?
DEXTER: Not the slightest.
TEMPLE: Were you surprised when you heard that she'd disappeared?
DEXTER: Good Lord, yes!
TEMPLE: But you're not unduly perturbed?
DEXTER: Well, I'm puzzled, of course, like everyone else, but –
TEMPLE: But not perturbed?
DEXTER: No. I think she'll turn up all right.
TEMPLE: Well, I hope you're right, Dexter. I hope you're right.

FADE SCENE.

FADE UP of a dance orchestra and the noise of people dancing in a crowded dance hall.
The dance orchestra stops playing and there is applause.
The dancers leave the floor during the following announcement by JOHNNY TEAKO.

TEAKO: (*He has an American accent and is very sure of himself*) Well, that's all, folks! Rest awhile, boys and girls – rest awhile. We'll be back with you again in just five minutes' time.

There are general noises from the dance hall.

STEVE: Does he like himself? It's almost indecent!
TEMPLE: Wait here, Steve, I'm going to have a word with him.

23

STEVE: Don't be long.

TEMPLE: I'll be back in a minute, don't move from the table.

FADE DOWN of the general noise.

JOHNNY TEAKO is strumming on the piano, amusing himself.

Several of the band are talking in the near background.

TEMPLE: Are you Johnny Teako?

TEAKO: (*At the piano*) I'm not Gregory Peck.

Several of the boys laugh.

TEMPLE: You don't sound like Gregory Peck. My name's Temple, I'd like to have a word with you.

TEAKO: Go ahead, Mac.

TEMPLE: This is private. Is there a dressing room somewhere?

TEAKO: Go ahead, I'm listening. I'm listening. (*To someone in the near background; ignoring TEMPLE*) Linda, we'll start with the new arrangement of Night and Day.

LINDA: (*From the background*) Yes, Johnny.

TEAKO: And get the thing straight this time, it was all boxed up last night.

LINDA: Yes, Johnny.

TEMPLE: Teako, I said I wanted to have a word with you …

TEAKO: Sure. I'm listening, Mac. I'm listening. (*To the band*) The guy wants to have a word with me and says nothing.

Several of the boys show their amusement.

TEAKO continues strumming the piano.

TEMPLE: On Tuesday night a girl sent you a note asking you to play a certain number …

TEAKO: Well?

TEMPLE: Do you remember that note?

TEAKO: Are you kiddin'? I get fifty notes every night.

TEMPLE: You haven't had fifty tonight. I've been here an hour and a half and you haven't had one.

The piano stops.

The conversation dies down.

TEAKO: (*Annoyed*) What is this?

TEMPLE: I've told you. A girl sent you a note …

TEAKO: Yeah, yeah, I know that. What about it?

TEMPLE: Do you remember the note?

A pause.

TEAKO touches the piano.

TEAKO: Maybe …

TEMPLE: Do you remember what the girl looked like?

TEAKO: Mac, I see hundreds of girls. Every afternoon, every night, I see hundreds of them. Why should I remember that particular girl?

TEMPLE: Because she sent you a note.

TEAKO: Okay.

TEAKO strums on the piano again.

TEAKO: She sent me a note. So what?

TEMPLE: Teako, this is important; do you remember that girl? Do you remember what she looked like?

Another pause.

TEAKO: (*Almost sentimental*) Yeah, I remember. She had a blue dress and a little grey hat and she wore a pink jacket. She was with a guy in a tuxedo. Nice looking guy.

TEMPLE: Would you recognise him again?

TEAKO: Sure I'd recognise him. His name's Dexter. Brian Dexter.

TEMPLE: How do you know?

TEAKO: I saw a picture of him in one of the glossy magazines, two days ago. (*A pause*) Anything else?

TEMPLE: Was that the first time you'd seen the girl?
TEAKO: Yeah …
TEMPLE: She hadn't been here before?
TEAKO: I'd never seen her before.
TEMPLE: Right. Thank you, Mr Teako. Oh – what was the number?
TEAKO: The number?
TEMPLE: Yes, the song she requested.

A pause.

TEAKO: It was – Goodbye, My Baby, My Baby Doll. (*Smiling*) Satisfied?
TEMPLE: Yes, I'm satisfied.

TEAKO laughs.

He starts to play the piano again.

TEAKO: Any time, Mac. Any time …

The piano continues.

SLOW FADE of the piano to the background.

TEMPLE returns to the table.

TEMPLE: Get your wrap, Steve – we're leaving.
STEVE: That girl was watching you the whole time, Paul.
TEMPLE: Which girl?
STEVE: The one in the orchestra.
TEMPLE: Are you sure?
STEVE: Yes; she was talking to someone but she had her eye on you the whole time.
TEMPLE: All right, Steve. Let's get out of here.

START FADE.

STEVE: The last time I came to one of these places was four years ago when Charlie won the local championship …

COMPLETE FADE.

FADE IN of the front hall of the Palais de Danse.
There is a background of street noises and traffic.

STEVE: Oh dear, it's raining!

COMMISSIONAIRE: Would you like a taxi, sir?

TEMPLE: Do you think you could find us one?

COMMISSIONAIRE: I'll try, sir.

TEMPLE: Right.

A pause.

LINDA: (*From the background; calling*) Mr Temple!

STEVE: Paul, it's that girl! The one I was telling you about!

LINDA TEAKO arrives.

LINDA: (*She is nervous and slightly out of breath. She has a very slight cockney accent*) Mr Temple, do you think I could have a word with you?

TEMPLE: Yes, of course.

LINDA: I'm Linda Teako, Johnny's wife. I'm also the vocalist with the orchestra and …

TEMPLE: Yes, I know, we've been listening to you …

LINDA: Mr Temple, please don't think me rude but … I … I overheard part of your conversation and … Johnny didn't tell you the truth.

TEMPLE: Didn't he, Mrs Teako?

LINDA: No … You see … that girl – the one you questioned him about?

TEMPLE: Yes?

LINDA: I saw the note she gave him …

TEMPLE: Well?

LINDA: (*Rather frightened*) It wasn't what you thought, it wasn't a request at all, it …

TEMPLE: Well, what was it?

LINDA: (*Obviously frightened*) Look, Mr Temple, if I tell you about the note you won't question Johnny about it, will you? …

TEMPLE: Don't worry, Mrs Teako; I shan't even mention it to your husband.

LINDA: Well, I saw the girl give him the note and I knew, by the way he looked at it, that there was something different about it. It was almost as if …

TEMPLE: As if what?

LINDA: As if he'd been expecting it.

TEMPLE: Go on …

LINDA: He read the note and put it in his waistcoat pocket; even that made me suspicious because normally when he gets a written request he puts on quite an act, holding the paper up and whispering into the microphone.

TEMPLE: Go on …

LINDA: Later that night, while I was changing, I looked at the note.

TEMPLE: Well?

LINDA: It had a name on it, just a person's name and an address.

TEMPLE: What was the name and address, do you remember?

LINDA: Yes, it was Lawrence.

TEMPLE: Lawrence.

LINDA: That's right. It said: Mr Clive Lawrence, Hotel Schweizerhof, Zermatt.

TEMPLE: Mr Clive Lawrence, Hotel Schweizerhof, Zermatt. Is that all it said?

LINDA: Yes, that's all.

TEMPLE: You haven't got the note?

LINDA: No, I put it back in his pocket. (*Faintly pathetic*) You see, in a way I was rather relieved, I thought perhaps it was a … different … kind of note.

STEVE: Your husband leads you quite a dance, doesn't he, Mrs Teako?

28

LINDA: Oh, Johnny's all right; he's going through a
            phase at the moment, he'll … grow out of it.
TEMPLE: Well, thank you very much, Mrs Teako, I'm very
            grateful to you.

The dance orchestra starts playing in the background in the
dance hall.

LINDA: You won't tell Johnny about this, will you?
TEMPLE: Don't worry, I shan't say a word to your
            husband, I promise you.
LINDA: That's the band! I've got to get back, Mr
            Temple, or he'll wonder where I am! Goodbye!
            Goodbye, Mrs Temple!
STEVE: Goodbye. The poor woman! She's terrified of
            that over-dressed slab of brilliantine.
CONCIERGE: Excuse me, sir. Your taxi …
TEMPLE: Thank you. Here you are …
CONCIERGE: (*Pleasantly surprised*) Oh, thank you, sir!

FADE DOWN of the dance music.

FADE UP the sound of breakfast cups and the pouring of
coffee.

STEVE: You're very interested in the paper this morning,
            Paul.
TEMPLE: I'm just looking to see if there's anything about
            Sylvia Ross.
STEVE: Is there?
TEMPLE: No; either the press haven't got on to it yet or
            they're deliberately playing it down.
STEVE: Would you like some more coffee?
TEMPLE: No, thanks.
STEVE: Paul, what sort of a man is Sir Carlton Ross?

The door bell rings in the background.

TEMPLE: I thought you met him, Steve. About a year ago.
STEVE: No, I don't think so.

TEMPLE: I rather like him, but he's a curious bird. He was a Don at Oxford for a time and then he suddenly … Wasn't that the door bell?

STEVE: Yes, I think it was.

TEMPLE: (*Rising*) It's probably Sir Graham. I phoned him last night after you went to bed.

The door opens.

CHARLIE: Excuse me, sir. A Miss Gardner would like to see you.

TEMPLE: Miss Gardner? (*To STEVE*) Who's Miss Gardner?

STEVE: It must be Mary Gardner, Bob Gardner's sister …

TEMPLE: Ask her in, Charlie.

CHARLIE: Yes, sir.

STEVE: Why on earth should Mary Gardner want to see you?

TEMPLE: What time is it, Steve?

STEVE: Twenty to ten.

TEMPLE: She must have left Downburgh pretty early to get here by twenty to ten.

CHARLIE: Miss Gardner, sir.

STEVE: Hello, Mary! This is a surprise. How are you?

MARY: (*Faintly embarrassed*) I do apologise, calling like this, Mrs Temple. I wouldn't have done it but …

STEVE: That's all right, Mary. We're delighted to see you.

TEMPLE: Would you like some coffee?

MARY: (*Hesitantly*) It's very kind of you, but –

TEMPLE: Bring another cup, Charlie.

CHARLIE: Yes, sir.

STEVE: Sit down, Mary.

TEMPLE: Did you come up to London this morning?

MARY: Yes, I caught the seven-ten from Felixstowe – there isn't an early train from Downburgh.

TEMPLE: What made you come up to Town so early?

MARY: A man called Bristow telephoned me yesterday morning and said he wanted to see me. He asked me if I could see him this morning at eleven o'clock.

TEMPLE: Bristow?

MARY: Yes, I believe they're a firm of solicitors. Bristow, Thompson and …

TEMPLE: Bristow, Thompson, and Dawson?

MARY: Yes! Do you know them, Mr Temple?

TEMPLE: I've heard of them. They're a very good firm. Harrogate Buildings, Lincolns Inn.

MARY: That's right.

STEVE: What do they want to see you about, Mary? Do you know?

MARY: I haven't the slightest idea; I just can't imagine, Mrs Temple.

STEVE: Is it something to do with Bob?

MARY: I don't know, Mrs Temple. All I know is I feel awfully worried. I don't like the idea of seeing a solicitor, especially in London.

STEVE: Is that why you wanted to see my husband?

MARY: Oh, no. I found this letter yesterday afternoon in an old deed box. It's addressed to you, Mr Temple.

TEMPLE: To me?

MARY: Yes. I think Bob must have written it just before the accident …

TEMPLE takes the letter.

TEMPLE: Thank you.

TEMPLE opens the letter.

A pause.

31

STEVE: What is it, Paul?

TEMPLE: (*Reading*) "Dear Mr Temple, I wonder if you remember our conversation about the little things that later become so important. I have a feeling that this name and address is going to be … one of those little things …"

STEVE: What name and address? What does it say?

TEMPLE: (*Reading*) "Mr Clive Lawrence, Hotel Schweizerhof, Zermatt."

FADE IN closing music.

END OF EPISODE ONE

EPISODE TWO

SALTY WEST

OPEN TO:

MARY: A man called Bristow telephoned me yesterday morning and said he wanted to see me. He asked me if I could see him this morning at eleven o'clock.

TEMPLE: Bristow?

MARY: Yes, I believe they're a firm of solicitors. Bristow, Thompson and …

TEMPLE: Bristow, Thompson, and Dawson?

MARY: Yes! Do you know them, Mr Temple?

TEMPLE: I've heard of them. They're a very good firm. Harrogate Buildings, Lincolns Inn.

MARY: That's right.

STEVE: What do they want to see you about, Mary? Do you know?

MARY: I haven't the slightest idea; I just can't imagine, Mrs Temple.

STEVE: Is it something to do with Bob?

MARY: I don't know, Mrs Temple. All I know is I feel awfully worried. I don't like the idea of seeing a solicitor, especially in London.

STEVE: Is that why you wanted to see my husband?

MARY: Oh, no. I found this letter yesterday afternoon in an old deed box. It's addressed to you, Mr Temple.

TEMPLE: To me?

MARY: Yes. I think Bob must have written it just before the accident …

TEMPLE takes the letter.

TEMPLE: Thank you.

TEMPLE opens the letter.

A pause.

STEVE: What is it, Paul?

35

TEMPLE: (*Reading*) "Dear Mr Temple, I wonder if you remember our conversation about the little things that later become so important. I have a feeling that this name and address is going to be ... one of those little things ..."

STEVE: What name and address? What does it say?

TEMPLE: (*Reading*) "Mr Clive Lawrence, Hotel Schweizerhof, Zermatt."

STEVE: But, Paul, that's the name and address that ...

TEMPLE: Steve, please, just a moment. Mary, have you heard this name – Clive Lawrence – before?

MARY: Why, no ...

TEMPLE: Your brother never mentioned it?

MARY: No, never, Mr Temple ...

TEMPLE: What about the address: The Hotel Schweizerhof, Zermatt?

MARY: (*Bewildered*) I've never heard of the Hotel Schweizerhof or Mr Lawrence or even Zermatt for that matter. Where is Zermatt, anyway?

TEMPLE: It's a mountain village in Switzerland. A holiday resort at the foot of the Matterhorn.

MARY: I've never been to Switzerland. But neither had Bob so far as I know. (*Puzzled*) Mr Temple, what does he mean – the little things that later become so important?

TEMPLE: (*Deliberately vague*) Oh, it's a reference to a conversation we had, the first time we met.

The door opens.

STEVE: Ah, here's Charlie with the coffee. Now let me pour you a cup, Mary.

STEVE pours the coffee.

CHARLIE: Excuse me. Sir Graham Forbes is here, sir. He's in the study.

TEMPLE: Yes, all right, Charlie. Excuse me, Mary – I won't be a moment.

START FADE.

STEVE: Do you take sugar?

MARY: Yes, please. This is very kind of you, Mrs Temple ...

STEVE: Nonsense, Mary! How many lumps – two?

MARY: Yes, please.

COMPLETE FADE.

FADE UP TEMPLE.

TEMPLE: Good morning, Sir Graham! Sorry to have kept you waiting.

FORBES: That's all right, Temple!

TEMPLE: Any news?

FORBES: No, I'm afraid not. We had a bit of a scare during the night. A report came through from Hammersmith that they'd picked a girl out of the river ...

TEMPLE: And you thought it was Sylvia Ross?

FORBES: Yes; fortunately it wasn't. Well, I gather you saw Dexter.

TEMPLE: Yes, I saw him.

FORBES: What do you make of him?

TEMPLE: He's pleasant enough, a little irresponsible perhaps, but ...

FORBES: Irresponsible? I shouldn't have said that.

A slight pause.

TEMPLE: Sir Graham, he didn't go to that concert at the Festival Hall.

FORBES: What do you mean – he didn't go? Of course he did! He took Sylvia Ross.

TEMPLE: No. No, that's just the point, he didn't. They changed their minds and went to a dance hall.

FORBES: A dance hall? I can't believe that, Temple, why …

TEMPLE: It's true. Dexter told me himself. In any case I've checked the story.

FORBES: Then why in heaven's name didn't he tell us that in the first place?

TEMPLE: One, because he didn't want you to tell Lady Ross; two, because he didn't really consider it important.

FORBES: He didn't consider it important?

TEMPLE: No, and strangely enough I can see his point of view. He told the truth about going to the restaurant, about taking Sylvia home in a taxi. So far as he was concerned that's all that mattered.

FORBES: If he lied about the concert how do we know that he didn't lie about everything else?

TEMPLE: Didn't the waiter and the taxi driver confirm his story?

FORBES: (*Reluctantly*) Yes. Nevertheless, he should have told us about the dance hall.

TEMPLE: I agree; unfortunately he didn't.

FORBES: Which dance hall was it?

TEMPLE: The one in the Strand. Steve and I went there last night. But before I tell you about our visit, there's something I want to ask you.

FORBES: Well?

TEMPLE: Do you remember the Burford case?

FORBES: Burford? Yes, I think so. He was an accountant and was arrested for housebreaking. He swore he was innocent but three people identified him.

TEMPLE: That's right. I gave evidence. Burford got four years.

FORBES: Well?

TEMPLE: What's happened to him since then, Sir Graham?

38

FORBES: I'm afraid I don't know.
TEMPLE: Could you find out?
FORBES: Yes, of course.
TEMPLE: I'd like you to.
FORBES: You mean – now?
TEMPLE: If you could, Sir Graham.
FORBES: Has Burford got anything to do with the disappearance of Sylvia Ross?
TEMPLE: I don't know, but I'd like to know where he is and what he's doing.
FORBES: All right, Temple.

FORBES dials a number.

There is a pause.

FORBES: (*On the telephone*) Extension 17, please … (*A tiny pause*) Vosper? … This is Forbes … Vosper, listen: you remember Max Burford? … no, Burford … Yes, that's right, that's the man … Well, what's he doing now, do you know? (*A long pause*) I see … Well, do you think you could get me more details? … No, I'm with Mr Temple … Yes … All right, Vosper, do that and ring me back. (*He replaces the receiver*) He's making inquiries and ringing back.
TEMPLE: Thank you, Sir Graham.
FORBES: Why are you interested in Burford, Temple?
TEMPLE: Sit down, Sir Graham, and I'll tell you. (*A pause, then:*) Just over a fortnight ago Steve and I went to Downburgh; it's a little fishing village on the east coast.
FORBES: Yes, I know it.
TEMPLE: Well, while we were there we went out in a boat with one of the local fishermen, a young fellow called Bob Gardner. It was quite a pleasant trip until someone suddenly decided to use the boat

39

for target practice. Gardner was hit; fortunately it wasn't serious. However, a week later – the day Steve and I left Downburgh – Gardner had an accident and was killed.

FORBES: Did anyone witness the accident?

TEMPLE: Yes, one of the locals, an old boy called Salty West.

FORBES: Did you talk to him?

TEMPLE: No, I didn't, but I gather – from what Salty told Inspector Ivor – that there was no doubt about it being an accident.

FORBES: Go on, Temple.

TEMPLE: When we arrived in Town you told us about the disappearance of Sylvia Ross and, at your suggestion, I questioned Brian Dexter, who is a friend of Sylvia's. He told me that they'd been to a dance hall and that Sylvia had sent a note to Johnny Teako.

FORBES: Who on earth is Johnny Teako?

TEMPLE: He's the dance band leader.

FORBES: Oh, I see.

TEMPLE: I questioned Teako about the note and he confirmed what Dexter had told me. That it was simply a request to play a certain dance tune. Later, when Steve and I were leaving the dance hall, Teako's wife, Linda, told me that she had seen the note and that it contained a name and an address. The name was: Clive Lawrence. The address: Hotel Schweizerhof, Zermatt.

A pause.

FORBES: Is that the complete story?

TEMPLE: No, not quite. This morning Mary Gardner – Bob Gardner's sister – arrived with this letter. She found it in a deed box after her brother was killed. It's addressed to me. Read it, Sir Graham.

A pause while SIR GRAHAM reads the letter.

FORBES: But this letter mentions the same name – Clive Lawrence – and the same address!

TEMPLE: Yes.

FORBES: In other words, the death of Bob Gardner might, in some way or other, be connected with the disappearance of Sylvia Ross.

TEMPLE: It looks very much like it.

FORBES: Well, how does Max Burford fit into all this?

TEMPLE: I'm not sure that he does; but while we were staying at Downburgh, Steve suddenly had the feeling that she was being watched. She gave me a description of the man and …

The telephone rings.

FORBES: It reminded you of Max Burford.

TEMPLE: Yes, it did. Excuse me.

TEMPLE lifts the receiver.

TEMPLE: Hello? … Yes … Oh, hold on, will you, please? (*To FORBES*) It's for you, Sir Graham – it's Vosper.

FORBES: Thanks. (*On the phone*) Hello, Vosper … (*Listening*) Yes … Yes, I see … Are you sure about that? … Who did you speak to? … (*Pause*) Yes, all right, Vosper. Thank you for ringing.

SIR GRAHAM replaces the receiver.

FORBES: Apparently Max Burford's living at Bray, near Maidenhead. According to Vosper he's running a boat-building firm called Harper Brothers.

TEMPLE: Thank you, Sir Graham.

FORBES: (*Looking at the letter*) Clive Lawrence, Hotel Schweizerhof … You know, I think M.I.5. ought to see this letter, Temple.

TEMPLE: All right, Sir Graham.
START FADE.
FORBES: I'll let you have it back some time tomorrow.
COMPLETE FADE.

A door opens.
TEMPLE: Hello, Steve – where's Miss Gardner?
STEVE: She's just left, Paul.
TEMPLE: But her appointment wasn't till eleven o'clock.
STEVE: Yes, I know, but the poor dear was terrified she'd be late. (*Laughing*) I've never seen anyone so nervous; she made me so jumpy I spilt a cup of coffee all over her.
TEMPLE: Oh, dear!
STEVE: I had to lend her a coat. She's bringing it back at four o'clock.
TEMPLE: Oh, good, I wanted to see her again. (*A pause*) Steve …
STEVE: Yes, dear?
TEMPLE: You remember that man you saw at Downburgh, the one who came into the shop …
STEVE: Yes.
TEMPLE: Do you think you'd recognise him again?
STEVE: Yes, I think so.
TEMPLE: Aren't you sure?
STEVE: I'm pretty sure – yes.
TEMPLE: Well, get dressed, Steve. We're going out.
STEVE: Going out? Where?
TEMPLE: To Maidenhead.
STEVE: Why Maidenhead, for goodness' sake?
TEMPLE: I want you to take a look at a man called Max Burford.
FADE IN of incidental music.

42

FADE DOWN music.
FADE IN the sound of a car.
It is travelling along a country lane.
STEVE is driving.

STEVE: When did you last see this man – Burfield?

TEMPLE: Burford? I told you – it was several years ago.
          He was arrested for housebreaking and I was a
          witness.

STEVE: And you think it was Burford I saw at
          Downburgh?

TEMPLE: I've got a feeling it was. Your description
          certainly reminded me of him.

STEVE: You never said anything about Burford to the
          Inspector. I told him about the man on the cliff
          and the man in the shop and you said …

TEMPLE: The Inspector irritated me; besides, it's just a
          hunch, Steve, I'm not really sure.

STEVE: Supposing you're right; what are you going to
          do?

TEMPLE: Slow down, dear – this is a nasty bend.

The car slows down.

TEMPLE: If I'm right I want to know what he was doing in
          Downburgh; I want to know if he was a friend of
          Bob Gardner's.

STEVE: It was me he was interested in, Paul – not Bob
          Gardner. (*A slight pause*) What sort of a man is
          Burford?

TEMPLE: Well, the first time I met him I quite liked him.
          He seemed intelligent and amusing. Later he
          changed rather and became … faintly aggressive.
          When the case was over he completely lost
          control of himself and went for me, of all people.
          I don't know why. I was just a witness.

43

STEVE: What do you mean – he went for you? You mean, he threatened you?

TEMPLE: Yes.

STEVE: And you think that's why he went to Downburgh, because he wanted to …

TEMPLE: Darling, I don't know why he went to Downburgh, always assuming that he did.

STEVE: But it seems a long time to nurse a grievance, surely by now …

TEMPLE: (*Suddenly*) Here we are, Steve! Pull in on the right, dear!

The car slows down and turns off the country lane.

TEMPLE: That's it.

STEVE: Harper Brothers – is that the place?

TEMPLE: Yes.

STEVE: It's quite a nice looking building.

TEMPLE: Yes, if he owns this he's done very well for himself.

STEVE switches off the car engine.

STEVE: Is that the river at the bottom of the lane?

TEMPLE: Yes.

The car door opens.

TEMPLE: Stay here, Steve. I shan't be long.

STEVE: But I thought you wanted me to see him. After all, if I don't see him I shan't be able to tell you whether he was the man …

TEMPLE: Yes, I know, Steve, I know. But just wait in the car just now. I shan't be long.

FADE SCENE.

FADE UP background noises of a country lane.
As TEMPLE approaches the building there are the sounds of workshop activities. Background noises of a saw drill and general activity.

FADE UP of noise.

TEMPLE: (*Shouting above the roar*) Excuse me! I'm looking for Mr Burford.

NORMAN: (*Shouting back*) You'll find him in the drawing office, sir.

TEMPLE: Where is that?

NORMAN: Through the paint shop and first door on your left. Mind your coat as you go through, sir!

TEMPLE: Thank you.

Hold the factory noises.

TEMPLE reaches the door and knocks.

BURFORD: (*Calling from inside*) Come in!

The door opens and TEMPLE enters the office.

As he closes the door the factory noises FADE to the background.

BURFORD: (*An Irish accent; on the telephone; not recognising TEMPLE*) I'll be with you in just a minute. All right, Bert, change the gauge and have a word with Morgan about the veneer. Don't stand any nonsense – you know Morgan … Right, Bert – I leave it with you.

BURFORD replaces the receiver.

BURFORD: Sorry about that. Now, what can I do for you?

TEMPLE: (*Quietly*) I hope you can give me some information.

BURFORD: (*The Irish accent becoming more pronounced*) Information? What kind of … (*He stops dead; peers at TEMPLE*) I've seen you before somewhere …

TEMPLE: Yes, that's right. We met some time ago. Several years, in fact.

BURFORD: (*Remembering*) Good Lord! … You're Temple!

TEMPLE: Didn't you recognise me, Mr Burford?

BURFORD: No; no, my eyesight's pretty bad these days. I can hardly recognise … (*His manner changes; curt and unfriendly*) What is it? What do you want?

TEMPLE: I told you. I want some information.

BURFORD: Look, Temple, if you've come down here to poke your nose into my affairs I can tell you right now …

TEMPLE: I'm not interested in you or your affairs, Burford; providing, of course, you're not interested in me – or mine.

BURFORD: What do you mean by that?

TEMPLE: Last time we met you threatened to kill …

BURFORD: Look, that must be all of eight years ago and I was a damn fool. I made a mistake and I paid for it. So far as I'm concerned that's dead and buried.

TEMPLE: I hope you mean that.

BURFORD: Why shouldn't I mean it? Look, Temple, I've made no bones about the past. There isn't a man in this workshop who doesn't know who I am and what I am. I've built up a first-class business during the past three years; I've built it by working hard and being strictly honest. Now, I don't know why you came here this morning, but if you're out to make trouble for me I warn you …

TEMPLE: I'm not out to make trouble for anyone. Take the chip off your shoulder, Burford, and relax. (*A pause*) Now to start with, I went into that witness box because I'd no alternative; there was nothing personal about it.

BURFORD: I've told you, I'm no longer interested in what happened eight years ago!

TEMPLE: All right, tell me what happened – a week ago.
BURFORD: A week ago?
TEMPLE: Yes, in Downburgh.
BURFORD: Downburgh?
TEMPLE: Yes.
BURFORD: I've never been to Downburgh.
TEMPLE: You were there a week ago; unless I'm mistaken, my wife saw you there.
BURFORD: You're mistaken, Temple, and so's your wife!
TEMPLE: All right, Burford.
BURFORD: You don't believe me, do you? It's a pity you didn't bring your wife down here – we could have had another identity parade.
TEMPLE: My wife's outside, in the car.
Pause.
BURFORD: All right – let's have a word with Mrs Temple.
The door opens and we hear the noises of the workshop again.
FADE DOWN the noises of the workshop.

FADE UP the sound of a car radio.
TEMPLE and BURFORD arrive at the car.
TEMPLE: Hello, Steve!
STEVE: Oh, hello!
The radio is switched off.
TEMPLE: Steve, I want you to meet Mr Burford.
BURFORD: Good morning, Mrs Temple.
STEVE: Good morning.
TEMPLE: Steve, is Mr Burford the man you saw at Downburgh? The man you saw on the cliff, the morning you went for a walk?
A pause.
BURFORD: Well – am I, Mrs Temple?
Another pause.

47

STEVE: No.

TEMPLE: (*Surprised*) You're sure?

STEVE: Yes, I'm quite sure, Paul.

BURFORD: Thank you, Mrs Temple.

TEMPLE: Burford, I'm sorry.

BURFORD: There's nothing to be sorry about; mistakes happen. Is there anything else, Temple?

TEMPLE: No.

BURFORD: Well, if you'll excuse me, I've got rather a busy morning. Goodbye, Mrs Temple.

STEVE: Goodbye.

BURFORD walks away.

TEMPLE: (*Calling after BURFORD*) Burford! Wait a minute!

TEMPLE joins BURFORD.

BURFORD: Yes, what is it?

TEMPLE: Look, Burford, don't get any silly ideas – about this morning, I mean. I was simply making a routine inquiry and … Well, what I'm trying to say is, forget this morning – don't let it worry you.

BURFORD: I won't. Apparently I've other worries, Mr Temple. Goodbye.

TEMPLE: Goodbye, Burford – and good luck.

BURFORD: (*Walking towards the factory*) Thank you.

A pause.

TEMPLE returns to STEVE.

STEVE: Well, I don't think much of your hunches!

TEMPLE: What do you mean – you don't think much of them?

STEVE laughs.

TEMPLE: Move over, Steve. I'll drive.

STEVE: No, it's all right, I'll drive.

TEMPLE: Steve, move over!

STEVE: Now, it's no good being irritable.

TEMPLE: I'm not irritable – I'm not the least irritable.

STEVE: (*Laughing*) Jump in!

TEMPLE gets into the car.

STEVE: Well – where do we go from here?

TEMPLE: We'd better have some lunch. There's a hotel
            just round the corner.

STEVE presses the starter.

STEVE: Yes, all right.

TEMPLE: Steve, you're sure it wasn't Burford you saw at
            Downburgh?

STEVE: I'm positive, darling. He looked very much like
            Burford; he wore the same sort of glasses and he
            had the same rather peculiar way of looking at
            you, but it – wasn't Burford.

TEMPLE: You're sure?

STEVE: Yes, I'm sure.

STEVE starts to laugh.

TEMPLE: What are you laughing at?

STEVE: (*Amused*) Oh, nothing.

TEMPLE: Steve, what are you laughing it?

STEVE: I was just thinking. I've rather enjoyed this
            morning. It isn't often you make mistakes, is it,
            dear?

TEMPLE: Lunch!

STEVE laughs again.

*FADE UP the sound of STEVE laughing and the car being
driven back to the country lane.*

FADE DOWN.

*FADE IN the noise of a fairly crowded restaurant in a
country hotel.*

*TEMPLE and STEVE are shown to a table by an elderly
WAITER.*

49

WAITER: I'm afraid this is the only table we've got, sir. We're very crowded today.

STEVE: It's a very nice table; thank you very much.

TEMPLE: My wife adores eating in the dark.

WAITER: Would you care for the wine list, sir?

TEMPLE: By all means; the wine list and a torch.

STEVE: Paul, please. (*Sitting down*) Oh dear, this chair isn't very comfortable.

TEMPLE: Would you like to sit here, Steve? There's a superb view of the kitchen.

STEVE: Paul, there's someone waving to you.

TEMPLE: It's probably the chef.

STEVE: No, darling, I mean the young man standing over there … Oh, he's coming over.

BRIAN DEXTER arrives at the table.

DEXTER: Hello, Mr Temple! This is a surprise. Are you lunching here?

TEMPLE: Eventually. Oh, I beg your pardon – I don't think you know my wife. Brian Dexter.

DEXTER: How do you do, Mrs Temple?

STEVE: How do you do?

TEMPLE: What are you doing in this part of the world, Dexter?

DEXTER: Oh, I'm frequently down here. I'm interested in a publishing firm at Henley.

TEMPLE: I see.

DEXTER: I suppose there isn't any news – about Sylvia, I mean?

TEMPLE: No, I'm afraid not.

DEXTER: Inspector Vosper phoned me this morning. My word, he was pretty angry. I suppose you told him about the dance hall?

TEMPLE: I told Sir Graham; I had to.

DEXTER: Yes, of course. You know, I didn't take this thing very seriously at first. It seemed to me that Sylvia had simply tootled off somewhere and was probably staying with some aunt or other. Now, I'm not so sure.

STEVE: Why aren't you so sure, Mr Dexter?

DEXTER: Well, the police are making such a devil of a fuss. They've questioned me twice and this morning I heard they'd been making inquiries about me from a chap I was at Oxford with. I mean, they don't go to those lengths unless they're pretty worried.

TEMPLE: They're pretty worried, Dexter.

DEXTER: Well, let's hope there's some news fairly soon. Goodbye, Mrs Temple.

STEVE: Goodbye.

TEMPLE: (*Stopping DEXTER*) Oh, Dexter! When I saw you last night I think you told me that you first met Sylvia in Switzerland.

DEXTER: That's right, at the winter sports.

TEMPLE: Where were you staying – St Moritz?

DEXTER: Good Lord, no! That's not my cup of tea. I was at Zermatt.

TEMPLE: And Sir Carlton and Lady Ross were at the same hotel?

DEXTER: That's right; I told you. That's how I met Sylvia. (*A little laugh*) It was funny really. I never dreamt her father was the head of M.I.5. One night I made a complete ass of myself. Talked about our incompetent secret service. The old boy must have been highly amused.

TEMPLE: What was the name of the hotel, do you remember?

DEXTER: Where we were staying you mean?

TEMPLE: Yes.

DEXTER: Of course I remember. It was the Schweizerhof. Why do you ask?

TEMPLE: I wondered, that's all. Ah, here's the waiter!

DEXTER: Well – goodbye, Mrs Temple. I hope we shall meet again.

STEVE: I hope so, too.

TEMPLE: Goodbye, Dexter.

DEXTER: Goodbye, sir.

A pause.

STEVE: (*When DEXTER is out of hearing*) That's an extraordinary coincidence!

TEMPLE: What is?

STEVE: The fact that he met Sylvia Ross at Zermatt and they were both staying at the Schweizerhof hotel.

TEMPLE: Yes; it's also quite a coincidence that we should find Dexter within half a mile of Max Burford. Steve, I know I've asked you this before; you're quite sure about Burford, aren't you?

STEVE: Quite sure, Paul. He wasn't the man I saw at Downburgh. The man looked like him; very much like him – but it wasn't Burford.

TEMPLE: All right, Steve.

STEVE: In future, leave the hunches to me, dear.

TEMPLE: Some of your hunches aren't so hot! Why, I remember …

WAITER: Excuse me, sir, is that your car outside, the Bentley?

TEMPLE: Yes.

WAITER: I wonder if you would mind moving it, sir? The gentleman you were talking to won't be able to get his car out; he's hemmed in.

TEMPLE: Yes, of course.

STEVE: (*Rising*) It's all right, Paul. I'll do it. I've got the key. You order the lunch. Nothing to start with for me, dear.

START FADE.

WAITER: Would you like the wine list, sir?

TEMPLE: I should prefer the menu.

COMPLETE FADE.

FADE IN the sound of a car engine ticking over.

STEVE arrives.

DEXTER: Oh, I didn't realise it was your car, Mrs Temple!

STEVE: I'm sorry. I'm afraid I'm always doing this sort of thing.

DEXTER: If you unlock it, we can release the brake and I can push it back.

A pause.

STEVE: (*She has been looking at DEXTER's car*) I beg your pardon?

DEXTER: I said: if you unlock it, we can release the brake and push it back.

STEVE: No, no, it's quite all right. I'd better move it in case someone else wants to park here.

DEXTER: All right. I'll move forward a bit.

STEVE: Thank you.

DEXTER accelerates and his car moves forward slightly.

FADE OUT the noise of the car.

FADE IN TEMPLE speaking.

TEMPLE: By Timothy, Steve, I thought you were never coming!

STEVE: I'm sorry; it took rather longer than I thought.

TEMPLE: I've ordered you the Plat du Jour!

STEVE: (*Her thoughts elsewhere*) Yes, all right, Paul.

TEMPLE: Well, don't you want to know what it is?

STEVE: M'm?

TEMPLE: I said, don't you want to … Steve, is anything wrong?

STEVE: No, darling, why?

TEMPLE: You look miles away. Did Dexter say anything to you?

STEVE: No, no, he just moved his car.

TEMPLE: What did you make of him?

STEVE: Who?

TEMPLE: Dexter, Steve. Dexter

STEVE: Oh, he seems quite a pleasant young man. What did you say you'd ordered?

TEMPLE: The Plat du Jour, dear. That's French for …

WAITER: Steak and kidney pie, sir.

TEMPLE: Oh. Oh, thank you very much.

FADE IN of incidental music.

FADE DOWN music.

We hear the sound of a key in a lock, followed by the opening of a door.

The door closes.

CHARLIE: Oh, hello. I didn't expect you back this early, sir.

TEMPLE: We rang the bell, Charlie.

CHARLIE: Did you, sir?

STEVE: Any messages, Charlie?

CHARLIE: Yes – Miss Gardner telephoned about ten minutes ago. She said she wouldn't be able to see you this afternoon, Mrs Temple. She's catching an early train.

STEVE: Is that all she said?

CHARLIE: Yes.

TEMPLE: All right, Charlie.

STEVE: There's nothing else – no letters or telegrams or anything?

CHARLIE: No – would you like some tea, Mrs Temple?

STEVE: Yes. Yes, I think we would. We'll have it in the drawing room.

TEMPLE and STEVE enter the drawing room.

TEMPLE: Are you expecting a telegram, Steve?

STEVE: (*Innocently*) Me?

TEMPLE: Yes, you.

STEVE: No. No, of course not.

In the background the door bell rings.

TEMPLE: You know, it's a curious thing, but all the way back from Maidenhead you've acted like someone with …

STEVE: Is that the front door bell?

TEMPLE: If it is, Charlie can answer it.

STEVE opens the drawing room door.

STEVE: (*Calling*) It's the front door, Charlie!

TEMPLE: What is it? What's come over you, Steve?

STEVE: (*A shade too pleasant*) What do you mean, dear?

TEMPLE: You know perfectly well what I mean! All the way back from Maidenhead you've behaved as if …

STEVE: (*Determined to change the subject*) Paul, you're grumpy You've been grumpy the whole afternoon.

TEMPLE: I haven't been anything of the sort!

STEVE: You're annoyed because you made a mistake about Burford. It was a perfectly natural mistake, darling.

TEMPLE: Look, Steve, I am not annoyed because I made a mistake about … What is it, Charlie?

CHARLIE: Excuse me, sir – there's a telegram for you.

STEVE: I'll take it, Charlie!

TEMPLE: (*Stopping STEVE*) It's all right, Steve – It's for me! I'll take it.

TEMPLE takes the telegram from CHARLIE.

A pause.

TEMPLE opens the telegram.

TEMPLE: There's no reply.

CHARLIE: Thank you, sir.

CHARLIE goes out.

The door closes.

STEVE: May I – see it, Paul?

TEMPLE: What the devil does this mean, Steve?

STEVE: I don't know, darling. I haven't seen it.

TEMPLE: It's from Inspector Ivor at Downburgh. He says: "Thanks for telegram …" I didn't send him a telegram!

STEVE: Go on, finish it!

TEMPLE: "Thanks for telegram. Stop. Salty West left here two days ago. Stop. Regards. Ivor."

STEVE: Then I was right! I knew jolly well I was right!

TEMPLE: Steve, what is this?

STEVE: Paul, listen! You know when I moved the car so that Dexter could get out of the car park?

TEMPLE: Yes, yes …

STEVE: Well, there was a car next to Dexter's – a huge Rolls – and sitting in the front seat on his own was a spruce, clean shaven, smartly dressed little man …

TEMPLE: Well?

STEVE: Well, I was under the impression I'd seen him before somewhere.

TEMPLE: Well, go on.

STEVE: While Dexter had his back turned, the little man caught me looking at him and he …

TEMPLE: He what?

A pause.

STEVE: He winked.

TEMPLE: He winked?

STEVE: (*Very seriously*) Yes.

A pause.

TEMPLE starts to laugh.

STEVE: No, Paul, I'm not joking. I'm serious. Do you know who it was? (*Pause*) It was Salty West.

TEMPLE: Salty West?

STEVE: Yes.

TEMPLE: Steve, now I ask you! What would Salty West be doing sitting in a Rolls Royce at Maidenhead?

STEVE: There you are, you see! I know you wouldn't believe me! I knew you'd ridicule me! That's why I sent Inspector Ivor the telegram!

TEMPLE: What did you put in the telegram?

STEVE: I simply said: "Is Salty West still in Downburgh? Paul Temple."

A slight pause.

TEMPLE: When did you see Salty West?

STEVE: I saw him several times while we were in Downburgh. He was nearly always down at the quay.

TEMPLE: Did you ever speak to him?

STEVE: Yes, we always said "good morning" to each other. I very nearly arranged for us to go out with him instead of Bob Gardner.

TEMPLE: But, Steve, from what you've told me – the man you saw – the man in the Rolls – looked very different from Salty.

STEVE: Of course he did! Salty always wore dirty trousers and a black sweater and he looked as if he hadn't shaved for a week. The little man I'm telling you about was as smart as a band-box – but it was Salty West!

TEMPLE: You're sure?

STEVE: I'm absolutely sure!

TEMPLE: It's a pity you didn't tell me about this at the time, Steve.

STEVE: And what would you have said?

TEMPLE: I shouldn't have said anything but I'd have made a note of the car number.

STEVE: Well, I made a note of it. It was UPF – four eight five.

TEMPLE: Oh!

STEVE: I'm not quite so stupid as I look, darling. (*A pause*) Paul, don't you believe me? Don't forget Salty was with Bob Gardner when the accident happened – if it was an accident.

TEMPLE: Yes, I know. I hadn't forgotten that. (*He looks at the telegram*) "Salty West left here two days ago" …

STEVE: What are you thinking?

TEMPLE: (*Quite seriously*) I was just wondering why he winked …

FADE IN incidental music.

FADE DOWN the music.
FADE IN the sound of TEMPLE snoring.
TEMPLE and STEVE are in bed.
A pause.
The telephone rings.
It continues to ring.
STEVE wakes up with a start.

STEVE: Paul! Paul!

TEMPLE: (*Sleepily*) M'm?

STEVE: The telephone!

TEMPLE: What?

STEVE: The telephone!

TEMPLE: Oh …

TEMPLE stretches out and picks up the receiver.

TEMPLE: Hello? … Yes? … What? … Yes, speaking … I'm sorry I can't hear you, can you speak a little … That's better …

STEVE: Who is it?

TEMPLE: (*Not quite so sleepy now*) Yes … Yes, I'm listening … Tonight? … Isn't it rather late, it's a quarter past two … Well, you may not think so, but I do … Can't you tell me over the phone? … I see. All right, Teako – give me the address …

STEVE: I've got the pad, darling …

TEMPLE: (*On the phone*) Yes … What? … Sixteen – what's that? … Sixteen, Darlington … Oh, Barrington … Sixteen, Barrington Mews … Yes, I know it, it's in Kensington … All right, Teako – in about an hour.

TEMPLE replaces the receiver.

TEMPLE: That was Johnny Teako – he wants to see me.

STEVE: Tonight?

TEMPLE: Yes.

STEVE: But why on earth tonight?

TEMPLE: He says it's urgent; apparently it's about Sylvia Ross.

STEVE: But it's a quarter past two!

TEMPLE: That doesn't mean anything to characters like Johnny Teako. I doubt whether he ever gets to bed much before four.

STEVE: Paul, do you think he's found out?

TEMPLE: Found out – what about?

STEVE: About his wife. Do you think he knows she spoke to us at the dance hall?

TEMPLE: It's possible.

STEVE: What did he say, exactly?

TEMPLE: He simply said, "I've got to see you, Mr Temple
            – I want to talk to you about Sylvia Ross."
STEVE: Paul, why don't you ring Sir Graham?
TEMPLE: It's very late, Steve, and –
STEVE: Paul, please! Go on, darling. You ring Sir
            Graham and I'll tell Charlie to get the car.

A pause.
TEMPLE: All right, Steve.
TEMPLE picks up the telephone and starts to dial.
FADE OUT on the dialling.

FADE UP the sound of a key in a lock.
A front door opens and closes.
FORBES: Hello, Carson! I didn't expect to find you up!
CARSON: I came down to answer the telephone, Sir
            Graham. May I take your coat?
FORBES: Thank you.
They pass into the drawing room.
CARSON: I trust it was a pleasant dinner, sir?
FORBES: I'm afraid it wasn't, Carson. The dinner was too
            short and the speeches too long.
CARSON: Oh dear, sir. Not an ideal combination.
FORBES: Well since you're up you can mix me a nightcap.
CARSON: What would you like, sir – a whisky and soda?
FORBES: Please. (*Casually*) Who was it in the telephone?
CARSON: Mr Temple, sir. He asked me to tell you that he'd
            just received a call from Johnny Teako.
FORBES: From Johnny Teako?
CARSON: Yes; I understand it was an urgent call, sir. He's
            meeting him at sixteen, Barrington Mews. Mr
            Temple particularly asked me to tell you that, sir.
FORBES: Barrington Mews? That's in Kensington.
CARSON: That's right, sir. Curiously enough I worked in
            Barrington Mews for four years – Lady

Derbyshire's. Number ten. I don't remember a number sixteen, sir.

FORBES: You don't?

CARSON: No, sir.

START FADE.

FORBES: Never mind the drink, Carson. Get my coat ...

COMPLETE FADE.

FADE IN the sound of TEMPLE's car.

It draws to a standstill.

The car doors open and close.

STEVE: Are you sure this is it, Paul?

TEMPLE: Yes, this is it. Look – Barrington Mews ...

STEVE: It's terribly dark; it's a good job you brought the torch.

TEMPLE and STEVE are walking on the cobbles of the mews courtyard.

TEMPLE: I don't know why the devil you came, Steve – you'd be far better off in bed.

STEVE: And miss the opportunity of meeting Mr Teako! I'll bet he's got the most ravishing dressing gown!

TEMPLE: Yes, with pictures of himself all over it.

A slight pause.

STEVE: Did you leave a message for Sir Graham?

TEMPLE: Yes, they said they were expecting him back at any moment. (*Hesitating*) I say, that's funny ... This house is number three ... Let's see what's on the other side ...

TEMPLE and STEVE cross the courtyard to the other side of the mews.

STEVE: This is number five.

TEMPLE: There aren't sixteen houses down here, there can't be ...

STEVE: Well, perhaps they're not numbered
           consecutively …
TEMPLE: That wouldn't make any difference. Let's walk
           to the end, Steve.

A pause.

The footsteps continue.

TEMPLE: … This is number nine … and that's eight on the
           other side. There isn't a sixteen …
STEVE: It's always the same in a mews, you can never
           find the number you want. We shall probably
           find sixteen sandwiched between number four
           and …
MARY: (*Interrupting STEVE; she is calling to them from
           the other end of the mews; a note of desperation
           in her voice*) Mr Temple! Mr Temple!
STEVE: Who's that?
MARY: (*From the background*) Mr Temple! Where are
           you?
STEVE: Paul, it's Mary Gardner!

*In the background the sound of a car approaching the mews
is heard.*

MARY: (*Anxiously*) Mr Temple, are you there?
STEVE: Paul, you've put the torch out, she can't see us!
TEMPLE: Stay where you are, Steve! Don't move!
MARY: Mr Temple!

*In the background the car passes the corner of the mews and
as it does so there is the sound of revolver shots.*

MARY screams.

The car gathers speed and FADES AWAY.

FADE on the sound of the car.

*FADE UP on MARY. She has been hit by the bullets and is in
obvious pain.*

TEMPLE and STEVE are breathless, having run from the other end of the mews.

STEVE: Paul, is she badly hurt?

TEMPLE: Steve, wait here! Stay with her … There's a phone box on the corner. I'm going to ring for an ambulance …

STEVE: Paul!

TEMPLE: What is it?

STEVE: She's wearing my coat! They thought it was me …

FADE UP closing music.

END OF EPISODE TWO

EPISODE THREE

THE HANDBAG

OPEN TO: *The sound of a car passing the corner of the mews and as it does so there is the sound of revolver shots.*
MARY screams.
The car gathers speed and FADES AWAY.
FADE on the sound of the car.

FADE UP on MARY. She has been hit by the bullets and is in obvious pain.
TEMPLE and STEVE are breathless, having run from the other end of the mews.

STEVE: Paul, is she badly hurt?

TEMPLE: Steve, wait here! Stay with her … There's a phone box on the corner. I'm going to ring for an ambulance …

STEVE: Paul!

TEMPLE: What is it?

STEVE: She's wearing my coat! They thought it was me …

TEMPLE: Don't be silly! It's just a coincidence.

STEVE: It isn't, Paul. You know it isn't!

We hear the sound of a car arriving at the mews. It brakes to a standstill.

TEMPLE: Here's Sir Graham. Stay here, I'll be with you in a moment.

The car doors open and close.
There is a background of noises.

MARY: (*Suddenly tries to speak but she is in great pain*) Mrs Temple – I – listen, please –

STEVE: Yes, Mary – yes, I'm listening …

FADE TO TEMPLE meeting FORBES at the entrance to the mews.

FORBES: What's happened, Temple?

TEMPLE: It's Mary Gardner – Bob Gardner's sister – she's been shot. We need an ambulance, Sir Graham!

FORBES: Right! (*Turning*) Vosper, get an ambulance here
            – straight away!
VOSPER: (*In the near background*) Yes, sir!
FADE the background of voices.
MARY: (*She is still trying to speak to STEVE*) Mrs
            Temple, I want … I want to tell you …
            something …
STEVE: It's all right, Mary. We've sent for a doctor, he
            won't be long now.
MARY: Mrs Temple, please listen to me …
STEVE: Yes, I'm listening, Mary, what is it?
MARY: (*With an effort*) Watch your handbag … Don't
            leave it, Mrs Temple … Watch … your …
            handbag …
STEVE: I haven't got a handbag, Mary. I didn't bring one
            with me.
MARY is unable to reply.
FORBES and TEMPLE join STEVE.
TEMPLE: What is it, Steve?
FORBES: Was she trying to say something?
STEVE: Yes, she said something about my handbag …
            She said: "Watch your handbag, Mrs Temple …"
TEMPLE: Where is your bag?
STEVE: I haven't got one, Paul. I didn't bring one with
            me.
TEMPLE: Are you sure?
STEVE: Yes, of course.
TEMPLE: Then why should she mention your handbag?
            That's very odd.
START FADE.
FORBES: The poor girl's delirious.
COMPLETE FADE.

FADE IN the sound of coffee cups and the pouring of coffee.
In the background a clock chimes the hour: five o'clock.

STEVE: Would you like some more coffee, Sir Graham?

FORBES: (*Sounding tired*) No, not for me, thank you, Steve. (*Looking at his watch*) I make it ten to five, is that clock fast?

TEMPLE: Yes, about six minutes.

STEVE: (*Yawning*) Oh dear, I'm tired.

TEMPLE: There's no reason for you to sit up, darling. I should go to bed.

FORBES: Vosper ought to have been here hours ago.

TEMPLE: He's probably staying at the hospital.

FORBES: I told him to leave someone there and report straight back here.

STEVE: Coffee, Paul?

TEMPLE: No, thank you, dear.

Pause.

FORBES: Temple, you're sure it was Teako on the telephone?

TEMPLE: Well, he said it was Teako and it sounded exactly like him.

FORBES: M'm. When you questioned him about the note did he admit that he knew Sylvia Ross?

TEMPLE: No; he simply said he remembered her; he also remembered Dexter, apparently he'd seen a photograph of him in The Tatler. (*Pause*) Sir Graham, did you make inquiries about the name that was on the note – Clive Lawrence?

FORBES: Yes, of course. I've been through to the Swiss people; they're contacting the Schweizerhof Hotel.

STEVE: (*Stifling a yawn*) Paul, I'm taking your advice and going to bed.

TEMPLE: Yes, all right, dear. I'll be up shortly.

STEVE: Good night, Sir Graham – or good morning – or whatever it is.

FORBES: Good night, Steve.

The door opens and closes.

TEMPLE: Cigarette, Sir Graham?

FORBES: Thank you, Temple.

They light cigarettes.

FORBES: I gather you saw Max Burford?

TEMPLE: Yes; I saw him this morning, or rather yesterday morning – but I was wrong about him. He's never been to Downburgh.

FORBES: Well, what made you suspect him in the first place?

TEMPLE: Steve's description. She said the man was about my height, wore bi-focal glasses, and had an Irish accent.

FORBES: That certainly sounds like Burford.

TEMPLE: That's what I thought, but I was wrong. (*Taking a diary from his pocket*) Sir Graham, I've got a car registration number here, do you think you could get one of your people to check it for me?

FORBES: Yes, of course.

TEMPLE: It's UPF 485.

FORBES: (*Taking a note*) UPF 485 …

TEMPLE: Yes; it's a Rolls. I'd like to know who the car belongs to.

FORBES: Is it urgent?

TEMPLE: I'd like to know as soon as possible.

FORBES: It isn't the car that drove past the mews; the one that Mary Gardner …?

TEMPLE: No, no, no, it was parked outside a hotel at Maidenhead. There was someone in the car and Steve was under the impression it was someone she'd seen at Downburgh – an old boy called Salty West.

There is a knock on the door and CHARLIE enters with INSPECTOR VOSPER.

FORBES: Salty West?

TEMPLE: Yes, apparently …

CHARLIE: Inspector Vosper's here, sir.

TEMPLE: Oh, come in, Vosper! That's all right, Charlie.

CHARLIE: Thank you, sir.

VOSPER: I'm sorry to have been so long, Sir Graham. I didn't leave the hospital until three o'clock and then …

TEMPLE: How is Miss Gardner?

VOSPER: Not too good, I'm afraid. She was still unconscious when I left, sir.

FORBES: If you left the hospital at three where on earth have you been, Vosper? It's nearly five o'clock.

VOSPER: I've been having a talk with a friend of Mr Temple's.

TEMPLE: A friend of mine?

VOSPER: Yes – Johnny Teako.

FORBES: Where did you find Teako?

VOSPER: Well, I finally ran him to earth at a rehearsal room in Baker Street.

FORBES: What, at this hour of the morning?

VOSPER: Those boys never go to sleep, sir.

TEMPLE: Did you ask him about the telephone call?

VOSPER: Yes, of course.

TEMPLE: Well, what did he say?

VOSPER: Let me tell you what happened, Mr Temple. The night watchman at the Palais de Danse told me about the rehearsal room. I had difficulty in finding it though, because the address he gave me was Baker Street and the actual entrance was

71

in an alley off Consort Road. However, I arrived there at about a quarter to four and the first person I saw was a dark, rather good-looking girl …

During the preceding speech FADE IN dance music: a rehearsal of a dance orchestra.

VOSPER: Excuse me. I'm looking for Johnny Teako.

LINDA: I'm Mrs Teako. Can I help you?

VOSPER: Is that your husband, Mrs Teako – on the platform?

LINDA: Yes. (*Stopping VOSPER*) No, wait a minute – please! What is it you want to see my husband about?

VOSPER: It's purely a private matter.

LINDA: Have you written a song?

VOSPER: No …

LINDA: Because if you have …

VOSPER: I haven't written a song, Mrs Teako. My name is Vosper – Detective Inspector Vosper.

LINDA: Oh. Oh, one moment, please.

Pause.

TEAKO: Okay, break it up! Break it up! I've heard some pretty dicey noises in my time but – (*Annoyed*) What is it, Linda?

LINDA: There's someone to see you, Johnny.

TEAKO: (*Angrily*) What do you mean – someone to see me?

LINDA: It's a police Inspector …

TEAKO: Well, where is he? Why doesn't someone put some lights on in this place?

VOSPER: Mr Teako? Can I have a word with you, sir? I'm Detective Inspector Vosper.

TEAKO: Oh, there you are! You must be the original invisible man!

VOSPER:	Not the original one.
TEAKO:	Well, what can I do for you?
VOSPER:	You seem to be a glutton for work, Mr Teako.
TEAKO:	Sure.
VOSPER:	Do you usually rehearse all night?
TEAKO:	When we've an early morning broadcast we do.
LINDA:	What is it you want, Inspector?
TEAKO:	Take it easy, Linda. Let the guy get round to it. He's doing a nice build up.
VOSPER:	I wanted to ask you a question.
TEAKO:	Well, go ahead.
VOSPER:	Why didn't you keep your appointment with Mr Temple?
TEAKO:	What appointment?
VOSPER:	The one you made by telephone.
TEAKO:	What is this? Do you know what he's talking about, Linda?
LINDA:	No.
VOSPER:	You telephoned Mr Temple and said you had something to tell him about a girl called Sylvia Ross. You arranged to meet him at a house in Kensington.
TEAKO:	I did?
VOSPER:	Yes.
TEAKO:	Who told you that?
VOSPER:	Mr Temple did.
TEAKO:	Why, the guy's nuts!
VOSPER:	You deny it?
TEAKO:	Of course I deny it! In the first place I've never heard of a girl called Sylvia Ross and in the second place ...
VOSPER:	I'm afraid that's not strictly true. You told Mr Temple that Miss Ross handed you a note asking you to play ...

TEAKO:	Oh, was that the kid? There seems to be an awful lot of fuss over that youngster! Who is she anyway – and what's happened to her?
VOSPER:	We don't know what's happened to her.
LINDA:	You mean – she's disappeared?
VOSPER:	Yes, Mrs Teako, she's disappeared.
TEAKO:	So what? Kids disappear every day. They get tired of the old man, or the old woman, or the boyfriend, or …
LINDA:	Wait a minute, Johnny! You say Mr Temple told you that my husband phoned him …
VOSPER:	Your husband telephoned him and said he had some information about Sylvia Ross. He asked Mr Temple to meet him at an address in Kensington – sixteen, Barrington Mews. Temple kept the appointment but …
TEAKO:	But I didn't! You bet I didn't! I know nothing about it – for the simple reason that I didn't phone Mr Temple or anyone else!
VOSPER:	Temple says you did, Teako.
TEAKO:	Okay, it's his word against mine.
LINDA:	What time was this phone call made, Inspector?
VOSPER:	I should imagine about a quarter to two. Where were you at a quarter to two, Mr Teako?
TEAKO:	Well, I wasn't playing canasta!
LINDA:	Johnny …
TEAKO:	I was in a taxi travelling to this God-forsaken place.
VOSPER:	Was anyone with you?
TEAKO:	Sure. There were five of us – not counting Linda.
VOSPER:	Where did you pick the taxi up?
TEAKO:	I didn't pick it up; it picked me up at the Palais.
LINDA:	Inspector, what happened at Barrington Mews?

VOSPER: Well, Mr Temple kept the appointment and while he was looking for number sixteen a girl called Mary Gardner turned up.

TEAKO: (*Without thinking*) Mary Gardner!

VOSPER: Yes; you've heard of Miss Gardner, Mr Teako?

TEAKO: No, no, I just wondered what she …

LINDA: Who's Mary Gardner?

VOSPER: She's a girl Mr and Mrs Temple met while they were staying at Downburgh.

LINDA: Well, what was she doing at Barrington Mews?

VOSPER: Your guess is as good as mine, Mrs Teako.

LINDA: But didn't she tell you – or Mr Temple – what she was doing there?

VOSPER: Unfortunately she didn't have an opportunity – she was shot.

TEAKO: What!

VOSPER: Yes.

TEAKO: (*Apparently perturbed*) You mean someone deliberately …

LINDA: How dreadful! But what happened, Inspector?

ED: (*Calling from the background*) Johnny, when are we going to start again? Is this a rehearsal or a vacation?

TEAKO: I'll be with you in a moment, Ed! Go on, Inspector – what happened to Mary Gardner?

In the background a piano starts.

VOSPER: Well, a car came round the corner just as she entered the mews; someone fired from the car and Miss Gardner was hit.

LINDA: Was she killed?

VOSPER: No, but I'm afraid it's very serious. (*Closing the subject*) However, this obviously doesn't concern you if you don't know Miss Gardner and you didn't phone Mr Temple –

75

TEAKO: I certainly didn't make that phone call, Inspector.

VOSPER: I see. Well, thank you. I'm sorry to have interrupted your rehearsal.

FADE ON the piano being played in the background.

FADE UP of VOSPER speaking.

VOSPER: … It was about a quarter to five when I left Baker Street. I came straight here.

TEMPLE: Well, your experience of Mrs Teako seems to have been a very different one from mine, Inspector.

VOSPER: How do you mean?

TEMPLE: Well, the night I saw her she seemed tense and worried and – quite frankly, scared to death of her husband.

VOSPER: Yes, I can understand anyone thinking that.

TEMPLE: But that's not what you think?

VOSPER: No. I think Teako talks loud and acts loud – but she's the brains of the outfit.

TEMPLE: Well, you may be right, Inspector.

FORBES: But what about Teako himself, do you think he was telling the truth?

VOSPER: Not about Mary Gardner. It's obvious they both know her; on the other hand I do think he was telling the truth about the phone call.

TEMPLE: I'm inclined to agree with you, Inspector.

The telephone rings.

FORBES: Well, if Teako didn't phone you, Temple – who did?

TEMPLE: Excuse me.

TEMPLE lifts the receiver.

TEMPLE: (*On the phone*) Hello?

BELL: (*On the other end of the line*) Mr Temple?

TEMPLE: Yes.

BELL: This is Sergeant Bell, sir. I'm speaking from St Matthew's Hospital.

TEMPLE: Yes, Sergeant?

BELL: Would you deliver a message to Inspector Vosper, sir?

TEMPLE: Yes, certainly.

BELL: I'm afraid it's bad news, sir. Miss Gardner died ten minutes ago.

TEMPLE: Oh. Thank you, Sergeant. I'll tell the Inspector.

BELL: Very good, sir.

TEMPLE: Did she regain consciousness?

BELL: Only for a few moments, sir. She said something, but I'm afraid it didn't make sense.

TEMPLE: What did she say, Sergeant?

BELL: (*Puzzled*) It was something about … Mrs Temple's handbag, sir …

FADE UP incidental music.

FADE DOWN the music.
FADE IN TEMPLE speaking.

TEMPLE: Where's my dressing gown, Steve?

STEVE: (*Rather sleepily*) It's on the bed … Paul, I just can't imagine what Mary Gardner was referring to. I didn't take a handbag out with me.

TEMPLE: She said: "Watch your handbag …"

STEVE: "Watch your handbag … Don't lose it, Mrs Temple."

TEMPLE: Steve, how many handbags have you got?

STEVE: Oh dear! Here we go!

TEMPLE: No, seriously, Steve.

STEVE: Well, I've got about six or seven altogether but there are two I use fairly regularly.

TEMPLE: Where are they?

STEVE: They're in this drawer.

STEVE opens a drawer.

A slight pause.

TEMPLE: That's the black one …

STEVE: Yes, that's the one you bought me when we had the row about …

TEMPLE: Yes, I remember, darling.

STEVE: I use that more than any of the others.

TEMPLE: Is that the one you took to Downburgh?

STEVE: Yes.

TEMPLE: So if Mary Gardner was referring to a particular handbag she was probably referring to this one?

STEVE: I suppose so. I doubt if she's ever seen any of the others.

TEMPLE: Open it, Steve.

STEVE opens the handbag.

TEMPLE: Is there anything missing?

STEVE: (*Looking in the bag*) Lipstick, mirror, hanky … No, everything's here. I expect Sir Graham was right, Paul.

TEMPLE: What do you mean?

STEVE: The poor girl was delirious. She didn't know what she was saying.

TEMPLE: She knew what she was saying all right.

STEVE: (*Yawning*) Put the light out, Paul, and come to bed. It's after half past five.

TEMPLE: Yes, all right.

STEVE: Have you told Charlie not to call us?

TEMPLE: M'm?

STEVE: (*Sleepily*) I said, have you told Charlie not to call us?

TEMPLE: (*His thoughts elsewhere*) Yes, I've told Charlie.

FADE IN incidental music.

FADE music.

A door opens.

CHARLIE: I've brought you some more toast, sir.

TEMPLE: (*As he finishes drinking*) Oh, thank you, Charlie. Is Mrs Temple awake yet?

CHARLIE: No, sir, I don't think so. Shall I make her a cup of tea?

The telephone rings.

TEMPLE: No, you'd better wait until she rings. It's all right, I'll answer it.

TEMPLE lifts the receiver.

TEMPLE: (*On the phone*) Hello?

VOSPER: (*On the other end of the line*) Mr Temple?

TEMPLE: Speaking.

VOSPER: This is Vosper.

TEMPLE: Good morning, Inspector! What can I do for you?

VOSPER: I understand from Sir Graham you're interested in a certain registration number …

TEMPLE: UPF 485?

VOSPER: That's right.

TEMPLE: Well?

VOSPER: It's a Rolls Royce.

TEMPLE: Yes, I know that, Vosper.

VOSPER: It belongs to a Mr de Silva.

TEMPLE: Mr de Silva?

VOSPER: Yes – Ernest de Silva. He's an eye specialist; he's got rooms in Harley Street.

TEMPLE: Do you know him?

VOSPER: No, but he's got a very good reputation – as an eye specialist.

TEMPLE: I see. Well, thank you, Vosper.

VOSPER: Not at all. Goodbye.

TEMPLE: Goodbye.

TEMPLE replaces the receiver.

TEMPLE: Charlie …
START FADE.
CHARLIE: Yes, sir?
TEMPLE: I want the telephone directory – A to D.
CHARLIE: Very good, sir.
COMPLETE FADE.

FADE IN ERNEST de SILVA speaking.
DE SILVA: (*He is in his late fifties; well spoken, a faintly precise manner; the suggestion of a foreign accent*) … And see that Dr Walters gets the report by four o'clock; if it doesn't reach the hospital by four there's no point in sending it.
NURSE: Yes, Mr de Silva.
De SILVA is turning the pages of a diary.
DE SILVA: Now let me see; I've got Lady Merson at eleven o'clock, Mr Carruthers at eleven-thirty, Lord Handleford at twelve-fifteen …
NURSE: And there's a Mr Temple, sir – he telephoned this morning.
DE SILVA: Mr Temple?
NURSE: Yes, sir.
DE SILVA: Is he from Dr Rogers?
NURSE: I don't think so, sir. He said it was a private matter but rather urgent.
DE SILVA: Temple? The name's familiar.
NURSE: It's Mr Paul Temple, sir.
DE SILVA: Is he here?
NURSE: Yes, he's been waiting about ten minutes.
DE SILVA: All right – send him in.
NURSE: Yes, sir.
DE SILVA: And tell Barker I want to see him.
NURSE: Yes, Mr de Silva.
Pause.

The door opens.

NURSE: (*Announcing*) Mr Temple, sir.

DE SILVA: Oh, good morning, Mr Temple. I'm sorry to have kept you waiting. I only heard about your appointment a few moments ago. Do sit down … Yes, nurse?

NURSE: I'll tell Barker now, sir.

DE SILVA: Thank you.

The door closes.

TEMPLE: I imagine you're a very busy man, Mr de Silva, so I'll come straight to the point.

DE SILVA: (*Smiling*) Obviously you don't want to consult me professionally, Mr Temple.

TEMPLE: Why do you say that?

DE SILVA: None of my patients ever come straight to the point.

TEMPLE: No. I wanted to have a word with you about your car. I understand you have a Rolls. UPF 485.

DE SILVA: That's correct – yes.

TEMPLE: Yesterday afternoon your car was parked outside the Stags Head Hotel at Maidenhead.

DE SILVA: (*Surprised*) Yesterday afternoon?

TEMPLE: Yes.

DE SILVA: Are you sure?

TEMPLE: Quite sure.

DE SILVA: Go on, Mr Temple.

TEMPLE: There was a man sitting in the car; I should like to know who he was and if, by any chance, he's a friend of yours?

DE SILVA: (*With a little laugh*) Well – this is a most unusual request. I – I don't quite know what to say.

TEMPLE: (*Pleasant*) Supposing you answer the question.

DE SILVA: Very well. First of all, I don't think you did see the car outside …

81

TEMPLE: I didn't see it. My wife saw it.

DE SILVA: Very well. I don't think your wife did see my car outside the Stags Head Hotel but, if by any chance she did, then obviously the man sitting in the car must have been my chauffeur.

TEMPLE: No, it wasn't your chauffeur, Mr de Silva.

DE SILVA: (*Laughing*) Then it wasn't my car, Mr Temple!

TEMPLE: My wife doesn't usually make mistakes, and she has very good eyesight.

DE SILVA: (*Curious*) She made a note of the registration number?

TEMPLE: Yes.

DE SILVA: Well, that's extraordinary.

TEMPLE: Did you use the car yesterday?

DE SILVA: Yes – now let me see. My chauffeur took me to St John's Hospital at eleven o'clock and picked me up again at about – about a quarter to four.

TEMPLE: Then it could very easily have been your car my wife saw.

DE SILVA: It could have been, yes. But – what was my car doing at Maidenhead?

TEMPLE: That's a question for your chauffeur, Mr de Silva.

DE SILVA: Yes. Yes, indeed. But tell me, I'm intrigued. Why are you so interested in this man?

TEMPLE: My wife thought she recognised him; I think she was mistaken. Last night we had a few words about it; this morning at breakfast, we had a little bet. I'd like to settle the matter once and for all.

There is a knock on the door.

DE SILVA: (*Laughing*) But tell me, how can you possibly win if you bet against your wife? It's an impossibility, Mr Temple!

The door opens.

BARKER: You wanted to see me, sir?

DE SILVA: Ah, yes! Come in, Barker! (*To TEMPLE*) This is my chauffeur. (*To BARKER*) Barker, what did you do yesterday afternoon after you dropped me at the hospital?

BARKER: I called at Harridges, sir, and picked up some parcels for Mrs de Silva.

DE SILVA: And after that?

BARKER: (*A moment's hesitation*) After that I took the car back to the garage, sir.

DE SILVA: What time was that?

BARKER: About twelve o'clock, sir.

DE SILVA: What did you do then?

BARKER: Well, I started to clean the car, sir, then I had lunch.

DE SILVA: And after lunch?

BARKER: I finished cleaning the car, did one or two odd jobs, and then picked you up at the hospital.

DE SILVA: You didn't go out to Maidenhead?

BARKER: Maidenhead? Did you want me to go to Maidenhead, sir?

DE SILVA: That's not what I asked you, Barker. Did you go to Maidenhead?

BARKER: Why, no, sir.

DE SILVA: Thank you, Barker. Pick me up at four-thirty.

BARKER: Yes, sir.

The door closes.

DE SILVA: Well, there you are, Mr Temple. Either my chauffeur's lying or your wife made a mistake.

TEMPLE: How long have you had your chauffeur?

The door opens.

DE SILVA: About three months. He seems very reliable; he's an excellent driver; had first-class references. Of course, one can never tell. (*Looking up*) Yes, what is it, nurse?

NURSE: Mr Dexter's telephoned, sir. Can you see him tomorrow afternoon at three o'clock?

A pause.

DE SILVA: Yes, all right, nurse. Well, goodbye, Mr Temple. I'm sorry not to have been more helpful.

TEMPLE: On the contrary, you've been most helpful, Mr de Silva.

COMPLETE FADE.

FADE IN a door bell ringing.

STEVE: (*From the background*) I'm coming! I'm coming!

The front door opens.

TEMPLE: Hello.

STEVE: Haven't you got your key?

TEMPLE: No, I left it on the desk.

The door closes.

STEVE: Brian Dexter's here, Paul. He wants to see you.

TEMPLE: Dexter? How long has he been here?

STEVE: About five minutes, that's all. Did you see de Silva?

TEMPLE: Yes.

STEVE: What happened?

TEMPLE: I'll tell you later, Steve. Where's Dexter?

STEVE: He's in the study. He seems a bit worried.

TEMPLE: What's he worried about?

STEVE: I don't know. I think Inspector Vosper's been on to him again.

TEMPLE: All right, Steve. Are there any other messages?

STEVE: No, nothing, dear.

FADE.

84

FADE UP.

DEXTER: (*He is surprised and irritated*) ... But I just don't see the point of all these questions.

TEMPLE: I should have thought the point was fairly obvious. You were the last person to see Sylvia Ross, so obviously ...

DEXTER: Yes, I know, but just because I was the last person to see her it doesn't mean to say I know what's happened to her!

TEMPLE: You know, your attitude seems to have changed, Dexter. When I first saw you, you didn't appear a bit worried about this business.

DEXTER: Yes, I know, but I never realised the police would begin to suspect me of all people. Look, Temple, would you mind having a word with Vosper?

TEMPLE: Me?

DEXTER: Yes. Ask him point blank what's at the back of his mind.

TEMPLE: Why don't you ask him?

DEXTER: I have done.

TEMPLE: Well?

DEXTER: I can't get any sense out of the man; all he does is ask a lot of questions. Do you know what he asked me this morning?

TEMPLE: No.

DEXTER: He asked me where I first met Sylvia. I told him Zermatt. He asked me which hotel. I told him the name of ... (*He stops; a sudden thought*) By the way, you asked me the name of the hotel, didn't you?

TEMPLE: Yes, I did – but what did Inspector Vosper ask you?

85

DEXTER: Oh, he went one better. You leave that to Vosper! He wanted to know if I remembered the number of my room. The number of my room, for Pete's sake! It's over a year since I stayed at the place.

TEMPLE: Did he ask you anything else?

DEXTER: Good heavens above, isn't that enough?

TEMPLE: All right, Dexter. I'll have a word with the Inspector. I'll see if I can find out what he's up to.

DEXTER: Thank you. Forgive me if I lost my temper, but really – it's infuriating to keep answering the same questions over and over again.

TEMPLE: Yes, I know. (*Pause*) Dexter, you remember when my wife moved my car for you – yesterday afternoon at Maidenhead?

DEXTER: Yes.

TEMPLE: I understand there was another car in the car park, quite close to yours.

DEXTER: There were several cars.

TEMPLE: Yes, but this was actually next to yours.

DEXTER: I think there was a Rolls next to mine.

TEMPLE: Yes, that's right. Did you take particular note of it?

DEXTER: No; it was black; fairly new. I don't remember anything else about it.

TEMPLE: Was there anyone sitting in it?

DEXTER: Oh dear. If there was, I don't remember.

TEMPLE: You don't remember whether it was the chauffeur or …

DEXTER: I honestly don't. I have a feeling there was someone in the car, but I don't really remember what the person looked like.

TEMPLE: You don't know whether it was a man or a woman?

DEXTER: I'm afraid I don't.

TEMPLE: It's not important. He bumped my car and I simply thought I'd like to have a word with him.

DEXTER: It's infuriating, isn't it? I thought that sort of thing only happened to me. Well, goodbye, Mr Temple. I'm sorry to have bothered you, but if you can have a word with Vosper ...

TEMPLE: I certainly will.

DEXTER: Thank you.

TEMPLE: This way ... Oh, Dexter! Don't think I'm trying to emulate the Inspector, but – do you mind if I ask you a personal question?

DEXTER: Well?

TEMPLE: Do you wear glasses?

DEXTER: Glasses?

TEMPLE: Yes.

DEXTER: Why, no! (*Faintly amused*) I didn't notice anyone in the Rolls because I didn't take the trouble to look at it. If I had I should have seen them all right. My eyesight's excellent I can assure you.

TEMPLE: I'm delighted to hear it.

The door opens.

TEMPLE: (*Pleasantly*) This way.

FADE IN incidental music.

FADE DOWN music.

FADE IN the sound of a police launch on the Thames.

There is a background of river noises.

The sound of the launch continues.

VOSPER: What time do you make it, Sergeant?

THOMAS: (*A Cockney police sergeant*) Just after six, sir.

VOSPER: We should have reached them by now, surely?

THOMAS: (*Peering ahead*) Yes, I should have thought so, sir.

VOSPER: Is it always as misty as this?

THOMAS: No; it's a bad night, sir. Wouldn't surprise me if we don't get a bit of fog later on.

VOSPER: (*Shivering*) I can't imagine anything worse than being permanently posted …

THOMAS: Here she is, sir! That's it … (*Turning; calling*) Starboard, sarge! Starboard!

GEORGE: (*In the background, calling across the launch*) Steady down, Fred! Steady!!!!

FADE IN the sound of a cargo boat approaching the police launch.

THOMAS: (*Calling through a megaphone from the police launch*) Captain Jansen!

JANSEN: (*A Norwegian sea captain; calling through a megaphone from the approaching cargo boat*) This is Captain Jansen – have you a police officer on board?

THOMAS: (*Calling*) Yes … We're coming closer, Captain!

The launch draws level with the cargo boat.

There is a great deal of noise and activity.

GEORGE: (*In the background*) Steady, Fred! Mind the rope!

THOMAS: (*Calling*) Watch out for the rope, Captain!

A rope is thrown from the police launch.

CUT DOWN the noise of the engine of the police launch.

VOSPER: I can manage, Sergeant.

THOMAS: Careful, sir! It's not as easy as it looks!

GEORGE: (*In the background*) Okay, Fred! Keep her like that!

We hear the sound of water swishing against the side of the launch.

FADE DOWN background noise.
FADE UP VOSPER.

VOSPER: Captain Jansen?

JANSEN: Yes, I am Captain Jansen. You are the police officer, yes?

VOSPER: Inspector Vosper, C.I.D.

JANSEN: Glad to meet you, Inspector, and sorry to bring you out on such an unpleasant errand.

VOSPER: Where is he?

JANSEN: Down below, in one of the cabins. This way, if you would be so good …

VOSPER: Thank you.

FADE.
FADE background noises from the river.

FADE UP.

JANSEN: Well, there you are … Poor devil …

VOSPER: M'm.

JANSEN: You recognise him, perhaps?

VOSPER: No, I've never seen him before. Where did you pick him up?

JANSEN: About a mile from Cooper's Wharf. Why do they do these things always on the river? For me, I say, if I have to do this a nice warm room and a gas fire. You agree, perhaps, Inspector?

VOSPER: Yes, I do.

JANSEN: There is a wallet. It fell out of his pocket. I keep it for you, Inspector. (*Pause*) Here it is …

VOSPER: Thank you.

JANSEN: I look inside for the name, but there is nothing, no information, just some money and some – what do you call them, snapshots, photographs?

VOSPER: Photographs?

JANSEN: Yes. I put them on my desk because they are wet and I thought perhaps it would be better for you, and for the photographs.

VOSPER: How many are there?

JANSEN: Six. All snapshots of the same person. But, go – see for yourself. (*Pause*) She is, what you say – a good looker?

VOSPER: Yes.

JANSEN: You know this lady?

VOSPER: Yes, I know her, Captain. I know her.

FADE.

FADE UP of STEVE.

STEVE is sitting at her dressing table singing to herself.

The bedroom door opens.

STEVE: I'm nearly ready, Paul.

TEMPLE: Yes, all right, Steve. I'll get the car out. (*Suddenly*) By Timothy, Steve, you're not putting that hat on!

STEVE: What do you mean?

TEMPLE: We're going to the pictures – not a garden party.

STEVE: You say that every time I buy a new hat!

TEMPLE: Now, Steve, I ask you …

STEVE: Don't ask me anything, darling, just get the car out!

TEMPLE: If I were you, I should put on that little …

STEVE: That little black one! Yes, I know, darling. We are having a night out I presume and not going to the morgue?

TEMPLE: Well, so long as I don't have to sit behind you.

The door opens.

TEMPLE: Yes, Charlie?

CHARLIE: Inspector Vosper's here, sir – he'd like a word with you.

TEMPLE: Vosper? All right, Charlie. I'll see you downstairs, Steve.
STEVE: For goodness' sake get rid of him, Paul – the big film starts at eight-twenty.
FADE.

FADE UP of TEMPLE speaking.
TEMPLE: Hello, Vosper! This is an unexpected pleasure!
VOSPER: Have I interrupted your dinner?
TEMPLE: No, as a matter of fact we're just going out.
VOSPER: (*Disappointed*) Oh. Oh dear.
TEMPLE: What's the matter?
VOSPER: I was hoping you'd be able to spare me an hour or so.
TEMPLE: An hour or so?
VOSPER: Yes, I'd like you to come out to Rotherhithe with me.
TEMPLE: This evening?
VOSPER: Yes.
TEMPLE: But why Rotherhithe?
VOSPER: A man was picked out of the river late this afternoon – I'm hoping you might be able to identify him.
TEMPLE: What makes you think I can identify him?
VOSPER: Well, I don't know for certain that you can, but I'd like you to try.
TEMPLE: Yes, all right, Vosper.
The door opens.
STEVE: Good evening, Inspector!
VOSPER: Good evening, Mrs Temple.
STEVE: Are you ready, Paul?
TEMPLE: Steve, I'm terribly sorry, but –
STEVE: But what?
TEMPLE: I'm afraid you'll have to go on your own, dear.

91

STEVE: But why?

TEMPLE: Something's happened, Steve. I'll tell you later.

STEVE: Oh, all right.

TEMPLE: Take the car. I'll meet you for supper. I'll book a table at Luigi's.

STEVE: Are you going with the Inspector?

TEMPLE: Yes; I'll see you at Luigi's at about half-past ten.

STEVE: I'm not really mad about this film, you know. I could come with you …

VOSPER: I would have suggested that, Mrs Temple – but – I don't think it's a very good idea.

TEMPLE: No, you're not exactly dressed for the morgue, darling.

STEVE: Oh …

STEVE starts laughing; a nervous, uncertain laugh.

FADE.

FADE IN the sound of pouring rain.

A car draws to a standstill on a gravel path.

The car doors open and close, followed by the sound of hurried footsteps.

FADE UP the sound of a bell clanging.

A heavy door is unbolted and opened.

SMITH: Oh, good evening, Inspector!

VOSPER: Good evening. This is the gentleman I was telling you about – Mr Temple.

SMITH: Yes, sir. This way, if you please. Not a pleasant evening, I'm afraid.

We hear more footsteps.

A heavy key is inserted, and a door is unlocked.

SMITH: Mind the step, sir.

More footsteps on a stone floor.

SMITH: Here we are … If you'll just stand over there, Mr Temple, please.

We hear the sound of a sliding door.
There is the noise of steel rollers and the removal of a sheet.
A pause.

VOSPER: Well, do you recognise him?

A pause.

TEMPLE: Yes, I saw him this morning. His name's Barker
– he's chauffeur to a man called de Silva.

VOSPER: Thank you. That's all, Smith – thank you.

SMITH: Good night, Inspector. Have a pleasant weekend.

VOSPER: Good night.

We hear the sound of the sliding door etc again followed by
TEMPLE and VOSPER crossing the stone floor.

TEMPLE: Was it suicide?

VOSPER: It looks like it; it looks remarkably like it.

TEMPLE: But you don't think it was?

VOSPER: No. (*Pause*) Barker had a wallet in his pocket
containing twenty-seven one-pound notes, two
fivers, and six photographs – snapshots. I've got
the photographs here somewhere. I'd like you to
take a look at them. Here we are!

TEMPLE: (*A slight pause*) Why, that's my wife! That's
Steve! They're – they're all photographs of
Steve!

VOSPER: Yes. (*Significantly*) I thought you'd be interested,
Mr Temple.

FADE IN incidental music.

FADE music.
FADE UP background noises and conversation of a crowded
restaurant.

TEMPLE: Good evening, Luigi!

LUIGI: Oh, good evening, Mr Temple! Your table's
ready, sir.

TEMPLE: Has my wife arrived?

LUIGI: No, not yet, sir.

TEMPLE: (*Surprised*) Are you sure?

LUIGI: Yes, quite sure, sir. This way please ...

They cross to a corner table.

TEMPLE: I make it a quarter to eleven – is that right?

LUIGI: Yes – it's about twelve minutes to, to be exact, sir.

TEMPLE: My wife should be here by now.

LUIGI: There's so much traffic these days. I'll have madam shown to your table the moment ... Ah, here is Mrs Temple! Good evening, madam!

STEVE: Hello, Luigi! How are you?

LUIGI: I'm very well, thank you, madam. It's nice to see you again.

STEVE: It's nice to see you again.

LUIGI: I'll send the waiter straight away, Mr Temple.

TEMPLE: Thank you.

STEVE: Sorry I'm late, Paul. I had an awful job parking the car.

TEMPLE: Yes, I expect you did.

STEVE: I got caught in the theatre traffic. I think I'd like a drink, darling.

TEMPLE: Yes, all right. I'll get the wine waiter.

STEVE: You look very serious – is something wrong?

TEMPLE: Yes.

STEVE: What is it?

TEMPLE: I'll tell you after supper, Steve.

STEVE: Why not now?

TEMPLE: (*Hesitating; then:*) No, I'll tell you afterwards, dear – while we're having coffee.

STEVE: Paul, you're not feeling ill?

PAUL: No, I'm fine, darling. Don't worry, Steve – I'll tell you all about it afterwards.

94

STEVE: All right. I'm going to powder my nose, darling, and while I'm away you can order me the largest dry Martini you've ever … (*She stops dead*)

TEMPLE: What is it?

A definite pause.

TEMPLE: Steve, what is it?

STEVE: Paul … I've lost my handbag!

FADE IN closing music.

END OF EPISODE THREE

EPISODE FOUR

RETURN TO DOWNBURGH

OPEN TO: A background of restaurant noises.

STEVE: Sorry I'm late, Paul. I had an awful job parking the car.

TEMPLE: Yes, I expect you did.

STEVE: I got caught in the theatre traffic. I think I'd like a drink, darling.

TEMPLE: Yes, all right. I'll get the wine waiter.

STEVE: You look very serious – is something wrong?

TEMPLE: Yes.

STEVE: What is it?

TEMPLE: I'll tell you after supper, Steve.

STEVE: Why not now?

TEMPLE: (*Hesitating; then*:) No, I'll tell you afterwards, dear – while we're having coffee.

STEVE: Paul, you're not feeling ill?

PAUL: No, I'm fine, darling. Don't worry, Steve – I'll tell you all about it afterwards.

STEVE: All right. I'm going to powder my nose, darling, and while I'm away you can order me the largest dry Martini you've ever … (*She stops dead*)

TEMPLE: What is it?

A definite pause.

TEMPLE: Steve, what is it?

STEVE: Paul … I've lost my handbag!

TEMPLE: You've what?!

STEVE: I've lost my handbag!

TEMPLE: Steve, are you sure?

STEVE: Of course I'm sure. (*Searching*) It's very funny, because I had it in the cinema. I distinctly remember …

TEMPLE: Which one was it …

STEVE: Which one?

TEMPLE: (*Quickly*) Yes – which bag was it?

STEVE: Why, the black one. The one I showed you earlier this evening …

TEMPLE: The one you took to Downburgh?

STEVE: Yes. (*Puzzled*) Paul, this is very odd … You remember what Mary Gardner said about …

TEMPLE: Yes, I do.

STEVE: It's an extraordinary coincidence!

TEMPLE: A little too extraordinary for my liking!

STEVE: What do you mean?

TEMPLE: Mary Gardner warned you! She knew perfectly well that sooner or later someone would make an attempt to get the handbag from you.

STEVE: But why? It was just an ordinary handbag.

TEMPLE: What was in it – do you remember?

STEVE: Just the usual things. A hanky, a powder compact, a letter from … (*Suddenly*) Oh dear!

TEMPLE: What is it?

STEVE: My earrings, Paul! My gold earrings!

TEMPLE: Were they in your handbag?

STEVE: Yes. One was hurting slightly so I took them off and put them in my bag.

TEMPLE: While you were in the cinema?

STEVE: Yes.

TEMPLE: Steve, when did you last see the bag?

STEVE: It's difficult to say. I certainly had it in the picture house …

TEMPLE: You don't remember bringing it out with you?

STEVE: No, I don't.

TEMPLE: Was there anyone sitting next to you?

STEVE: Yes, a man came and sat down while the picture was on, but I didn't see him properly.

TEMPLE: You're sure there was nothing else in the bag – besides what you've told me?

STEVE: No, I'm sure there wasn't.

TEMPLE: Well, there's nothing we can do at the moment. We'll call in the cinema on the way home.

STEVE: (*Watching TEMPLE*) You think it's been stolen, don't you, Paul?

TEMPLE: Well – don't you?

STEVE: Yes. And what's more, I think it must have been done deliberately.

TEMPLE: You mean – someone wanted that particular handbag?

STEVE: Yes.

TEMPLE: (*Thoughtfully*) But why?

STEVE: (*Quietly*) I don't know why, but Mary Gardner knew …

TEMPLE: (*Softly; thoughtfully*) Yes …

STEVE: Paul, tell me: what happened tonight?

TEMPLE: A man called Barker committed suicide, or was murdered – we're not sure which. Anyway, Vosper had a hunch that I might be able to identify him. He was right.

STEVE: Well, who was he?

TEMPLE: He worked for Ernest de Silva: he was his chauffeur.

STEVE: (*Surprised*) His chauffeur?

TEMPLE: (*Quietly*) Yes. (*A moment*) Steve, there's something I've got to tell you, darling   it's not going to be easy.

STEVE: What do you mean?

TEMPLE: I want you to go away for a little while.

STEVE: Go away?

TEMPLE: Yes.

STEVE: Where to, exactly?

TEMPLE: The South of France if you like. Have a holiday – enjoy yourself.

STEVE: But I've just had a holiday!

TEMPLE: Well – have another one, it won't do you any harm.

STEVE: What is this? What's it all about, Paul?

TEMPLE: Steve, I'm worried; I'm terribly worried about this Lawrence affair.

STEVE: Well, that's no reason for trying to get rid of me!

TEMPLE: I'm not trying to get rid of you. You're no fool, Steve – you know what I'm referring to, don't you?

STEVE: (*A moment*) You're worried because Mary Gardner was shot wearing my coat. You think those shots were intended for me, don't you?

TEMPLE: Yes, I do, but – that isn't everything.

STEVE: (*Seriously*) Go on.

TEMPLE: Well, this afternoon when they fished Barker out of the river they found a wallet on him; there were half a dozen photographs in the wallet – snapshots.

STEVE: Well?

TEMPLE: They were snapshots of you.

STEVE: (*Astonished*) Of me?

TEMPLE: Yes.

STEVE: But why on earth should Barker carry photographs of me?

TEMPLE: Why, indeed?

STEVE: Do you know why?

TEMPLE: There's only one possible explanation; he carried the photographs as a means of identification. There was going to be no mistake next time, Steve!

STEVE: But why on earth should they bother their heads about me? Surely you're the one they should worry about, you're investigating the case!

TEMPLE: Yes, but for some unknown reason you're the one they're interested in.

STEVE: Paul, where were the photographs taken, in London?

TEMPLE: It was difficult to tell, they were mostly street photographs; you obviously didn't realise you were being taken.

STEVE: Was I carrying a handbag?

TEMPLE: (*Interested*) Yes, I think so.

STEVE: Was it the black one; the one I've just lost?

TEMPLE: Yes, I believe it was.

STEVE: Then isn't it possible that it wasn't me they were interested in, but the handbag?

TEMPLE: Yes, that's quite a point, Steve.

STEVE: Isn't there some means of enlarging a photograph, and getting a close-up of a particular section of it?

TEMPLE: Yes, that can be done. But it still doesn't explain why Barker was carrying the photographs.

STEVE: He wanted to make sure he got the right handbag.

TEMPLE: In other words, the photographs were still a means of identification …

STEVE: Yes, but not of me, of the handbag.

TEMPLE: Well, it's certainly an interesting theory. You know, I ought to have thought of that!

STEVE: (*Smiling*) Yes, dear, you should. And there's something else you ought to have thought of too.

TEMPLE: What's that?

STEVE: I'm just as interested in this Lawrence affair as you are. We'll <u>both</u> go to the South of France – when it's all over.

There is a tiny pause, then TEMPLE starts to laugh.

TEMPLE: (*Laughing*) Yes, all right, Steve. All right!

FADE IN incidental music.

FADE music.

FADE IN street noises; with a background of traffic.

TEMPLE and STEVE are walking towards their car which is parked in a busy thoroughfare.

STEVE: There's the car, Paul – on the corner.

TEMPLE: Yes, I'd spotted it. By Timothy, you were lucky to find a parking meter.

A slight pause.

STEVE: Do you think we should tell the police?

TEMPLE: What do you think?

STEVE: I think we'd better. After all, they may have found the bag.

TEMPLE: Yes, all right, dear, but I'm not very optimistic.

STEVE: Well, one thing is certain, if they haven't found it, it was definitely stolen.

TEMPLE: Yes, unless …

STEVE: Unless what?

TEMPLE: Unless you forgot to take it out with you in the first place and we find it on the bed when we get home!

STEVE: (*Laughs*) How do you think I got into the cinema if I didn't have my handbag with me?

TEMPLE laughs and opens the car door.

TEMPLE: I'll drive, Steve.

STEVE: All right, dear – here's the key …

TEMPLE: (*Pleasantly*) And next time you park the car I suggest you lock it.

STEVE: I was in such a hurry and so delighted to find a place to park that … (*She stops*)

TEMPLE: What is it?

STEVE: (*Softly; astonished*) Paul! Look – on the back seat … my handbag!

104

TEMPLE: (*A moment; then amused*) Well, really, Steve! You are the limit!

STEVE: Paul, I'm sure I didn't put it there!

TEMPLE: Of course you put it there! Steve, you really do take the prize!

STEVE starts to laugh.

TEMPLE: For the last hour we've discussed nothing but that wretched handbag and all the time it's been here, in the car.

STEVE: But, Paul, I know I didn't put it there.

TEMPLE: Well, if you didn't, who did? Were you in a hurry when you left the cinema?

STEVE: Yes. I knew I was late and …

TEMPLE: And you jumped into the car and tossed your bag on to the back seat!

STEVE: (*Hesitantly*) Well …

TEMPLE: (*Laughing*) Come on, you goof!

TEMPLE and STEVE get into the car.

TEMPLE presses the starter.

The car starts.

FADE the sound of the car engine.

FADE IN the sound of the car travelling along the Thames Embankment.

STEVE: The Festival Hall looks very gay. I've never seen it like that before.

TEMPLE: There must be a dance on or something … (*Pause*) Tired?

STEVE: (*About to sneeze*) A … little …

TEMPLE: (*Amused*) What's the matter?

STEVE: I – I thought I was going to sneeze. (*A moment*) You know, it's a curious thing, when we drive by here during the day I always think the river looks

	so … so … (*About to sneeze again*) so … Atishoo!
TEMPLE:	I hope you haven't caught a cold, Steve.
STEVE:	No, I'm all right, it's just a … Oh dear! I do sound thick, don't I?
TEMPLE:	You certainly do!
STEVE:	I'd better get my hanky; it's in my handbag.
TEMPLE:	(*Significantly*) Which is on the back seat, darling.
STEVE:	(*Laughing*) Oh, shut up!

A moment.

TEMPLE:	Can you reach?
STEVE:	(*Stretching over the seat*) Yes, I think so.
TEMPLE:	I always remember the first time I drove down the Embankment, many years ago. I had an old ten-horsepower … (*He hesitates*) What is it?
STEVE:	(*Quietly; puzzled*) Paul, this isn't my handbag!
TEMPLE:	What do you mean?
STEVE:	It looks like it; it looks exactly like it; the same material and the clasp is the same, but it's so heavy and it feels as if …
TEMPLE:	(*Suddenly; tensely*) Don't open it, Steve! For goodness' sake don't open …

As TEMPLE speaks STEVE opens the handbag and there is a loud report of a revolver shot from within the car.
It is followed by the smashing of the windscreen.
The shot causing the car to swerve off the road and mount the pavement.

| STEVE: | (*Frightened*) Look out, Paul! We'll be over the Embankment! Careful! |

TEMPLE jams on the brakes and the car skids to a standstill, coming to rest against the Embankment wall.
During the following dialogue gradually register background voices; a gathering of people; curious sightseers; and the arrival of police.

STEVE: (*Breathlessly*) Paul, are you hurt?

TEMPLE: No … I couldn't see a confounded thing … the bullet splintered the windscreen …

STEVE: You've cut your hand!

TEMPLE: It's nothing, Steve. Now don't worry about it …

STEVE: … That shot might have killed you …

TEMPLE: Yes, but it wasn't intended for me.

STEVE: What actually happened?

TEMPLE: The revolver fired when you touched the clasp and opened the bag; fortunately it was pointing the other way.

STEVE: They must have stolen my bag in the cinema and planted this thing in the car while we were having supper.

TEMPLE: Yes, and Mary Gardner knew about it. She knew they were going to do this.

STEVE: But why, Paul? Why do they want to get rid of me?

TEMPLE: I don't know, Steve – but by Timothy, I'm going to find out!

FADE UP the background noises and voices.

FADE IN of incidental music.

FADE DOWN the music.

We hear the sound of a key in a lock.

The door opens.

TEMPLE: (*Surprised*) Oh, hello, Charlie! I thought you'd be in bed by now.

CHARLIE: I was in bed, sir, but a Mr Burford called to see you. He said it was urgent so I asked him to wait.

STEVE: (*Surprised*) Mr Burford!

CHARLIE: Yes, Mrs Temple.

TEMPLE: (*To STEVE*) It's Max Burford. (*To CHARLIE*) Where is he, Charlie – in the drawing room?

CHARLIE: Yes, sir.

TEMPLE: Right!

STEVE: Paul, you've got to do something about that hand!

TEMPLE: Yes, all right, Steve. Offer Burford a drink. I'll be with you in two or three minutes. Get me some of that antiseptic ointment, Charlie, it's in the bathroom.

FADE SCENE.

FADE UP a door opening.

TEMPLE: Hello, Burford! Sorry to have kept you waiting.

BURFORD: Good evening, Mr Temple.

TEMPLE: Didn't my wife offer you a drink?

STEVE: Of course I did, Paul, but Mr Burford …

BURFORD: If you don't mind I'd rather not, Temple, thank you very much.

TEMPLE: Well, what can I do for you?

BURFORD: I don't know that you can do anything for me, but – (*To STEVE*) You remember that man you saw at Downburgh, Mrs Temple, the man you thought was me?

STEVE: Yes?

BURFORD: Would you recognise him again?

STEVE: I think so.

BURFORD: I'd like you to take a look at this photograph.

A slight pause.

STEVE: Yes … Yes, this is the man …

BURFORD: Are you sure?

STEVE: I'm positive. But who is he, Mr Burford – he's terribly like you.

BURFORD: His name's Freeman – Dan Freeman. He's a cousin of mine although curiously enough

108

	we've always looked more like brothers – twin brothers in fact – than cousins.
TEMPLE:	Why didn't you tell me about Freeman when I questioned you? Obviously, you must have thought of him.
BURFORD:	Yes, I did, Temple, but I didn't want to say anything about him until – well, until I was quite sure.
TEMPLE:	And now you're quite sure?
BURFORD:	Yes, it was Freeman your wife saw at Downburgh, I don't think there's any doubt about that.
TEMPLE:	What was he doing there?
BURFORD:	I don't know.
TEMPLE:	Have you asked him?
BURFORD:	Yes. He denies going to Downburgh, and he says he's not interested in you or Mrs Temple. But he's not telling the truth, I'm sure he's not …
TEMPLE:	Supposing you tell us something about this cousin of yours?
BURFORD:	I'm afraid he's something of a mystery. He always seems to be fairly well off and yet no one seems to know what he does for a living.
TEMPLE:	Is he married?
BURFORD:	No, he's a bachelor; keeps himself very much to himself.
STEVE:	Where does he live?
BURFORD:	He travels a great deal, mostly on the Continent, but he has a cottage just outside Felixstowe. I went down there this morning.
TEMPLE:	Go on …
BURFORD:	I told him about your visit and the fact that Mrs Temple was under the impression she'd seen

109

	me at Downburgh. I suggested that the only possible explanation was that we'd been mistaken for each other.
TEMPLE:	But he denied it?
BURFORD:	Most emphatically; a little too emphatically, in fact. That's what made me suspicious.
TEMPLE:	Did anything else make you suspicious, Burford?
BURFORD:	Yes. (*Thoughtfully*) Dan's up to something; I don't know what it is but his whole manner implies a certain – well, a certain caution. I've a shrewd suspicion that whatever it is he's mixed up in he's out of his depth.
TEMPLE:	Why do you say that?
BURFORD:	He's using another name, Mr Temple …
TEMPLE:	Another name?
BURFORD:	Yes; a telephone call came through for him while I was in the cottage. It was a personal call but the operator didn't ask for Dan Freeman.
TEMPLE:	Who did she ask for?
BURFORD:	The name sounded to me like Lawrence – Clive Lawrence.

A pause.

TEMPLE:	And Freeman took the call?
BURFORD:	Yes.
TEMPLE:	What did he say?
BURFORD:	He said: "Is that you, Teako? There's nothing to worry about, she's been taken to the Isle of Skye."
TEMPLE:	"There's nothing to worry about, she's been taken to the Isle of Skye?"
BURFORD:	Yes.
TEMPLE:	Is that all he said?

BURFORD: Yes; he didn't even give the other person time to reply. That may have been because I was there, of course.

TEMPLE: You're sure he called this other person – the man who made the call – Teako?

BURFORD: Well, it sounded like Teako. It's an unusual name, isn't it?

TEMPLE: It is indeed. Have you heard it before?

BURFORD: Yes, I believe I've heard it over the radio. Isn't there a dance band fellow called Teako – Johnny Teako?

STEVE: Yes, I believe there is.

TEMPLE: You'd better give me Freeman's address, Burford.

BURFORD: It's – Redstone Cottage, Denford Heath, near Felixstowe.

TEMPLE: (*Making a note*) Thank you. It was very decent of you to come along with this information.

BURFORD: I'm afraid I had no alternative.

TEMPLE: Why do you say that?

BURFORD: Dan's up to something; I don't know what it is, but whatever it is I don't want you to think I'm mixed up in it.

TEMPLE: I see. (*Pleasantly*) Well, change your mind and have a drink. I'm going to have a whisky and soda.

BURFORD: (*After a moment; relaxing slightly*) All right, Temple – I'll join you. A whisky and soda …

FADE IN incidental music.

FADE music.
A door opens.

SERGEANT: Mr Temple is here, sir.

VOSPER: (*Rather tired*) Right – send him in, Sergeant.

111

SERGEANT: Yes, sir.

VOSPER: And don't forget the coffee I ordered; black coffee.

SERGEANT: Very good, Inspector.

A moment.

SERGEANT: (*To TEMPLE*) This way, sir, please …

TEMPLE enters.

TEMPLE: Good morning, Vosper!

VOSPER: Hello, Temple! That's all right, Sergeant. Oh, you might tell the Superintendent I'll be at the twelve o'clock meeting.

SERGEANT: Very good, sir.

The door closes.

TEMPLE: You look tired, Inspector!

VOSPER: It's not surprising; I haven't had any sleep for thirty-six hours.

TEMPLE: When did you get back?

VOSPER: About an hour ago.

TEMPLE: Did you fly?

VOSPER: Yes. I left Edinburgh at seven o'clock. Twenty-four hours ago I was in the Isle of Skye.

TEMPLE: I understand from Sir Graham it was a wild goose chase. I'm sorry, Vosper.

VOSPER: My dear Temple, it wasn't your fault. It sounded a pretty good lead; obviously we had to follow it up.

TEMPLE: Was it a complete blank?

VOSPER: Yes. We combed Skye with a fine tooth-comb; if Sylvia Ross is on the island heaven knows where they're keeping her.

TEMPLE: What about Dan Freeman?

VOSPER: Well, our Felixstowe people report that he left the cottage a few days ago; he certainly isn't there at the moment.

112

TEMPLE:	A few days ago?
VOSPER:	Yes.
TEMPLE:	Then he must have left shortly after Burford saw him.
VOSPER:	I believe it was the same night.
TEMPLE:	Is the cottage empty at the moment?
VOSPER:	I understand so. Freeman certainly isn't there.
TEMPLE:	Who's in charge at Felixstowe?
VOSPER:	A man called Ivor; Inspector Ivor. He's a very good man. If you find yourself in that part of the world I should look him up.
TEMPLE:	I've met Ivor. He came over to Downburgh while I was staying there.
VOSPER:	That's right. We put him on to this business because he knew Mary Gardner and was au fait with the general situation.
TEMPLE:	(*Thoughtfully*) I may go down to Felixstowe and have a word with Ivor.
VOSPER:	I certainly think you could do worse. (*A moment, then:*) Temple, do you think Burford was telling the truth?
TEMPLE:	Do you mean about the telephone call, or the fact that he visited Freeman?
VOSPER:	Both.
TEMPLE:	Yes, I believe he was, Vosper. You see, when I saw him – the first time – and questioned him about the Downburgh incident he was obviously worried; he'd something at the back of his mind.
VOSPER:	You mean he was thinking about Freeman?
TEMPLE:	Yes.
VOSPER:	Then why didn't he mention him to you? He must have known that he was the obvious explanation. You're not going to tell me that

113

this is the first time they've been mistaken for each other.

The door opens.

VOSPER: Yes, Sergeant?

SERGEANT: A Mr Teako would like to see you, sir. He says it's important.

VOSPER: All right. Tell him to come up.

SERGEANT: Yes, sir.

The door closes.

VOSPER: We've been watching Teako ever since we got your message, Temple. He's made no attempt to contact Freeman; so far as we can tell the only thing he's interested in is that wretched dance orchestra.

TEMPLE: Nevertheless, Teako's mixed up in this business; I'm sure of that.

VOSPER: I agree – but to what extent, exactly?

TEMPLE: When you saw Teako, the night Mary Gardner was shot, you expressed the opinion that his wife was the brains and Teako merely a line-shooter.

VOSPER: Yes, I still think that.

TEMPLE: But it was Teako, remember – not his wife – that contacted Freeman.

VOSPER: Yes … but if Burford was telling the truth the phone call seems to imply that Teako wasn't at all happy about things. Freeman said: "There's nothing to worry about, she's been taken to the Isle of Skye."

The door opens.

TEMPLE: You mean Teako probably made the call because …

SERGEANT: Mr Teako, sir.

The door closes.

VOSPER:	Come in, Teako! I think you know Mr Temple.
TEAKO:	(*Surly*) Yeah – I know Mr Temple!
VOSPER:	Won't you sit down?
TEAKO:	Look, Inspector, I guess we're both pretty busy so I won't beat about the bush. Have you got someone tailing me?
VOSPER:	Tailing you?
TEAKO:	You know what I mean – following me around?
VOSPER:	Sit down, Teako.

A pause.

TEMPLE:	What makes you think someone's following …
TEAKO:	(*Interrupting TEMPLE*) Look, don't give me this "what makes you think" technique. I've asked a simple question, I want a simple answer. Is someone tailing me?
VOSPER:	(*Quietly*) Yes.
TEAKO:	One of your own?
VOSPER:	Yes, one of my men.
TEAKO:	(*Obviously relieved*) Okay, at least we know where we are. Now what's this all about?
TEMPLE:	Supposing you tell us what it's all about?
TEAKO:	I don't get this?
VOSPER:	Teako, a girl called Sylvia Ross disappeared; the night she disappeared she sent you a note.
TEAKO:	I know, I told you about it; I told you what was on the note.
VOSPER:	You said it was a request for your orchestra to play a certain dance number.
TEAKO:	So it was!
VOSPER:	Are you sure the note didn't contain something quite different?
TEAKO:	What, for instance?
VOSPER:	Well – a name and an address.
TEAKO:	What name? What address?

115

VOSPER: The name: Mr Clive Lawrence. The address: Hotel Schweizerhof, Zermatt.

TEAKO: (*Surprised; yet angry*) I've never heard of anyone called Lawrence. Who the hell's Lawrence?

VOSPER: Teako, we're under the impression you're mixed up in this business. That's why I put one of my men on to you. Now, if you've got any sense, you'll talk.

TEAKO: Talk? Talk, about what? Get wise to yourself, for Pete's sake! I'm an entertainer, a public figure, if a girl wants to send me a note there's nothing I can do about it. I've told you, I'd never set eyes on Sylvia Ross until she came to the Palais that night.

TEMPLE: And what about Brian Dexter?

TEAKO: Who's Dexter?

TEMPLE: He's the man she was with.

TEAKO: I don't even remember the guy! Now look, Inspector, so far I've been very patient about all this, but if you don't stop this malarky and call off your bloodhound I shall write to the powers that be.

TEMPLE: And what will you tell them, Mr Teako?

TEAKO: I shall tell them that an innocent man is being persecuted; I shall tell them the whole story!

TEMPLE: Well, that's more than you've told us.

TEAKO: (*Angrily*) What do you mean?

TEMPLE: (*Politely*) Teako, you say you've never heard of a Mr Lawrence.

TEAKO: No.

TEMPLE: Have you heard of a man called Freeman – Dan Freeman?

TEAKO: No!

TEMPLE: Didn't you telephone Freeman the other day? Didn't Freeman tell you not to worry? Didn't he say: "There's nothing to worry about, she – meaning Sylvia Ross – has been taken to the Isle of Skye?"

TEAKO: (*Angrily*) I tell you I've never heard of Freeman; if I've never heard of him how the hell could I telephone him?

VOSPER: For an entertainer, a public figure, it's surprising the number of people you've never heard of.

TEAKO: (*Rising; extremely angry*) Now listen, policeman, don't get too clever or …

TEMPLE: (*Interrupting TEAKO*) Teako, do you happen to know a Mr de Silva, by any chance?

TEAKO: (*Taken by surprise*) De Silva?

TEMPLE: Yes.

TEAKO: (*Hesitantly*) Yes, I know de Silva; he's an eye specialist.

TEMPLE: That's right.

TEAKO: I consulted him about six months ago.

TEMPLE: Why?

TEAKO: I – I was having headaches; I thought perhaps I needed glasses.

TEMPLE: Who recommended de Silva?

TEAKO: My – my wife did.

TEMPLE: Your wife?

TEAKO: Yes. She went to him before we were married.

TEMPLE: Oh. (*Pleasantly*) Oh, I see. Thank you.

TEAKO: (*Puzzled*) Why are you smiling?

TEMPLE: Am I smiling?

TEAKO: (*Irritated*) Yes! Have I said something funny?

TEMPLE: (*Still smiling*) On the contrary, my dear fellow, on the contrary …

FADE IN incidental music.

FADE DOWN music.

FADE IN a slight background of traffic noises then the sound of a car door being opened and closed.

TEMPLE: No, don't put that on the back seat, Steve – put it in the boot.

CHARLIE: I'm afraid the boot's full, sir.

TEMPLE: (*Surprised*) The boot's full!

CHARLIE: Yes, sir.

TEMPLE: Good heavens, Steve, how many suitcases are we taking? We're only going for two or three days remember.

STEVE: You say that every time we go away! And the moment we get there you say – "Didn't you pack my brown suit, dear!"

TEMPLE: (*Laughing*) All right, Steve! All right!

STEVE gets into the car.

CHARLIE: I think you've got everything now, sir.

TEMPLE: Yes. You know the address, Charlie – in case you want me. Downburgh, same hotel as before, the telephone number's on the pad.

CHARLIE: Yes, sir. Have a good trip.

TEMPLE: Ready, dear?

TEMPLE starts the car.

STEVE: Yes, I'm ready. Bye, Charlie!

CHARLIE: Goodbye, Mrs Temple.

TEMPLE accelerates and then changes gear.

FADE SCENE.

FADE UP a telephone ringing.

A door opens.

CHARLIE answers the telephone.

CHARLIE: (*On the phone*) Hello?

OPERATOR: (*On the other end of the line*) Hold the line a moment please … Go ahead, caller …

DE SILVA: (*On the other end of the line*) Hello?

CHARLIE: Hello?

DE SILVA: Can I speak to Mr Temple, please?

CHARLIE: I'm sorry, sir, you've just missed him.

DE SILVA: Just missed him? You mean he's gone out for a while?

CHARLIE: No, sir. Mr and Mrs Temple have gone away for two or three days.

DE SILVA: (*Pleasantly; curious*) Oh, I see. Perhaps you could give me their address.

CHARLIE: (*Without thinking*) Certainly, sir, they're staying at … (*He thinks better of it*) … some place in the country.

DE SILVA: Some place in the country?

CHARLIE: Yes, sir.

DE SILVA: Well, where exactly?

CHARLIE: I'm afraid I don't know where exactly, sir.

DE SILVA: (*Angrily*) That's not very helpful.

CHARLIE: No, sir. Who shall I say called?

DE SILVA: Mr de Silva. Mr Ernest de Silva.

CHARLIE: (*Unruffled*) Thank you, Mr de Silva. I'll deliver your message.

CHARLIE replaces the receiver.
FADE IN incidental music.

FADE DOWN music.
FADE IN noises associated with the bar parlour of a small hotel.

IVOR: I'd like another pint, please, Doris.

DORIS: Yes, sir.

IVOR: No, on second thoughts you'd better make it half a pint.

DORIS: (*Laughing*) Yes, all right, Inspector.

TEMPLE: Good evening, Inspector!

119

IVOR: Oh, hello, Mr Temple! My word, you must have stepped on it! I didn't expect you here as soon as this.

TEMPLE: You know my wife, don't you?

IVOR: Good evening, Mrs Temple.

TEMPLE: Steve, you remember Inspector Ivor.

STEVE: Yes, of course.

IVOR: Can I offer you a drink, Mrs Temple?

STEVE: No, thank you, Inspector.

IVOR: Temple?

TEMPLE: May I have a light ale?

DORIS: A light ale? Very good, sir. I'll bring them across to the table.

IVOR: Thank you, Doris.

START FADE.

IVOR: Come along, Mrs Temple – let's sit over there in the corner.

COMPLETE FADE.

FADE UP INSPECTOR IVOR.

IVOR: … As soon as I got the message I went out to the cottage, but there was no sign of Freeman.

TEMPLE: I understand it's at a place called Denford Heath?

IVOR: That's right; it's about four miles from here. Quite a nice looking cottage but rather isolated. It's on the fringe of Lanamoor Wood.

TEMPLE: Was the cottage deserted?

IVOR: Completely. It was about half past four when I got there and Mrs Hanson had just left.

TEMPLE: Who's Mrs Hanson?

IVOR: She's the daily woman; she's got a key and she goes in more or less every morning.

TEMPLE: Have you spoken to her?

IVOR: Yes; and she didn't say a great deal. Just between you and me she's got a bit of a soft job working for Freeman and she doesn't want to lose it.

TEMPLE: What does Freeman do while he's down here?

IVOR: So far as I can gather he spends most of his time reading and pottering about. He doesn't stay very long; two or three days at the most.

STEVE: Do the local people like him?

IVOR: Quite frankly, they've seen very little of him, Mrs Temple. He's only had the cottage for a few months.

STEVE: I see.

A moment.

IVOR: Are you staying the night here, in Felixstowe?

TEMPLE: No, we're on our way to Downburgh.

IVOR: Well, you go through Denford Heath, you can have a look at it. The cottage is off the main road about a mile and a half from Denford Church.

STEVE: Inspector, is Salty West in Downburgh?

IVOR: Yes; he's returned. He went away for a while – remember, you sent me a telegram.

TEMPLE: Yes.

IVOR: Salty's lived most of his life in Downburgh. I don't ever remember him leaving the place before.

STEVE: Where did he go to, do you know?

IVOR: I don't know; no one seems to know. It's something of a mystery.

STEVE: Is he just the same as ever; I mean, does he look the same, mix with the same people?

IVOR: (*Hesitantly*) Yes, I think so. Perhaps he's a little more independent than he used to be; drinks rather a lot – but then he always did.

TEMPLE: We sent you the telegram, Inspector, because my wife was under the impression she'd seen him in London – well, actually, at Maidenhead.

IVOR: At Maidenhead?

TEMPLE: Yes. He was sitting in a Rolls Royce outside the Stags Head Hotel. He looked very clean, very spruce, and I gather, very pleased with himself.

IVOR: Salty West?

TEMPLE: Yes.

IVOR: (*Laughing*) You must have been mistaken, Mrs Temple.

STEVE: I wasn't mistaken, I can assure you. In any case, he recognised me – he winked.

IVOR: (*Interested; seriously*) He winked?

STEVE: Yes.

IVOR: Then that was Salty all right; he just can't resist winking, it's a regular habit of his. But what on earth was he doing at Maidenhead?

TEMPLE: That's what I'd like to know – and what I intend to ask him.

DORIS: A pint of bitter and a light ale.

IVOR: I said half a pint, Doris.

DORIS: Oh – I'm sorry, sir.

TEMPLE: It's all right, this is on me. You can manage a pint, Inspector.

DORIS: Thank you, sir.

A moment.

IVOR: (*Raising his glass*) Well – good luck, Mr Temple. I hope you get more out of Salty West than I did.

FADE UP the background noises of the bar parlour.

FADE DOWN
FADE UP the sound of TEMPLE's car.

It is travelling fairly slowly.

A pause.

TEMPLE: We must have done over a mile and a half since we left the church.

STEVE: Yes. (*A moment*) It's a lovely night. I haven't seen a moon like this for ages.

TEMPLE: It's a new moon, Steve. Turn your money over.

STEVE: What money?

TEMPLE laughs.

A pause.

STEVE: There's a cottage over on the left, Paul.

TEMPLE: Where? … Oh yes, I see it …

The car slows down.

TEMPLE: Yes, this looks like it …

The car slows down and comes to a standstill during the following dialogue.

STEVE: Are you going to stop?

TEMPLE: Of course. What do you think I've come down here for?

STEVE: I thought you just wanted to have a look at the place. I doubt whether Freeman's there.

TEMPLE: Doesn't matter if he isn't, I still want to have a look round.

STEVE: How long will it take us to Downburgh from here?

TEMPLE: Oh, less than an hour.

The car stops.

TEMPLE: What does it say on the gate, Steve?

TEMPLE and STEVE get out of the car.

STEVE: Redstone Cottage … Yes, this is it, Paul.

We hear the sound of a wicker gate being opened.

There are background noises of the countryside at night; birds; the sound of an owl etc.

STEVE: It's rather pretty …

123

TEMPLE: Yes … It's a very nice porch …
STEVE: I agree with the Inspector, though, it is isolated. I shouldn't like to live here …
TEMPLE: It probably looks quite different in the daylight.

We hear the owl in the near background.

STEVE: (*A little nervous*) Paul, did you hear that?
TEMPLE: (*Laughing*) It's only an owl, Steve – don't be silly.
STEVE: I'll bet there's quite a lot of bats round here.
TEMPLE: (*Amused*) I shouldn't be a bit surprised.
STEVE: Oh dear …

A slight pause.

TEMPLE: There's obviously no one here at the moment or there'd be a light showing.
STEVE: What's that handle on the side of the door?
TEMPLE: Where? Oh, it's the bell pull …

TEMPLE pulls the handle and the bell starts to ring inside the cottage.

A slight pause.

He pulls the handle again; the sound of the bell continues.

TEMPLE: There's no one in …
STEVE: There's a window over on the right, Paul. I dare say we could see into the … What are you looking at?
TEMPLE: There's something sticking out of the letter box.

TEMPLE pulls an envelope out of the letter box.

STEVE: What is it – a letter?
TEMPLE: No, it's a telegram …
STEVE: Addressed to Freeman?
TEMPLE: Yes, Dan Freeman, Redstone Cottage …
STEVE: Well, you'd better put it back in the … Really, Paul!

TEMPLE has ripped open the telegram.

A pause.

124

STEVE: What does it say?

TEMPLE: (*Reading*) "S.R. arrived Isle of Skye. Operation successful." …

STEVE: S.R. – That's Sylvia Ross.

TEMPLE: Yes.

STEVE: Is there a signature – who sent the telegram?

TEMPLE: It doesn't say …

STEVE: You know, it sounds to me as if we ought to be going to Scotland, Paul – instead of Downburgh.

TEMPLE: Yes … Yes … Nevertheless, we're going to Downburgh, Steve!

FADE IN incidental music.

FADE DOWN music.

FADE IN a background of the sea.

A clock chimes the hour: it is eight o'clock.

STEVE: (*Speaking while the clock is still striking*) Do you know what time it is, Paul?

TEMPLE: (*In bed*) M'm?

STEVE: I said: Do you know what time it is?

TEMPLE: (*Sleepily*) No – what time is it?

STEVE: It's eight o'clock.

TEMPLE: Oh. (*A moment*) Goodnight, dear.

STEVE: What do you mean – goodnight? It's eight o'clock in the morning! Get up, you lazy…

STEVE picks up a pillow.

TEMPLE: Now, Steve, take it easy! Take it easy! Put that pillow down … (*He sits up*) My goodness, you're developing into one of those frightfully hearty women! Physical jerks, cold showers, eggs and bacon for breakfast …

STEVE: (*At the window*) M'm – sounds delicious!

STEVE opens the window.

STEVE: Paul, it's a lovely morning! The sun's out already ... (*A deep breath*) Darling, I adore Downburgh.

TEMPLE: Good. I'll remember that next time you want to go to the South of France.

STEVE: What are we going to do this morning?

TEMPLE: I know what I'm going to do. I'm going to track down Salty West and have a jolly good talk to the old boy. I've got a hunch that he knows a great deal more than ... What are you looking at?

STEVE: (*Impressed*) Isn't that a wonderful yacht?

TEMPLE: Where?

STEVE: In the harbour.

TEMPLE: Well, I didn't think it would be in the ... (*Equally impressed*) Yes, by Timothy, it is!

STEVE: It's a beauty!

TEMPLE: It certainly is.

They stand staring out of the window.

STEVE: And you're not the only one who gets up at eight o'clock ...

TEMPLE: Why do you say that?

STEVE: Look! There's someone on deck ...

TEMPLE: If I had a yacht like that I doubt whether I should ever go below ...

STEVE: (*A moment*) What's he doing?

TEMPLE: (*Slowly; watching*) There's a dinghy on the other side, I think he's trying to get hold of the rope so that the dinghy ... (*He hesitates; still watching*)

A pause.

STEVE: What is it, Paul?

TEMPLE: Did you see the way he walked across the deck? Did you see how he stooped as it ... Steve, I've seen that man before somewhere ...

STEVE: Now don't be silly, you couldn't recognise anyone from this distance ...

TEMPLE: But I'm sure I ... Where are my binoculars?

STEVE: I don't think you unpacked them, unless ... Oh, there you are!

A moment.

TEMPLE: (*Taking the binoculars*) Thanks, Steve.

A definite pause.

STEVE: Well? (*Another pause*) Well?

TEMPLE: (*Excited*) By Timothy!

STEVE: (*Intensely curious*) Paul, what is it?

TEMPLE: (*A note of tenseness in his voice*) Do you know what they call that yacht?

STEVE: No? ...

TEMPLE: It's called – The Isle of Skye ...

FADE IN closing music.

END OF EPISODE FOUR

EPISODE FIVE

A PRESENT FOR STEVE

OPEN TO STEVE's voice.

STEVE: Look! There's someone on deck …

TEMPLE: If I had a yacht like that I doubt whether I should ever go below …

STEVE: (*A moment*) What's he doing?

TEMPLE: (*Slowly; watching*) There's a dinghy on the other side, I think he's trying to get hold of the rope so that the dinghy … (*He hesitates; still watching*)

A pause.

STEVE: What is it, Paul?

TEMPLE: Did you see the way he walked across the deck? Did you see how he stooped as it … Steve, I've seen that man before somewhere …

STEVE: Now don't be silly, you couldn't recognise anyone from this distance …

TEMPLE: But I'm sure I … Where are my binoculars?

STEVE: I don't think you unpacked them, unless … Oh, there you are!

A moment.

TEMPLE: (*Taking the binoculars*) Thanks, Steve.

A definite pause.

STEVE: Well? (*Another pause*) Well?

TEMPLE: (*Excited*) By Timothy!

STEVE: (*Intensely curious*) Paul, what is it?

TEMPLE: (*A note of tenseness in his voice*) Do you know what they call that yacht?

STEVE: No? …

TEMPLE: It's called – The Isle of Skye …

STEVE: The Isle of … Paul, you're joking!

TEMPLE: No, I'm not. Take the binoculars and look for yourself.

A pause.

TEMPLE: Well?

STEVE: (*Peering through the binoculars*) Yes … yes, you're right.

TEMPLE starts laughing.

TEMPLE: And to think poor old Vosper went dancing up to Scotland!

STEVE: (*Seriously*) You think the telegram we found and the message Burford overheard referred to the yacht?

TEMPLE: Well, don't you?

STEVE: I suppose it must have done … I wonder who the yacht belongs to?

TEMPLE: That shouldn't be difficult to find out. Give me the binoculars. Thanks.

STEVE: Who did you think it was on board? You said you thought you recognised him …

TEMPLE: (*Peering through the glasses*) Well, I thought it was Brian Dexter, but … now … I'm … not … so … sure … (*A moment*) He's getting into the dinghy. (*A pause*) I think he's coming ashore. Steve, where's the telephone?

STEVE: It's over here.

TEMPLE picks up the receiver.

TEMPLE: (*On the phone*) Hello? … Hello? …

STEVE: Who are you telephoning?

TEMPLE: I'm sending Sir Graham a telegram. The sooner he knows about the yacht the better. (*On the phone*) Hello?

GIRL: (*On the other end of the phone*) Room service …

TEMPLE: Give me the operator, please. I want to send a telegram.

GIRL: Yes, sir. Hold on a moment, please.

TEMPLE: Steve, the last time we were down here you went about quite a bit on your own because I was busy on the novel.

132

STEVE:	Yes?
TEMPLE:	Well, tell me: is there a café down here or a coffee house, a sort of general meeting place?
STEVE:	There's Mrs Purdie's.
TEMPLE:	What's that?
STEVE:	It's a shop near the quay; she serves light refreshments, coffee and biscuits and that sort of thing. It's a very nice little shop.
TEMPLE:	Do the locals use it?
STEVE:	Yes, but it's chiefly for visitors, they adore it.
TEMPLE:	Is there a Mrs Purdie?
STEVE:	(*With a Scots accent*) Of course there's a Mrs Purdie! And who do you think makes the homemade scones?
TEMPLE:	(*Laughing*) Not Mrs Purdie, I'll bet. (*On the phone*) Hello?
2nd GIRL:	(*On the other end of the phone*) Telegrams …
TEMPLE:	I want to send a telegram to Sir Graham Forbes … Forbes, that's right. F-O-R-B-E-S …

FADE SCENE.

FADE UP the sound of a door bell ringing; a spring shop bell.

STEVE:	Good morning, Mrs Purdie.
MRS PURDIE:	(*A middle-aged Scotswoman*) Oh, good morning, Mrs Temple! How nice to see you again. This is a pleasant surprise.
STEVE:	I don't think you've met my husband.
MRS PURDIE:	No. Good morning, sir.
TEMPLE:	Good morning, Mrs Purdie.

133

MRS PURDIE:	Will this table by the window be all right for you?
STEVE:	Yes, splendid. We'd like some coffee and some biscuits, please.
MRS PURDIE:	Yes, certainly. My word, it's a bit cold this morning, isn't it?
STEVE:	I was just saying how nice it was!
TEMPLE:	My wife never feels the cold.
STEVE:	Oh, darling, that's not true.
TEMPLE:	There seem to be quite a few visitors in Downburgh for the time of year.
MRS PURDIE:	Yes, we've been quite busy just lately, it's surprising.
STEVE:	(*In the near background*) It's a lovely view from this window, Paul.
TEMPLE:	Yes, it is indeed. Who does that yacht belong to, Mrs Purdie, do you know?
MRS PURDIE:	The white one, sir?
TEMPLE:	Yes.
MRS PURDIE:	It belongs to a lady, I believe. A Mrs – Oh dear, now what do they call her. A peculiar, foreign sort of name. (*Suddenly*) De Silva … That's it! Mrs de Silva.
TEMPLE:	(*Surprised*) Mrs de Silva?
MRS PURDIE:	That's right, Mrs de Silva. A very nice lady; very smart. Pots of money, of course.
TEMPLE:	Is the yacht often down here?
MRS PURDIE:	Yes, I suppose it is. It's been here two or three times this year. They do say it's a wonderful boat, equipped with all kinds of things. (*Amused*) Salty West told a friend of mine they even had a cinema aboard, but I can hardly believe that.
STEVE:	Have you seen Salty West recently?

MRS PURDIE:	He pops in occasionally, looking more dishevelled than ever. Two coffees, you said?
TEMPLE:	That's right, Mrs Purdie – and some biscuits.
MRS PURDIE:	Yes, sir.

A moment.

STEVE:	(*Excited*) Paul, you were right!
TEMPLE:	What do you mean?
STEVE:	It was Dexter you saw!
TEMPLE:	How do you know?
STEVE:	Look – through the window!
TEMPLE:	He's coming in here!

A pause.

The door opens. We hear the sound of the bell.

MRS PURDIE:	(*In the background*) Good morning, sir.
DEXTER:	(*Pleasantly; quite brightly*) Good morning, Mrs Purdie. I'd like some scones, please.
MRS PURDIE:	Yes, certainly, sir.
DEXTER:	And some cream, Mrs Purdie – that delicious cream we bought yesterday morning.
MRS PURDIE:	Yes, sir.

DEXTER starts to hum a tune to himself.

TEMPLE:	Good morning, Dexter.
DEXTER:	(*Surprised*) Why, hello, Temple!
TEMPLE:	(*Smiling*) It's a small world, isn't it?
DEXTER:	(*Distinctly ill at ease*) How – how long have you been down here?
TEMPLE:	We arrived last night. You know my wife, of course?
DEXTER:	Yes, yes, rather. Good morning, Mrs Temple.
STEVE:	Good morning, Mr Dexter.

TEMPLE: Are you staying at the hotel?

DEXTER: No, I – I'm staying with some friends.

TEMPLE: In Downburgh?

DEXTER: No, well – yes – in a way I … As a matter of fact I'm staying on one of the yachts.

TEMPLE: Oh, indeed.

STEVE: It wouldn't be that heavenly looking one over there, Mr Dexter – the white one?

DEXTER: Er – yes.

STEVE: We were admiring it this morning from our bedroom window.

TEMPLE: You must have some very wealthy friends, Dexter.

DEXTER: (*A little laugh*) Yes, I suppose I have.

TEMPLE: Is this a frequent haunt of yours?

DEXTER: No, I don't think I've been in this part of the world before; it's very pleasant, isn't it?

TEMPLE: Yes, very pleasant.

STEVE: Are you staying long?

DEXTER: Well, I don't really know, it rather depends on … when … we … decide … to … move … on …

STEVE: (*Amused*) Yes, I suppose it must.

DEXTER: That sounds a bit stupid, doesn't it? What I really meant is, it doesn't depend on me at all, it depends on someone else.

TEMPLE: On Mrs de Silva?

DEXTER: Yes. (*Surprised*) Do you know Mrs de Silva?

TEMPLE: No; but we admired the yacht so much we inquired who it belonged to. We were told it belonged to a Mrs de Silva.

DEXTER: Yes, that's right. She's an old friend of my father's.

TEMPLE: Is she related to Ernest de Silva – the eye specialist – by any chance?

136

DEXTER:	Yes; yes, she's his wife but the yacht doesn't belong to Ernest, it belongs to …
TEMPLE:	His wife.
DEXTER:	(*A nervous little laugh*) Yes.
TEMPLE:	I see.
DEXTER:	(*A moment; still uncertain of himself*) Do you know Ernest?
TEMPLE:	We have met. Is he a friend of yours?
DEXTER:	No; no, you'd hardly call him a friend.
MRS PURDIE:	Here's your scones, sir – and the cream.
DEXTER:	Oh, thank you, Mrs Purdie.
MRS PURDIE:	That'll be four an' six, sir.

MRS PURDIE takes the money.

MRS PURDIE:	Thank you, sir. (*To STEVE*) The coffee won't be a few moments, Mrs Temple.
DEXTER:	(*Hesitantly*) Well – I'll be making a move. Nice to have seen you. Goodbye, Mrs Temple.
STEVE:	Goodbye, Mr Dexter.
DEXTER:	(*Almost an afterthought*) Oh, I suppose there's no news – about Sylvia, I mean?
TEMPLE:	(*Quietly*) No, there's no news, Dexter.
DEXTER:	I haven't been questioned lately. I gather you must have spoken to the Inspector.
TEMPLE:	Yes, I did.
DEXTER:	Thank you, Temple. I'm very grateful.
TEMPLE:	(*Pleasantly*) Well, if you're grateful, perhaps you wouldn't mind doing me a favour?
DEXTER:	Why, yes, of course. What is it?
TEMPLE:	I'd like to meet Mrs de Silva.
DEXTER:	(*Taken aback*) Oh … well –
TEMPLE:	Do you think that could be arranged?
DEXTER:	Er – yes, I don't see why not.

TEMPLE: All right, I'll leave it with you, Dexter. We're staying at the Crescent Hotel.

DEXTER: I'll – I'll give you a ring, probably later in the day.

TEMPLE: Fine.

DEXTER: (*Hesitantly*) Perhaps you'd like to come out to the yacht for drinks?

TEMPLE: That would be very nice.

DEXTER: Well, I'll have a word with Julie – that's Mrs de Silva – and let you know.

TEMPLE: Splendid. Incidentally, you might tell her I was awfully sorry to hear about her chauffeur.

DEXTER: (*Puzzled*) Her chauffeur?

TEMPLE: Yes – Barker.

DEXTER: (*Puzzled*) I know Barker, he's often driven me to the theatre and places. What about him?

TEMPLE: He's dead; he's apparently committed suicide.

DEXTER: Barker did?

TEMPLE: Yes.

DEXTER: When?

TEMPLE: About four or five days ago, I believe it was.

DEXTER: Are you sure?

TEMPLE: Of course I'm sure. I identified the body.

DEXTER: But this is very odd. Julie can't know about it or she'd have mentioned it to me. (*A sudden thought*) But why did you identify the body? Was he a friend of yours?

TEMPLE: No, but when they fished him out of the river they didn't know who he was. They found some photographs on him; they were photographs of my wife.

DEXTER: Photographs of Mrs Temple?

TEMPLE: Yes.

DEXTER: But why should Barker carry photographs of Mrs Temple?

TEMPLE: Why, indeed? Yes, that puzzled me – at the time.

DEXTER: I'm quite sure Julie doesn't know about this. I'll – I'll give you a ring later.

TEMPLE: Yes, all right.

DEXTER: (*His thoughts elsewhere*) Goodbye.

TEMPLE: Goodbye, Dexter.

A pause.

We hear the sound of the door opening and closing and the door bell ringing.

STEVE: Did he know about Barker?

TEMPLE: If he did he's a pretty good actor.

STEVE: Paul, do you think he's in league with Freeman and this Mrs de Silva? Do you think Sylvia Ross is actually on that yacht?

TEMPLE: Well, the telegram we found and the phone message Burford overheard certainly must have referred to the yacht; on the other hand I certainly shouldn't have thought a yacht was a particularly good place to hide anyone.

STEVE: But I should have thought it was excellent!

TEMPLE: All the police need is a search warrant. Once they're on board they're bound to find the girl.

STEVE: Well, assuming she is on the yacht – assuming she's been kidnapped – I still don't understand why?

TEMPLE: You still don't understand why?

STEVE: If it's simply a question of money – a ransom – why haven't they contacted her father? And in any case, why pick on Sylvia Ross? There must be a considerable number of men a great deal better off than Sir Carlton.

139

TEMPLE: It isn't a question of money, Steve – I'm sure of that.

STEVE: You mean, it's tied up with the fact that her father's head of M.I.5.?

TEMPLE: Yes.

STEVE: (*Thoughtfully*) You know, Paul, I've often thought back to how this business first started.

TEMPLE: How did it start?

STEVE: Well, surely it really started the day we went out in that boat with Bob Gardner; the day the shots were fired at us.

TEMPLE: I think it started long before that.

STEVE: What do you mean?

TEMPLE: If Linda Teako was telling the truth the name Clive Lawrence was on the note that Sylvia Ross sent to Johnny Teako, also an address – The Hotel Schweizerhof, Zermatt.

STEVE: Well?

TEMPLE: Don't you remember what Bob Gardner said about that name and address? Don't you remember? He said – one day it's going to be very important. (*Thoughtfully*) Sylvia stayed at Zermatt over twelve months ago and that's when she first met this mysterious Mr Lawrence and when, in my opinion, this business first started.

STEVE: You don't think Dexter is Lawrence and he's simply pulling the wool over our eyes?

TEMPLE: It's possible, Steve, and I've thought of that. On the other hand Lawrence might be – someone else. One thing I'm sure of though …

STEVE: What's that, Paul?

TEMPLE: The key to this business, the solution to the whole mystery, is to be found here … in Downburgh …

FADE IN incidental music.

Slow FADE DOWN of music.
FADE IN background noises of the quay at Downburgh.
We hear the sound of footsteps on cobbles.

TEMPLE: There doesn't appear to be any sign of your
            friend Salty!

STEVE: He always used to be down here; usually
            lounging against one of the boats.

TEMPLE: Is that him over there?

STEVE: Where? Oh, no – he's much shorter than that.

TEMPLE: Let's walk further down, then I'll ask someone.

FADE UP the background noises.

We hear more footsteps.

TEMPLE stops a passer-by.

TEMPLE: Excuse me …

WALTERS: (*A man in his late thirties; a fisherman*) Yes,
            sir?

TEMPLE: Do you know Salty West?

WALTERS: (*Smiling*) Why, sure – I know Salty.

TEMPLE: You don't happen to know where he is at the
            moment?

WALTERS: Why, yes – that's him over there.

STEVE: Where?

WALTERS: In that boat, ma'am – out in the bay.

STEVE: I can see the boat but there doesn't appear to be
            anyone in it.

WALTERS: He's there all right. He's supposed to be
            fishing.

TEMPLE: Supposed to be?

WALTERS: Yes, if I know Salty he's asleep, been asleep
            for hours.

TEMPLE: Well, how long will he stay out there?

WALTERS: He'll wake up when the pubs open.

TEMPLE laughs.

TEMPLE: Could I hire a boat to take me out there? I want to have a chat with him.

WALTERS: You mean now?

TEMPLE: Yes.

WALTERS: (*A moment*) I'll row you out.

TEMPLE: Oh, thanks very much.

WALTERS: It'll cost you half-a-crown.

TEMPLE: That's all right.

WALTERS: (*Quickly*) Five bob return.

TEMPLE: (*Amused*) It's a deal.

START FADE.

WALTERS: Follow me, Mrs Temple. My boat's about a hundred yards further down.

FADE SCENE.

FADE UP the sound of the rowing boat on the water.

STAN WALTERS is rowing TEMPLE and STEVE out to SALTY WEST.

A pause.

STEVE: … It's further than I thought, Paul.

TEMPLE: Yes.

WALTERS: (*Rowing*) I should have made it ten bob.

STEVE laughs.

A pause.

WALTERS: Is Salty a friend of yours?

TEMPLE: No.

WALTERS: If you want a reliable boatman I don't recommend Salty.

TEMPLE: We just want to have a word with him, that's all.

WALTERS: He seems to be quite an attraction these days. This is the second time this has happened.

TEMPLE: What do you mean?

142

WALTERS: A gent came down here yesterday asking for Salty. Walked all over the village trying to find him.

TEMPLE: What was he like?

WALTERS: Who – the gent? Oh, tallish chap. Dark. Wore specs. Had a funny accent. Scotch or Irish; can never tell the difference myself.

STEVE: That sounds like Freeman, Paul.

TEMPLE: Did he find him?

WALTERS: Oh, he found him in the end. Salty was out in the bay. Pal o' mine rowed him out – the gent, I mean. (*Grinning*) Charged 'im twelve an' a tanner.

TEMPLE: What did he want exactly?

WALTERS: He wanted to see Salty.

TEMPLE: Yes, but why?

WALTERS: Don't know why … They 'ad quite a natter according to this pal o' mine.

TEMPLE: How long have you known Salty?

WALTERS: Oh, some few years. Can never make head or tail of him. Just don't know how he makes a living. Are you all right there, Mrs Temple? You're not getting wet?

STEVE: No, I'm all right, thanks. I've seen you before, haven't I?

WALTERS: Yes. I remember your being down here a few weeks ago. I was with Bob Gardner the morning you hired the boat.

STEVE: Yes, that's right, I remember now! Walters …

WALTERS: That's right, ma'am – Stan Walters.

STEVE: Was Bob Gardner a friend of yours?

WALTERS: (*A shade truculent*) He was my best friend.

TEMPLE: What was your opinion of the accident, Mr Walters?

143

WALTERS: Some as anyone else's – it ought never to have happened.

TEMPLE: You mean Bob should have left the dog, he shouldn't have rescued it?

WALTERS: (*Still faintly truculent*) He was a sick man; he'd already had one nasty experience. What the 'ell did he want to go climbing down the side of a cliff for?

TEMPLE: Did you talk to Salty about it?

WALTERS: (*After a pause*) No …

TEMPLE: I suppose you know what happened to Mary Gardner?

WALTERS: Yes, I know. I read about it. (*He stops rowing*) Here we are … It's all right, Mrs Temple – stay where you are …

WALTERS manipulates the oars in the water.

The boat draws close to the fishing boat.

STEVE: (*Amused*) You're right, he's asleep!

WALTERS: Salty! Salty, wake up!

WALTERS deliberately knocks the side of the fishing boat with his oar.

WALTERS: Salty!!!

TEMPLE: He certainly is asleep!

WALTERS hits the fishing boat again with the oar.

WALTERS: Salty!

WALTERS shakes the fishing boat.

WALTERS: What the devil's the matter with the man!

STEVE: He's waking up now.

SALTY stirs, yawns and stretches himself.

SALTY: What is this? What the devil's goin' on?

WALTERS: Salty, wake up!

STEVE: He's been drinking, Paul. Look at all the empty bottles!

SALTY: (*Irritated*) What is it? What do you want?

144

WALTERS: I've brought some friends out to see you.

SALTY: I haven't got any friends! Go away – vamoose!

WALTERS: Salty, wake up! D'you hear what I say – wake up!

SALTY: (*Shouting*) Go away – leave me alone – I want to sleep! Go away!

TEMPLE: Salty, we want to have a talk to you. We shan't keep you long …

SALTY: Who are you? You're no friend of mine. I haven't seen you before.

STEVE: You remember me, Salty. Mrs Temple.

SALTY: Mrs Who?

STEVE: Mrs Temple.

SALTY: Oh … Oh … (*He starts chuckling to himself; dazed with drink*) Yes, I remember you … I remember you … You looked surprised when you saw me … very – very surprised … Didn't think I could look smart, did you? Didn't think Salty West could look so … smart …

TEMPLE: Salty, I've one or two questions I want to ask you. I suggest Walters leaves us together for a little while and …

SALTY: I'm not answering any questions. I'm not talkin', I'm just not sayin' nothin' …

STEVE: Paul, he's drunk – you'll never get anything out of him while he's like this.

TEMPLE: Salty, listen; what were you doing at Maidenhead? Is de Silva a friend of yours or was it the chauffeur that took …

SALTY: (*Suddenly angry*) Go away! Leave me alone!

TEMPLE: Salty, I want to know what you were doing at Maidenhead.

SALTY: I tell you I'm not talking! Go away! Go away, blast you – leave me alone!

SALTY picks up a bottle and smashes it against the side of the boat.

STEVE: Paul, he's got hold of a bottle!

WALTERS: Put that bottle down, Salty!

SALTY: (*A threat*) Now will you leave me alone?

WALTERS: (*Tough*) Salty, put that bottle down!

A moment; then SALTY throws the bottle into the sea.

SALTY: (*Near to tears, sorry for himself*) Well, don't keep asking me a lot of questions … I don't know what the 'ell you're talking about – leave me alone.

STEVE: Paul, let's go back. You'll never get any sense out of him while he's like this.

WALTERS: I'm afraid she's right, sir.

TEMPLE: Yes, all right. (*To WALTERS*) Take us back.

WALTERS: Yes, sir.

WALTERS puts the oars back into the water and turns the boat round.

WALTERS: He's going to sleep again by the look of things!

FADE DOWN the sound of the oars in the water.

FADE UP a background of the noise of the sea.

Oars in the water; the boat has reached the shore.

TEMPLE: Can you manage?

WALTERS: Yes; just stay where you are, sir, I'll put the boat in.

WALTERS jumps into the water and pulls the boat onto the beach.

WALTERS: How's that?

TEMPLE: That's fine! Wait till I get out, Steve, then I'll give you my hand.

TEMPLE climbs out of the boat, then helps STEVE out.

TEMPLE: Ready?

STEVE: Yes …

146

TEMPLE: Steady … That's it!

WALTERS: I'm sorry it wasn't a more successful trip, sir.

TEMPLE: It couldn't be helped. Here we are, you can keep the change.

WALTERS: (*Pleased*) Oh, thank you, sir – that's very kind of you.

TEMPLE: Walters, tell me: do you see a great deal of Salty West?

WALTERS: Well, he always seems to be about, sir. As I told you before, he's a bit of a mystery. No one seems to know where he gets his money from, but he always seems to have plenty.

TEMPLE: Is he married?

WALTERS: No; heavens no, he lives on his own. He has a cottage at the top of Felston Cliff. I'm afraid you got rather a bad impression of him this morning, Mr Temple. He's not usually as bad as that.

STEVE: You mean, he's not usually so drunk?

WALTERS: Well, let's say, he's not usually so aggressive, Mrs Temple.

TEMPLE: Well, thank you, Walters. Ready, Steve?

STEVE: Yes, I'm ready …

WALTERS: (*Hesitantly*) Mr Temple …

TEMPLE: Yes?

WALTERS: Excuse me asking, sir; I know it's none of my business, but –

TEMPLE: Yes, Walters?

WALTERS: Why are you interested in Salty West, sir?

TEMPLE: I'll tell you why, Walters, if you'll tell me why *you're* interested.

WALTERS: Well, I know your reputation, sir, an' I was wondering if – (*He hesitates*)

TEMPLE: Go on …

147

WALTERS: I was wondering if you were dissatisfied in any way.

TEMPLE: (*Puzzled*) Dissatisfied?

WALTERS: With the verdict, sir.

TEMPLE: What verdict? Oh – you mean Bob Gardner?

WALTERS: Yes, sir. Was it an accident, or wasn't it?

TEMPLE: Well, if it wasn't, it must have been murder and if it was murder there must have been a motive. Can you suggest a possible motive?

WALTERS: (*A moment*) No. Everyone liked Bob. He was the most popular chap in Downburgh.

TEMPLE: Did Salty West like him?

WALTERS: Yes, I think so.

TEMPLE: What about his sister – Mary Gardner?

WALTERS: (*Truculently*) What about her?

TEMPLE: Was she popular?

WALTERS: (*A moment*) I 'ad very little to do with her. I don't know whether she was popular or not.

TEMPLE: I gather you were not particularly fond of Miss Gardner?

WALTERS: I've told you, I 'ad very little to with her. You still haven't answered <u>my</u> question, Mr Temple.

TEMPLE: Several days ago my wife saw Salty sitting in a Rolls Royce outside the Stags Head Hotel at Maidenhead.

WALTERS: (*Surprised*) Salty?

TEMPLE: Yes, Salty. The car belonged to a man called Ernest de Silva.

WALTERS: Yes, I heard you mention the name …

TEMPLE: His chauffeur, Barker, was found dead. He had some photographs on him, photographs of Mrs Temple. I wanted to question Salty about

	Barker and about his possible relationship with Mr de Silva.
WALTERS:	(*Thoughtfully*) De Silva …
TEMPLE:	Yes; Ernest de Silva.
STEVE:	Have you heard the name before, Mr Walters?
WALTERS:	(*Slowly*) Yes; there's a Mrs de Silva. She's often in Downburgh. That's her yacht over there …
STEVE:	Do you know her?
WALTERS:	I've seen her about. Good looking woman.
STEVE:	How old would she be?
WALTERS:	Oh, now you're asking me, Mrs Temple. Late forties.
TEMPLE:	What does she come down to Downburgh for, exactly? Has she got friends in this part of the world?
WALTERS:	I wouldn't know, Mr Temple.
TEMPLE:	Well, thank you, Walters. If we need you at any time …
WALTERS:	You can always find me down at the quay; if I'm not there, try the Hare and Hounds.
TEMPLE:	(*Smiling*) Right. (*To STEVE*) Ready, darling?
STEVE:	Yes, but wait a minute, there's some water in one of my shoes …

STEVE takes off one of her shoes and empties it.

| STEVE: | That's better … Goodbye … |
| WALTERS: | Goodbye, Mrs Temple. |

FADE SCENE.

FADE UP background voices in the entrance hall of the Crescent Hotel at Downburgh.
TEMPLE and STEVE enter the hall.
We hear the sound of the lift door opening and closing.

TEMPLE: I'm going up to the room, Steve – are you coming?

STEVE: No, I don't think so, dear. I'll see you in the lounge.

TEMPLE: Yes, all right. Order me a dry Martini.

GIRL: Excuse me, sir. Mr Temple?

TEMPLE: Yes?

GIRL: A Mr Dexter telephoned about a quarter of an hour ago, sir.

TEMPLE: Oh, did he leave a message?

GIRL: Yes, sir. He said he's spoken to Mrs de – er –

TEMPLE: De Silva.

GIRK: That's right, Mrs de Silva – and would you and Mrs Temple meet him down at the quay at about a quarter to six?

TEMPLE: I see. Thank you.

GIRL: Thank you, sir.

TEMPLE: There's no other message for me?

GIRL: No, sir.

STEVE: It's a wonder you haven't heard from Sir Graham; he must have got your telegram by now.

TEMPLE: Yes. I've got a hunch we shall see Vosper down here with half the Flying Squad!

STEVE: I wouldn't be surprised.

TEMPLE opens the lift door.

TEMPLE: I won't be long, Steve.

STEVE: Yes, all right.

STEVE enters the main lounge.

FADE UP background noises.

WAITER: Anything I can get you, madam?

STEVE: Yes, two dry Martinis, please.

WAITER: Yes, certainly, madam.

STEVE: (*Suddenly; surprised*) Why, hello!

LINDA: I beg your pardon?

STEVE: It is Mrs Teako, isn't it?

LINDA: Yes.

STEVE: Mrs Temple.

LINDA: Oh, hello, Mrs Temple! I'm sorry I didn't recognise you.

STEVE: Remember, we met the night my husband …

LINDA: Yes, of course, I remember.

STEVE: Are you staying here?

LINDA: No, we're just passing through – we stopped for lunch, that's all.

STEVE: Is your husband with you?

LINDA: (*Hesitantly*) Yes; he's just gone to get the car. We're in rather a hurry because he's got to be back in Town for a rehearsal at half past four.

STEVE: Did you come down last night?

LINDA: No, early this morning. Johnny's mother lives just outside Felixstowe and – well, she hasn't been well recently and we suddenly decided to pay her a flying visit.

STEVE: I see.

LINDA: You know how it is with old folks.

JOHNNY TEAKO enters the lounge.

TEAKO: (*From the background*) Linda, are you ready?

LINDA: Yes, I'm coming, Johnny.

STEVE: (*Pleasantly*) Hello, Mr Teako!

LINDA: Johnny, you remember Mrs Temple.

TEAKO: (*Faintly surprised*) Yeah – yeah, sure. How are you?

STEVE: I'm fine, but I'm sorry to hear about your mother, Mr Teako.

TEAKO: My mother?

LINDA: (*Without embarrassment*) I was just telling Mrs Temple about your mother being ill, Johnny.

TEAKO: Oh, yes …

LINDA: She asked me if we'd stayed the night here.

TEAKO: Oh, no! No, this is just a flying visit. I've got to be back in Town at four-thirty. Is your husband down here?

STEVE: Yes, we're staying for two or three days.

TEAKO: And very nice too! I wish I could take a break like that.

LINDA: (*With sarcasm*) What's stopping you?

TEAKO: Are you crazy? Where would the boys be without Johnny Teako?

LINDA: Don't tell him, Mrs Temple. Goodbye, have a nice time.

STEVE: Thank you.

TEAKO: Give your husband my regards.

STEVE: Yes, I will.

TEAKO: (*A sudden thought*) Incidentally, did he solve that little problem?

STEVE: Which little problem, Mr Teako?

TEAKO: You know, the one he was investigating. Did they find the girl?

STEVE: No, I'm afraid not.

TEAKO: M'm-m'm, that's too bad. Ah, well – goodbye.

STEVE: Goodbye, Mr Teako.

WAITER: Two gin and tonics, madam.

STEVE: No, two dry Martinis.

WAITER: Oh, I thought you said …

STEVE: I said two dry Martinis – but that's all right, you can leave those.

WAITER: I'll change them, madam.

STEVE: (*Suddenly, to TEMPLE*) Paul, do you know who I've just been talking to?

TEMPLE: Yes – the Teakos. I've just seen them. They were leaving the hotel as I came down the staircase.

152

STEVE: They're on their way back to Town.

TEMPLE: What were they doing here anyway; did they stay the night?

STEVE: No, apparently his mother's ill and they suddenly decided to pay her a flying visit.

TEMPLE: Does his mother live in Downburgh?

STEVE: Between here and Felixstowe; they called in here for lunch.

TEMPLE: M'm.

STEVE: The story sounded perfectly all right until the maestro himself appeared on the scene. Somehow I can't imagine him dashing down from Town just to see Mum.

TEMPLE: (*Thoughtfully*) No, I'm inclined to agree, Steve; besides it's too big a coincidence. I remember the first time we met … (*Looking up*) Yes?

GIRL: Excuse me, sir – you're wanted on the telephone.

TEMPLE: Oh, thank you. Is there a box down here?

GIRL: Yes, sir – just near the dining room.

TEMPLE: Thank you.

STEVE: This is probably Sir Graham. They've got your telegram.

TEMPLE: Yes. I shan't be a minute, Steve.

FADE the background noises of the lounge.

FADE UP the opening of a telephone box door.
The door closes.
TEMPLE lifts the receiver.

TEMPLE: (*On the phone*) Hello?

2nd OPERATOR: (*On the other end of the phone*) Mr Temple?

TEMPLE: Yes …

2nd OPERATOR: One moment, please.

The OPERATOR makes the connection.

153

2nd OPERATOR:　You're through – Mr Temple's on the line, caller.

TEMPLE:　Hello? (*A pause; irritated*) Hello?

2nd OPERATOR:　One moment, sir. (*To the caller*) Mr Temple's on the line, will you speak up, please?

SALTY:　(*On the other end of the line; very quietly*) Mr Temple?

2nd OPERATOR:　Speak up, caller!

SALTY:　(*Softly; tensely*) Is that you, Mr Temple?

TEMPLE:　Yes, this is Paul Temple. Who is that?

SALTY:　This is Salty West, sir.

TEMPLE:　Salty … Oh, hello! I didn't expect to hear from you.

SALTY:　I'm – I'm sorry about this morning, Mr Temple. I wanted to talk to you, but –

TEMPLE:　Don't worry about this morning, Salty. How's the hangover?

SALTY:　Oh, it – it could be worse, I think. I want to see you, Mr Temple, it's important.

TEMPLE:　Well, I want to see you, Salty.

SALTY:　Do you know where I live? Do you know Felston Cliff?

TEMPLE:　No, but I can find it.

SALTY:　It's up the hill past the quay; you fork right when you get to the Fox and Hounds. The cottage is called Roseberry. You can see it when you get to the pub.

TEMPLE:　I'll find it, Salty. What time?

SALTY:　Oh, any time this afternoon. About half past three …

TEMPLE:　Right …

SALTY:　And bring Mrs Temple with you.

TEMPLE:　(*Surprised*) Why Mrs Temple?

154

SALTY: (*Hesitantly; seriously*) I've – got – a – present for her. (*Suddenly; about to replace the receiver*) Half past three then …

SALTY replaces the receiver.

TEMPLE: (*Quickly; trying to stop SALTY from replacing the receiver, but he is too late*) Salty … Wait a minute … Salty!

FADE IN incidental music.

FADE music.

FADE UP background noises of a small garage and workshop.

JIM: Good afternoon, sir.

TEMPLE: Good afternoon. I'm taking my car out. I shall be back about five o'clock.

JIM: Yes, sir. Which one is it?

TEMPLE: The Bentley …

STEVE: (*Calling from the near background*) Paul …

TEMPLE: Just a minute, Steve. (*To JIM*) You might check the oil for me.

JIM: Certainly, sir. Shall I back the car out for you?

TEMPLE: Please.

TEMPLE joins STEVE.

TEMPLE: Yes, dear – what is it?

STEVE: (*Quietly*) Paul, that Rolls over there   that's the one I saw at Maidenhead.

TEMPLE: Are you sure?

STEVE: Yes, of course. UPF 485. It's de Silva's.

TEMPLE: Mrs de Silva's probably using it. I expect that's why it's down here.

STEVE: It wasn't here when we arrived.

TEMPLE: You're quite right, Steve. It wasn't.

We hear the sound of TEMPLE's car being moved from its parking space.

In the background, from the street, and during the following dialogue, there is the sound of a fire engine racing past the garage.

TEMPLE: (*To JIM*) Excuse me – that Rolls over there …
JIM: (*In TEMPLE's car*) Yes, sir?
TEMPLE: Was it brought in this afternoon?
JIM: Yes, about an hour ago. It belongs to a Mr de Silva.
TEMPLE: Did Mr de Silva drive it himself?
JIM: I believe so, sir.
TEMPLE: A short, dapper little man – grey hair.
JIM: That's right, sir.
TEMPLE: Is he staying in Downburgh?
JIM: I imagine so, sir. He's picking the car up tomorrow.
TEMPLE: I see.
JIM: You're pretty low on petrol, sir.
TEMPLE: Yes, all right. Fill her up.
JIM: Yes, sir.
FADE SCENE.

FADE UP the noise of TEMPLE's car travelling fairly slowly along a country lane.

TEMPLE is driving.

TEMPLE: … The Fox and Hounds should be at the top of the hill unless I've taken the wrong turning.
STEVE: I don't see how you could have done that, Paul.
TEMPLE: (*A moment*) What time do you make it, Steve?
STEVE: Just gone half past three.
TEMPLE: (*Suddenly*) There it is – the Fox and Hounds. Steve, when we reach the cottage I don't want you to get out of the car.
STEVE: Why not?
TEMPLE: I just don't, darling.

156

STEVE: Paul, are you sure that you understand what he said?

TEMPLE: Yes, I'm quite sure. He said – "And bring Mrs Temple, I've got a present for her."

STEVE: But why should Salty West want to give me a present? And what is it, anyway? What was he referring to?

TEMPLE: I don't know, but after that handbag I'm taking no chances.

STEVE: The old boy was probably still drunk.

TEMPLE: I don't think so, Steve.

A pause.

STEVE: Paul, I don't know whether you realise it or not, but within the last twenty-four hours every suspect in this affair …

TEMPLE: … Has visited Downburgh. Yes, I realise that.

STEVE: First of all we saw Brian Dexter, then Stan Walters told us about Freeman …

TEMPLE: We don't know for certain that it was Freeman.

STEVE: Well, it sounded like him. Then we bumped into the Teakos and finally we hear that Ernest de Silva … (*She stops*) What is it?

The car slows down.

TEMPLE: What's going on up there?

STEVE: It's a fire! Look!

TEMPLE: By Timothy, it certainly is a fire!

STEVE: It's a cottage, Paul … I wonder if … Slow down!

The car draws to a standstill.

FADE UP the noise of the fire burning in the distant background and the noise of water playing on the fire. There is a background of voices.

TEMPLE: That's Inspector Ivor!

STEVE: Where?

TEMPLE: Over there! (*Calling*) Inspector!

157

STEVE: He can't hear you, Paul!

TEMPLE: (*Calling louder*) Inspector!

STEVE: He's seen you.

TEMPLE: Come on, dear – let's get out of the car.

The car door opens and closes.

IVOR: Why, hello, Temple! What on earth are you doing here?

TEMPLE: What's more to the point, what are you doing here? Have you joined the local fire brigade?

IVOR: I happened to be in the station talking to a friend of mine when the message came through. I was curious.

STEVE: Whose cottage is it, Inspector?

TEMPLE: It's Salty West's. Am I right, Inspector?

IVOR: Yes – how did you know?

TEMPLE: We had an appointment with Salty, that's why we came up here.

STEVE: But what happened?

IVOR: It's difficult to tell at this stage, but it looks to me as if the cottage was deliberately set on fire.

TEMPLE: Where is Salty?

IVOR: He's over there, Temple, by the bank. He's in a pretty bad way, I'm afraid. We're waiting for an ambulance.

STEVE: Was he inside when …

IVOR: Yes, and they had a devil of a job getting him out. The thatched roof didn't exactly help.

TEMPLE: Do you mind if I have a word with him, Inspector?

IVOR: (*After a brief hesitation*) No, but I'm afraid you won't get much out of the poor devil.

TEMPLE: Stay with the Inspector, Steve.

FADE UP the background noises.

158

FADE DOWN slightly.
FADE IN SALTY WEST. He is in obvious pain.

TEMPLE: Salty, this is Temple …

SALTY: When – when are they going to take me away …?

TEMPLE: Soon, Salty. It won't be long now …

SALTY: I can't move my head, I … Oh, my head!

TEMPLE: Are you cold? Would you like me to fetch you a rug?

SALTY: No … No, don't touch me …

TEMPLE: (*Kneeling down by SALTY's side*) Salty, what did you mean on the phone when you said you'd a present for Mrs Temple?

SALTY: On – on the phone?

TEMPLE: Yes. This is Paul Temple, Salty. Remember – you telephoned me …

SALTY: Oh, yes … Yes, that's right …

TEMPLE: Well, what did you mean, Salty?

SALTY: Temple, feel … feel in my pocket … my coat pocket …

TEMPLE: Which one?

SALTY: (*Speaking with an effort*) The – the left …

A pause.

TEMPLE: In here?

SALTY: Yes. (*A pause*) Have – you – got – them?

TEMPLE: Yes … (*Surprised*) They're my wife's earrings! The ones that were in the handbag!

FADE IN closing music.

END OF EPISODE FIVE

EPISODE SIX

NEWS FROM SIR GRAHAM

OPEN TO: A background of noise: the fire burning; water playing on the fire and various voices.

TEMPLE is kneeling beside SALTY WEST.

TEMPLE: Salty, what did you mean on the phone when you said you'd a present for Mrs Temple?

SALTY: On – on the phone?

TEMPLE: Yes. This is Paul Temple, Salty. Remember – you telephoned me …

SALTY: Oh, yes … Yes, that's right …

TEMPLE: Well, what did you mean, Salty?

SALTY: Temple, feel … feel in my pocket … my coat pocket …

TEMPLE: Which one?

SALTY: (*Speaking with an effort*) The – the left …

A pause.

TEMPLE: In here?

SALTY: Yes. (*A pause*) Have – you – got – them?

TEMPLE: Yes … (*Surprised*) They're my wife's earrings! The ones that were in the handbag!

SALTY: Yes …

TEMPLE: But, how did you get them?

SALTY: I got them when I was in London, because I … Oh! … When are they going to take me to the hospital? (*In obvious pain*) Have they sent for the doctor?

We hear the sound of an approaching ambulance.

TEMPLE: Yes, here's the ambulance! You'll be all right in a minute.

SALTY: Help me to get my … I want to get on my feet so … that … I … can …

The ambulance brakes to a standstill. There are voices.

Car doors opening and closing.

TEMPLE: No, don't move, Salty. Stay where you are … They'll look after you …

SALTY: Mr Temple, come round to the hospital … when I'm better … I want to talk to you …

TEMPLE: Yes, all right. (*Quietly*) What is it you want to talk to me about?

SALTY: About Bob Gardner … I want to tell you what really happened that afternoon … (*His voice dies away, he is in great pain*)

MAN: (*To TEMPLE*) Excuse me, sir. (*To SALTY*) Now don't worry, you'll soon be all right. Fred, move round the other side so that I can get hold of his shoulders. That's better!

FADE voices and noises to the background.
FADE IN STEVE.

STEVE: …Paul, how is he?

TEMPLE: Pretty bad, I'm afraid.

STEVE: The ambulance took a long time getting here.

IVOR: Yes, there's isn't a hospital in Downburgh. You say you had an appointment with Salty, Mr Temple?

TEMPLE: Yes, he phoned me this morning and said he wanted to see me.

IVOR: (*Curious*) Have you any idea what he wanted to see you about?

TEMPLE: (*A moment*) No, I'm afraid I haven't, Inspector. Steve, I think we ought to get back to the hotel, there's nothing we can do here.

STEVE: Yes, all right, Paul.

TEMPLE: We're staying at the Crescent if you should want to get in touch with us, Inspector.

IVOR: Yes, all right, sir. I'll keep you posted about Salty.

TEMPLE: Thank you, Inspector. (*To STEVE*) Come along, darling.

IVOR: Goodbye, Mrs Temple.

STEVE: Goodbye, Inspector.

FADE DOWN the general background noises and the sound of the fire.

FADE IN the noise of TEMPLE's car driving into the entrance of the garage at Downburgh.

There are background noises of the garage.

JIM: Shall I put the car away, sir?

TEMPLE: If you would, please.

JIM: When shall you be needing it again, sir?

TEMPLE: Oh … We shan't want it tonight, shall we, Steve?

STEVE: What time are we meeting Dexter?

TEMPLE: A quarter to six at the quay.

STEVE: Oh, then we can walk.

TEMPLE: (*To JIM*) Say ten o'clock tomorrow morning then.

JIM: Very good, sir. Would you like the car washed?

TEMPLE: If you've got time, yes.

JIM: Thank you, sir.

TEMPLE: By the way, you're the only garage in Downburgh, aren't you?

JIM: There is another one, sir, but it's quite small and it's on the other side of the bay.

TEMPLE: I suppose you know most of the local people?

JIM: Well – most of them. I was born and bred here.

TEMPLE: Do you know Salty West?

JIM: Yes, I know Salty.

TEMPLE: He's just had a very bad accident; they've taken him to hospital.

JIM: Oh, I'm sorry to hear that. Is it serious?

TEMPLE: I'm afraid it might be.

JIM: (*Apparently not interested in pursuing the subject*) Ten o'clock tomorrow morning you said, sir?

TEMPLE: Yes, please.

JIM: Right! Thank you, Mr Temple.

TEMPLE: (*Stopping JIM*) One moment, Jim. (*Smiling*) It is Jim?

JIM: Yes, Jim Grant, sir.

TEMPLE: You know my name?

JIM: Yes, sir. I recognised you when you first arrived. There was a photograph of you in the local rag.

TEMPLE: When?

JIM: When you were here before, sir. Two or three weeks ago.

STEVE: Yes, that's right, Paul.

TEMPLE: Oh, I see. Jim, did you know Bob Gardner?

JIM: Yes, I knew him.

TEMPLE: Was he a friend of yours?

JIM: No. I don't mix much with the locals, most of my friends are in Felixstowe.

TEMPLE: But you knew Gardner?

JIM: Yes. He was a customer of mine.

TEMPLE: A credit customer?

JIM: (*Puzzled*) Yes – he had an account.

TEMPLE: Jim, have you got any chits that Bob Gardner signed?

JIM: I expect there's one or two on the file.

TEMPLE: Could I see them?

A pause.

JIM: All right. You'd better come in the office.

TEMPLE: Thank you. I'll see you back at the hotel, Steve.

STEVE: Yes, all right. I'll be in the room. Oh, have you got the key?

TEMPLE hands STEVE the key.

166

TEMPLE: Yes, here you are.

JIM: I'll just put the car on the wash, sir. The office is just over on the right, in the corner. I'll be with you in a minute.

TEMPLE: Right …

In the background JIM gets into the car and drives it into the garage.

TEMPLE: Oh, Steve!

STEVE: Yes?

TEMPLE: You remember that Salty West said he'd a present for you?

STEVE: Yes?

TEMPLE: Here it is …

A moment.

STEVE: My gold earrings! The ones that were in the handbag!

TEMPLE: Yes.

STEVE: Did Salty give them to you?

TEMPLE: Yes, he did. That was one of the reasons why he wanted to see me.

STEVE: But how did he get them?

TEMPLE: I don't know; but obviously he knew about the handbag. I'll see you back at the hotel, Steve. I shan't be long.

STEVE: Yes, all right, Paul.

FADE UP the sound of the car from the background.

FADE UP JIM speaking.

JIM: … Well, apparently I've only got two chits with Bob's signature. Now I come to think of it his sister signed for most of the stuff.

TEMPLE: If you've got one, that's all I want.

JIM: Yes, here you are – I think this one was signed by Bob. (*He looks at the chit*) Yes, that's right.

TEMPLE: Thank you. (*A pause*) May I keep this?

JIM: I don't see why not.
TEMPLE: You say Mary Gardner signed most of the time?
JIM: Yes.
TEMPLE: Why was that?
JIM: I don't know. I imagine she kept the accounts.
TEMPLE: Did you see much of her?
JIM: She popped in every now and again.
TEMPLE: Did you like her?
JIM: Mr Temple, why the questionnaire? I've told
          you, the Gardners weren't friends of mine.
TEMPLE: I'm not suggesting they were, Jim, but you must
          have seen a fair amount of them.
JIM: I saw Mary Gardner about once a week; Bob,
          perhaps two or three times.
TEMPLE: What was your opinion of Mary Gardner?
JIM: (*Faintly irritated*) Look, Mr Temple, forgive me
          if I sound rude, but – if you want the local gossip
          you've come to the wrong department. I've
          already told you I don't mix with the local
          people.
TEMPLE: Yes, you told me that, Jim. Were you surprised
          when you heard about Mary Gardner?
JIM: Of course; wouldn't you be surprised if you
          suddenly read in the newspapers that a customer
          of yours had been murdered?
TEMPLE: Yes, but unusual things seem to happen to people
          in this part of the world!
JIM: (*Drily*) They do indeed!
TEMPLE: I suppose you're thinking of Bob Gardner.
JIM: No, I was thinking of someone else.
TEMPLE: (*Interested*) Oh – who exactly?
JIM: (*A moment*) I was thinking of a young fellow
          called Andy Cross. He used to work for me; first
          class mechanic was Andy.

TEMPLE: What happened to him?

JIM: Oh, it's an old story. (*Dismissing TEMPLE*) Ten o'clock tomorrow morning, Mr Temple. Okay?

TEMPLE: (*Quietly*) What happened to Andy Cross?

JIM: I've told you; it's an old story.

TEMPLE: I haven't heard it.

JIM: (*A moment*) He committed suicide.

TEMPLE: When?

JIM: About a year ago.

TEMPLE: Why?

JIM: Well – they said it was over a girl he was going out with, Jill Chepstow. One night they had a row and Andy put his head in the gas oven.

TEMPLE: Well, that's not original. It's happened before.

JIM: Yes, I know.

TEMPLE: But you don't think he did put his head in the gas oven, is that it? You think he was murdered?

JIM: No; he committed suicide all right, but …

TEMPLE: But what?

JIM: But not because of Jill Chepstow.

TEMPLE: Well, why did he do it?

JIM: Your guess is as good as mine, Mr Temple.

TEMPLE: All right, Jim. Ten o'clock tomorrow morning.

JIM: Yes, sir.

The office door opens.

TEMPLE: And thanks.

JIM: For what?

TEMPLE: For telling me about Andy Cross.

FADE IN incidental music.

FADE DOWN the music.
FADE IN TEMPLE knocking on the bedroom door.
The door opens.

TEMPLE: Hello, Steve! Sorry I've been so long.

169

TEMPLE enters the bedroom.

The door closes.

STEVE: Did you get what you wanted?

TEMPLE: What do you mean?

STEVE: The chit you were talking about; Bob Gardner's signature.

TEMPLE: Oh yes. Yes, I got that all right.

STEVE: What did you want it for anyway?

TEMPLE: I wanted to compare the signature with the one on the letter; the one that Mary Gardner brought me.

STEVE: Have you still got that letter?

TEMPLE: Not here – at home. You've changed your dress.

STEVE: Of course. We're supposed to be meeting Brian Dexter at a quarter to six.

TEMPLE: What time is it now?

STEVE: It's just gone five.

TEMPLE: Oh, we've bags of time. It won't take us more than five minutes to walk down to the quay. I suppose there was no message for me when you got back to the hotel?

STEVE: No; I asked at the reception desk.

TEMPLE: I just can't understand why I haven't heard from Vosper or Sir Graham.

The telephone rings.

TEMPLE: You'd have thought that at least one of them would have …

TEMPLE lifts the receiver.

TEMPLE: (*On the phone*) Hello?

GIRL: (*On the other end of the line*) Mr Temple?

TEMPLE: Yes …

GIRL: There's a gentleman asking for you at the reception desk, sir.

TEMPLE: Well, who is it?

GIRL: One moment, sir.

The GIRL hands the receiver over to the visitor.

FORBES: (*On the other end of the line*) Temple, this is
            Forbes. May I come up to your room?

TEMPLE: (*Surprised*) Why, yes, of course!

GIRL: (*Back on the line*) Hello? Mr Temple …

TEMPLE: That's all right, send the gentleman up, please.

TEMPLE replaces the receiver.

STEVE: Who is it?

TEMPLE: It's Sir Graham.

STEVE: (*Surprised*) Sir Graham?

TEMPLE: Yes.

STEVE: Has he just come up from Town?

TEMPLE: It sounds like it.

STEVE: Is he alone?

TEMPLE: I imagine so.

STEVE: But surely he wouldn't come all this way without
            first …

TEMPLE: (*Laughing*) Steve, you know just as much about
            this as I do!

STEVE: Well, if he's motored all the way from Town I
            expect the poor darling could do with a drink. I
            should get the floor waiter, Paul.

TEMPLE: We'll deal with that problem later, Steve.
            (*Thoughtfully*) While we were staying down here
            before, did you ever hear anyone mention the
            name Andy Cross?

STEVE: Andy Cross?

TEMPLE: Yes.

STEVE: Do you know, I believe I did. I think Mrs Purdie
            mentioned him. Wasn't he a garage mechanic
            who committed suicide?

TEMPLE: Yes, that's right. Why didn't you tell me about
            him?

STEVE: I didn't think it was important. Surely, it's over a
            year since it happened?
TEMPLE: Yes, I think it was about a year ago.
STEVE: From what I remember he had a row with his
            fiancée and put his head in the gas oven.
TEMPLE: (*Thoughtfully*) Yes.
STEVE: Who told you about Andy Cross?
TEMPLE: Jim, the man at the garage. We were talking
            about Downburgh, and it suddenly came out.
STEVE: Well, it's a pretty commonplace story, isn't it?
            You can read that sort of thing every weekend in
            the Sunday newspapers.
TEMPLE: M'm.
There is a knock on the door.
STEVE: Here's Sir Graham!
The door opens.
TEMPLE: Come in, Sir Graham! Come in!
FORBES: Hello, Temple!
STEVE: Welcome to Downburgh, Sir Graham.
FORBES: Thank you, Steve! How are you?
STEVE: Oh, I'm fine.
FORBES: You certainly look fine! (*To TEMPLE*) Do you
            know, Temple, I don't think Steve's altered at
            all, not from the very first time we met way back
            in nineteen …
STEVE: Steady, Sir Graham! Steady!
They all laugh.
TEMPLE: (*Seriously*) I expect you got my telegram?
FORBES: About the yacht?
TEMPLE: Yes.
FORBES: I tried to phone you but we'd rather a hectic day
            and I decided … (*He stops; he is staring out of
            the window*) Is that the yacht – in the bay out
            there?

172

TEMPLE: Yes, that's the Isle of Skye. It belongs to a Mrs de Silva.

FORBES: De Silva? Is she any relation to Ernest de Silva?

TEMPLE: She's his wife.

FORBES: Oh. Is she aboard?

TEMPLE: Yes.

FORBES: Have you met her?

TEMPLE: Not yet; but we're going to. We've been invited for drinks.

FORBES: This evening?

TEMPLE: Yes.

FORBES: But if you haven't met her, how did you …

TEMPLE: Brian Dexter's invited us; he's a guest on board the yacht ..

FORBES: Is he? That's an interesting coincidence.

STEVE: And if you ask me he's not the only guest.

FORBES: What do you mean, Steve?

TEMPLE: Steve's thinking of Sylvia Ross.

FORBES: You think Miss Ross is on that yacht?

STEVE: Don't you, Sir Graham?

FORBES: Is that your opinion, Temple?

TEMPLE: I don't know. The conversation Burford overheard between Teako and Freeman certainly seemed to point that way, and so did the telegram I found. And yet –

FORBES: You're sceptical?

TEMPLE: Yes. Don't ask me why, Sir Graham, but I am. But look here, you didn't come all the way to Downburgh just to talk about my telegram.

FORBES: No, you're quite right, Temple. I didn't.

STEVE looks at FORBES.

STEVE: What is it, Sir Graham? What's happened?

TEMPLE: Is there a new development?

FORBES: Yes.

TEMPLE: Well?
FORBES: (*A moment; an announcement*) Sylvia Ross
             returned home about an hour after we received
             your telegram.
STEVE: (*Staggered*) What!
TEMPLE: What do you mean – she returned home?
FORBES: A taxi drove up to the house; Sylvia got out and
             rang the bell. It was as simple as that.
STEVE: (*Excitedly*) But surely someone must have seen
             …
TEMPLE: Just a minute, Steve! Sit down, Sir Graham. (*A
             moment*) Now take your time and let's have the
             whole story.
FORBES: (*Smiling*) Well, the whole story boils down to the
             simple fact that for days we've been searching
             for this girl and at half past eleven this morning
             she returned home. Fortunately her father was in
             the house, working in the library. Naturally, Sir
             Carlton was delighted to see her and pretty
             excited into the bargain …
STEVE: I can well imagine it!
FORBES: He telephoned us immediately and Vosper and I
             went round to Berkeley Square. I suppose it was
             about a quarter to twelve when we arrived. We
             were shown into the drawing room …

FADE SCENE.

FADE UP a door opening.
DAVIS: Sir Graham Forbes and Detective Inspector
             Vosper, sir.
ROSS: (*A cultured, dignified man in his early sixties*)
             Thank you, Davis. Come in, Sir Graham! Good
             morning, Inspector!
VOSPER: Good morning, sir.

ROSS: Well, this is excellent news, isn't it?

VOSPER: It certainly is, sir.

FORBES: Where is Miss Ross?

ROSS: She's in her room; but she knows you're here, she'll be down in a minute.

VOSPER: Is she all right, sir?

ROSS: (*Hesitantly*) Yes, I think so. A little pale, perhaps, but that's to be expected.

FORBES: (*Faintly irritated*) Yes, but what's the explanation? Where has she been?

ROSS: I don't know.

FORBES: Won't she tell you?

ROSS: Yes, she's told me – but it's not a very convincing story.

The door opens.

VOSPER: Well, where has she been, sir?

ROSS: Ah, here is Sylvia! I think she'd better answer your questions, Inspector. Come in, my dear! This is Sir Graham Forbes and Detective Inspector Vosper.

SYLVIA: (*She is self-possessed with a rather controlled tenseness*) Good morning, Sir Graham. Good morning, Inspector.

VOSPER: Good morning.

FORBES: Good morning.

ROSS: Do sit down, gentlemen, please! Sylvia, I think perhaps you'd better sit over here, dear – facing the Inspector.

SYLVIA: I'm all right where I am, there's no need to fuss, Daddy. (*Smiling*) I understand I've caused you a certain amount of embarrassment during the past week or so, Sir Graham. I'm terribly sorry.

FORBES: (*Irritated by SYLVIA*) It hasn't been just a question of embarrassment, Miss Ross. There

175

	have been certain developments which seemed to indicate that you were not entirely a free agent.
SYLVIA:	What do you mean?
FORBES:	From the moment you disappeared …
SYLVIA:	Oh, not disappeared, Sir Graham! I merely visited friends …
FORBES:	All right, we'll come to that point later. Certain things have happened, certain developments have taken place since you – visited your friends. We're interested in those developments and we need information about them. We believe that you can supply that information.
SYLVIA:	Forgive me, but I really haven't the slightest idea what you're talking about. My father told me that you wanted to see me because you were under the delusion that I'd disappeared.
FORBES:	Your father was under that delusion, Miss Ross; he contacted Scotland Yard. We didn't contact your father.
SYLVIA:	(*Laughing*) Yes, I'm afraid poor Daddy behaved rather stupidly because …
FORBES:	There was nothing stupid about your father's behaviour, Miss Ross. It's your behaviour that seems to me to warrant investigation.
SYLVIA:	My goodness, this is quite a third degree, isn't it! I never knew Scotland Yard went in for this sort of thing!
ROSS:	Sir Graham's annoyed, my dear, and I must confess with justification.
VOSPER:	Miss Ross, suppose you tell us exactly what happened that night; the night you went out with Brian Dexter?
SYLVIA:	(*A moment, then*) Well, we were going to a concert at the Festival Hall but at the last

moment we changed our minds and went to a dance hall in the Strand. On the way home Brian's car broke down, and we had to take a taxi. I got back to the house at about a quarter to twelve. Just as I let myself in the telephone was ringing. It was a girl called Doreen Beech. I hadn't seen Doreen for ages although at one time we used to be frightfully good friends.

VOSPER: Go on.

SYLVIA: Well, to cut a long story short she said she and her husband were throwing a party and she asked me to join them. I – decided to do so.

VOSPER: Where was the party?

SYLVIA: At a flat in Chelsea.

VOSPER: Go on.

SYLVIA: I left the house, caught a cab, and went to the party.

VOSPER: And then?

SYLVIA: The party didn't finish until a quarter to five and Doreen and her husband suggested I stayed the night with them. When I woke next morning I felt awfully ill; I think it must have been something I'd had to drink at the party. Doreen insisted that I stayed in bed. Naturally, I was worried about my father, but Gerald – Doreen's husband – was terribly sweet and said that he'd telephone Daddy and explain the whole situation.

ROSS: He didn't phone me, Sylvia, I never heard a word from you.

SYLVIA: That I simply can't understand.

VOSPER: That only accounts for one day, Miss Ross – what happened the rest of the time?

SYLVIA: I was ill; terribly ill.

VOSPER: Did you see a doctor?

177

SYLVIA: (*Hesitantly*) Yes.

VOSPER: What was his name?

SYLVIA: I – I don't remember his name; he was Doreen's doctor.

VOSPER: So your story, very briefly, is that you went to a party given by a Mr and Mrs – ?

SYLVIA: Beech.

VOSPER: Mr and Mrs Beech – you were taken ill and you stayed with Mr and Mrs Beech until you were better.

SYLVIA: Yes.

VOSPER: And during that time it never occurred to you to either telephone or write to your father?

SYLVIA: I've told you. Gerald phoned my father – at least, he said he did. He said he'd spoken to Daddy and that my father told him he was going abroad for two or three weeks and that I simply hadn't got to worry.

ROSS: But that's nonsense, my dear! Absolute nonsense!

SYLVIA: But how was I to know? You do go abroad, Daddy – quite frequently.

VOSPER: (*With quiet authority; he doesn't believe SYLVIA's story*) Miss Ross, these friends of yours – where do they live?

SYLVIA: I've told you – in Chelsea.

VOSPER: The address?

SYLVIA: (*Hesitantly*) There's no point in giving you their address because …

VOSPER: (*With authority*) What is the address, Miss Ross?

SYLVIA: Twenty-one Lansdale Mansions … (*Suddenly*) But I'm afraid you won't be able to get in touch with them because they left for Rome early this morning.

VOSPER: I see.

FORBES: Rather a convenient departure.

SYLVIA: What do you mean?

VOSPER: Sir Carlton, forgive me, but I just don't believe your daughter's story.

SYLVIA: (*A shrug*) Well, if you don't believe it, you don't believe it. I'm going to my room, Daddy, if you'd like to see me later …

FORBES: One moment, Miss Ross, please …

SYLVIA: Look, Sir Graham, there's no point in your asking me a lot of questions if you just don't believe what I tell you.

FORBES: (*Ignoring SYLVIA's remark*) The night you disappeared …

SYLVIA: You keep saying I disappeared; I tell you I didn't disappear, I simply visited friends!

FORBES: The night you visited your friends then, you also visited a dance hall. You sent a note to a man called Johnny Teako. What was on the note?

SYLVIA: It was simply a request for a particular dance number. Good heavens above, you're not going to make a mystery out of that, surely?

FORBES: Was that the first time you'd seen Johnny Teako?

SYLVIA: No; I'd seen him once or twice before.

FORBES: Where?

SYLVIA: (*Irritated*) Oh, I just forget where. Look, Sir Graham, what is this all about?

FORBES: Miss Ross, does the name Lawrence – Clive Lawrence – mean anything to you?

SYLVIA: (*Thoughtfully*) No.

FORBES: You never met a Mr Lawrence when you stayed at Zermatt twelve months ago?

SYLVIA: Not that I remember. Do you remember a Mr Lawrence, Daddy?

179

ROSS: No.

SYLVIA: Any more questions, Sir Graham?

FORBES: (*Quickly*) Yes. When did you last see Mr de
           Silva?

SYLVIA: (*Without thinking*) About a … (*She stops; a
           moment*) Mr de Silva?

FORBES: Yes.

SYLVIA: (*Hesitantly*) You mean the eye specialist?

FORBES: The eye specialist, Miss Ross.

SYLVIA: About a month ago.

FORBES: Is de Silva a friend of yours?

SYLVIA: No.

FORBES: Then why did you see him?

SYLVIA: Why do you usually see an eye specialist?
           Because I'd been having trouble with my eyes.

FORBES: Did you know about this, Sir Carlton?

ROSS: I knew that Sylvia had consulted a specialist and
           that he'd advised her to wear glasses but I'm
           afraid I couldn't have told you the name of the
           specialist.

FORBES: Well, apparently his name's de Silva. Ernest de
           Silva. Thank you, Miss Ross.

SYLVIA: No more questions?

FORBES: (*Unperturbed*) Not for the moment, thank you.

SYLVIA: I'll be in my room, Daddy, if you want me.

ROSS: Yes, all right, Sylvia.

SYLVIA goes out.

The door closes.

ROSS: I know exactly what you're thinking, Sir Graham
           – and I agree with you.

FORBES: Yes, but the point is why? Why is she lying? (*A
           moment*) Sir Carlton, forgive me if I ask a
           personal question.

ROSS: Go ahead, Sir Graham, please. Don't feel embarrassed about this; I understand your position perfectly. In a day or two when I've got over my feeling of intense relief I shall probably be just as annoyed with Sylvia as you are.

FORBES: Sir Carlton, your daughter knows, of course, that you're the head of M.I.5?

ROSS: Yes; but naturally she knows nothing about my work. She's never even met anyone in my department.

FORBES: Has she ever expressed any interest in what you do?

ROSS: Yes; I should have found it curious if she hadn't.

VOSPER: Have you ever heard of these people, sir – Mr and Mrs Beech?

ROSS: No, I haven't, but that doesn't necessarily mean that they don't exist. I must be frank with you, Inspector. I'm devoted to Sylvia and the past week or so hasn't exactly been easy for me; on the other hand, I don't want you to have any illusions. Sylvia and I have never been what you might call close to each other.

VOSPER: In other words, she's not going to confide in you, sir?

ROSS: No, she's not going to confide in me, Inspector.

FORBES: Thank you, Sir Carlton. You've been very frank with us and we appreciate it.

FADE SCENE.

FADE IN SIR GRAHAM's voice.

FORBES: … We left Berkely Square and went down to Chelsea. We had difficulty locating Lansdale Mansions but eventually we found it. It was a large old-fashioned block of flats near the

181

Embankment. No one had heard of a Mr and Mrs Beech. Number twenty-one was occupied by an elderly couple called Stimpson. They'd been there for sixteen years.

TEMPLE: Go on, Sir Graham.

FORBES: We had another talk to Sylvia but she stuck to her story. She was lying, of course, and she knew that we knew she was lying but there was nothing we could do about it.

STEVE: But, Sir Graham, now that you've found Sylvia Ross – or at any rate now that she's safe – surely the case is closed so far as you're concerned?

FORBES: That's Sir Carlton's point of view, Steve – but it's not mine. There are still certain things I don't understand about this business.

STEVE: For instance?

FORBES: Well – what did happen to Sylvia Ross?

STEVE: She spent the whole time with some boyfriend or other and she doesn't want her father to know anything about it.

FORBES: (*With a laugh*) That's what Vosper thinks, but I don't think the explanation is as simple as that.

TEMPLE: Neither do I.

FORBES: And what about the note she sent to Johnny Teako? Was the name Lawrence on the note – and if not what was the point of it? And how does a man like Ernest de Silva fit into all this?

TEMPLE: De Silva's in Downburgh, by the way. He arrived today, it seems.

FORBES: Oh, have you seen him?

TEMPLE: No, but his car's in the same garage as mine.

FORBES: Is he staying on the yacht?

TEMPLE: I should imagine so.

FORBES: You know, coming down here in the car I started thinking about all the people that are concerned in this affair. Brian Dexter. That man you saw at Maidenhead, Max …

TEMPLE: Max Burford …

FORBES: That dance band leader and his wife …

STEVE: Linda and Johnny Teako …

FORBES: This man de Silva; then that old boy you told me about – Salty something-or-other …

TEMPLE: Salty West. Incidentally, I don't suppose you heard about West. We had an appointment to see him this afternoon but his cottage caught fire and he was very badly burned.

FORBES: Was it an accident?

TEMPLE: So far as we know; though Inspector Ivor's not so sure, he thinks it may have been deliberate. They've taken Salty West to hospital.

There is a knock on the door.

FORBES: Did you talk to him?

TEMPLE: Yes, but he was very ill, it was hopeless trying to …

STEVE: I think there's someone at the door, Paul.

TEMPLE: Excuse me, Sir Graham!

TEMPLE opens the door.

IVOR: Mr Temple …

TEMPLE: Oh, Inspector Ivor! Come in!

The door closes.

IVOR: Good afternoon, Mrs Temple.

STEVE: Good afternoon, Inspector.

IVOR: (*Suddenly; seeing FORBES*) Oh, I'm sorry to disturb you, sir. I didn't realise you had a visitor.

TEMPLE: This is Sir Graham Forbes. Detective Inspector Ivor.

FORBES: (*Pleasantly*) Good afternoon, Inspector.

183

IVOR: Er – good afternoon, sir. (*Hesitantly*) Mr Temple,
            I thought you ought to know about Salty West …
TEMPLE: What's happened?
IVOR: He's dead, sir. He died before we reached the
            hospital.
TEMPLE: (*Quietly*) I'm sorry to hear that.
FORBES: Were you with him?
IVOR: Yes, sir. I was in the ambulance.
TEMPLE: Was he conscious at all?
IVOR: For part of the time, sir.
STEVE: Did he know that he was going to die, Inspector?
IVOR: Yes, towards the end I think he did. He asked me
            to deliver a message to you, Mr Temple.
TEMPLE: What was the message?
IVOR: He said: "Tell Paul Temple there isn't a Mr
            Lawrence, he was a decoy …"
TEMPLE: … There isn't a Mr Lawrence, he was a decoy?
IVOR: Yes, sir.
FORBES: Are you sure that's what he said?
IVOR: Yes, sir. I'm quite sure.
TEMPLE: Thank you, Inspector.
FADE IN incidental music.

FADE DOWN music.
*FADE UP background noises associated with the quay at
Downburgh.*
STEVE: I don't see any sign of our friend Dexter.
TEMPLE: Nor do I.
STEVE: Is it going to be foggy, do you think?
TEMPLE: I don't think so; it's just the sea mist.
STEVE: You can hardly see the yacht.
TEMPLE: That's it over there …
STEVE: Yes, but you can hardly see it.
TEMPLE: I expect it'll clear.

STEVE: What time do you make it, Paul?

TEMPLE: It's nearly six; he's late.

FADE IN the sound of an approaching dinghy with an outboard motor.

STEVE: There's someone coming now, Paul. I can hear the motor.

A pause.

TEMPLE: I don't see … Yes, there it is! It's a small dinghy by the look of things. This can't be Dexter …

A moment.

STEVE: It is, Paul!

A pause.

The dinghy draws nearer to the quay.

DEXTER: (*Calling from the approaching dinghy*) Hello, there!

TEMPLE: (*Calling back*) Here we are, Dexter! Over here!

The dinghy arrives at the landing stage.

DEXTER stops the motor.

DEXTER: (*From the dinghy*) I'm a bit late, I'm afraid. It's pretty misty out in the bay.

STEVE: Yes, it looks like it.

DEXTER: Sorry I had to bring this wretched little thing, but we've been having a spot of bother with the launch.

STEVE: (*Nervously*) Do you think the three of us can get in that?

DEXTER: (*Laughing*) Yes, we'll be all right. (*With a serious manner*) Can you swim, Mrs Temple?

STEVE: Well –

TEMPLE: (*Laughing*) He's only joking, Steve!

DEXTER laughs.

DEXTER: Give me your hand, Mrs Temple.

TEMPLE: Careful, Steve.

DEXTER helps STEVE into the dinghy.

STEVE: Keep hold of my hand!

DEXTER: I've got you, Mrs Temple. Don't worry. (*A moment*) Steady! … That's fine … Can you manage, Temple?

TEMPLE: (*Climbing into the dinghy*) Yes, I'm used to this sort of …

The boat commences to rock.

TEMPLE: Whoa!

DEXTER laughs.

STEVE: You'd better sit down here, Paul!

TEMPLE: (*Laughing*) I very nearly did!

STEVE: I suppose Mrs de Silva is expecting us because if she isn't …

DEXTER: (*Tinkering with the outboard motor*) Yes, indeed. She's looking forward to meeting you both. By the way, Temple, I believe you've met Ernest – her husband?

TEMPLE: Yes. Is he on board?

DEXTER: Yes; he arrived this afternoon. Curiously enough I'd never met him before. (*Still trying to start the motor*) Now what's the matter with this confounded thing?

A pause.

DEXTER still tinkers with the motor.

There are several false starts from the motor.

DEXTER: Sorry for the delay. It should be all right in a moment …

TEMPLE: Can I give you a hand?

DEXTER: No, I think I can …

DEXTER pulls the starting cord and the motor starts.

DEXTER: That's it!

DEXTER revs up the motor.

DEXTER: All set?

TEMPLE: Yes.

DEXTER: Mrs Temple?

STEVE: Er – yes …

DEXTER: Hold tight! Here we go!

We hear the sound of the outboard motor on the dinghy.

FADE DOWN as the dinghy races away.

Slow FADE IN of the sound of the outboard motor.

The dinghy is now travelling at normal speed.

A pause.

DEXTER: Are you getting wet, Mrs Temple?

STEVE: No, I'm fine.

DEXTER: Good. Because I'm afraid there's nothing I can do about it.

TEMPLE laughs.

A pause.

TEMPLE: How long are you staying on the yacht, Dexter?

DEXTER: Probably three or four days. I don't see any sense in rushing back to Town just to be buttonholed by Scotland Yard. And that's probably what would happen.

TEMPLE: (*Matter of fact*) I doubt whether Vosper will bother you again.

DEXTER: I wish I could think so. Still, I'm grateful to you for having a word with him.

TEMPLE: I wasn't referring to that. You see, since we saw you last there's been a new development.

DEXTER: (*Curious*) Really? What kind of a development?

TEMPLE: (*A moment, then:*) Sylvia Ross has returned home.

DEXTER: Sylvia … Temple, are you joking?

TEMPLE: No. No, I'm quite serious.

DEXTER: But – but how do you know? Who told you this?

TEMPLE: Sir Graham Forbes told me.

DEXTER: Why – this is wonderful news! Absolutely wonder … (*Suddenly; quietly*) Is she all right? I mean, she's not ill or …

TEMPLE: No, no, no, she's perfectly all right.

We hear the sound of an approaching motor launch.

It is racing towards the dingy at a tremendous speed.

DEXTER: But what on earth did she say? Where has she been?

TEMPLE: Well, apparently after you dropped her at the house she received an invitation from some people called Beech …

TEMPLE's words are drowned by the roar of the passing speedboat.

STEVE cries out in alarm, frightened.

The dinghy is tossed about on the water like a cork.

DEXTER: (*Angrily*) Why the fool! What's he trying to do!

TEMPLE: (*Quietly; alarmed*) By Timothy, if he does that again we've had it!

DEXTER: Are you all right, Mrs Temple?

STEVE: (*Breathlessly*) Yes. Yes, I'm sorry I screamed, but –

DEXTER: That's all right.

TEMPLE: Who was it? Have you any idea?

DEXTER: I couldn't see …

STEVE: There was a man sitting in the front with goggles on, but I doubt whether I should recognise him again.

DEXTER: (*Suddenly*) My God, he's coming back!

We hear the sound of the approaching speedboat.

STEVE: (*Alarmed*) He's going to do it again! He's coming at us!

TEMPLE: (*Quickly*) Keep the boat straight, Dexter! Don't swerve!

DEXTER: But if I don't swerve he'll run us down!

TEMPLE: (*Alarmed*) If you do you'll turn it over! Keep it straight!

DEXTER: But there's no point in …

DEXTER's voice is drowned by the sound of the approaching speedboat.

TEMPLE: Look out!

STEVE: (*Shouting*) Paul, we're turning over!!!!

The dinghy is struck by a gigantic wave and immediately overturns.

FADE AWAY the noise of the departing speedboat.

FADE UP the sound of the dinghy being tossed about by the waves.

FADE UP TEMPLE struggling in the water.

He is trying to swim against the heavy waves.

TEMPLE: (*Breathlessly*) Steve! Steve, where are you?

TEMPLE continues to struggle.

TEMPLE: Steve! Where are you?

TEMPLE continues swimming, desperately searching for STEVE.

TEMPLE: Steve, can you hear me?

We hear the sound of the water lapping against the overturned dinghy.

TEMPLE: (*Desperately*) Steve!

The sound of the water continues.

FADE IN closing music.

END OF EPISODE SIX

EPISODE SEVEN

ANOTHER SUSPECT

OPEN TO: *The sound of the dinghy being tossed about on the water.*

We hear the sound of an approaching speedboat.

STEVE: (*Alarmed*) He's going to do it again! He's coming at us!

TEMPLE: (*Quickly*) Keep the boat straight, Dexter! Don't swerve!

DEXTER: But if I don't swerve he'll run us down!

TEMPLE: (*Alarmed*) If you do you'll turn it over! Keep it straight!

DEXTER: But there's no point in …

DEXTER's voice is drowned by the sound of the approaching speedboat.

TEMPLE: Look out!

STEVE: (*Shouting*) Paul, we're turning over!!!!

The dinghy is struck by a gigantic wave and immediately overturns.

FADE AWAY the noise of the departing speedboat.

FADE UP the sound of the dinghy being tossed about by the waves.

FADE UP TEMPLE struggling in the water.

He is trying to swim against the heavy waves.

TEMPLE: (*Breathlessly*) Steve! Steve, where are you?

TEMPLE continues to struggle.

TEMPLE: Steve! Where are you?

TEMPLE continues swimming, desperately searching for STEVE.

TEMPLE: Steve, can you hear me?

We hear the sound of the water lapping against the overturned dinghy.

TEMPLE: (*Desperately*) Steve!

The sound of the water continues.

FADE SCENE.

FADE IN the noise of the sea and of a fishing boat.

STAN WALTERS and ARTHUR MAIN are gathering in their nets.

WALTERS: (*In a friendly, argumentative mood*) … You'll have to work harder, Arthur , or we shall never get the nets in …

ARTHUR: (*Pulling on the nets*) The blessed things seem to get heavier every night …

WALTERS: Yes, an' you know why …

ARTHUR: It isn't the catch!

WALTERS: You don't have to tell me that, you lazy son of a gun! It's the fact that you're too confoundedly lazy to … (*He stops speaking*)

ARTHUR: What is it? What are you staring at?

WALTERS: (*Peering*) What's that? Over to starboard …

A moment's pause.

ARTHUR: I don't see anything …

WALTERS: Look, man!

ARTHUR: It's a porpoise …

WALTERS: That's no porpoise! It looks to me like a man – swimming.

ARTHUR: Now I ask you, who the devil would want to go swimming at this time o' night?

WALTERS: I tell you it's a man! Reach me the oars …

ARTHUR: What are you going to do?

WALTERS: Do as I tell you – reach me the oars!

ARTHUR: And what about the nets?

WALTERS: The nets can wait!

START FADE.

ARTHUR: Yes, an' won't us look a couple o' fools if it turns out to be a porpoise!

WALTERS: (*Angrily*) Do as I tell you, and don't argue!

ARTHUR hands over the oars.

ARTHUR: Two bright shining oars coming over, chum, an' they're all yours, I'm not sweatin' my guts out …

COMPLETE FADE.

FADE UP STAN WALTERS rowing.

ARTHUR: (*Excited*) Slow down, Stan – steady …

WALTERS: Well – is that your idea of a porpoise?

ARTHUR: Where did he come from, that's what I'd like to know? (*Leaning over the side of the boat; calling*) Over here, mate! Over here …

WALTERS: I'll turn her round …

ARTHUR: It's all right. I think I can reach him … He's whacked, he's proper done in … (*Leaning over the side of the boat*) Here we are, mate – give me your 'and. That's it … Hold on!

WALTERS: Have you got him?

ARTHUR: (*Holding TEMPLE's hand*) Yes, but I don't know how I'm going to get back into the boat …

WALTERS: I'll give you a hand …

ARTHUR: (*Gasping for breath; holding on*) He's a dead weight … Steady! Steady!

WALTERS struggles.

WALTERS: (*Struggling*) We'll never get him in this way, we'll have to try …

ARTHUR: Wait a minute! He's coming to life a bit … That's it, chum! Good man! That's it! Get hold of his legs, Stan!

WALTERS pulls TEMPLE over the side of the boat.

WALTERS: (*Excited*) I've got him …

TEMPLE is hauled out of the water into the boat.

WALTERS: (*Breathlessly*) There!

A pause.

WALTERS: (*Regaining breath*) I know this chap, Arthur! His name's Temple …

ARTHUR: (*Regaining his breath*) Well, he picked a ruddy good time to go for a swim!

WALTERS: He didn't go for a swim, man! Use your head … Look at him, he's fully dressed …

ARTHUR: We'd better get to work on him, he's not too good.

WALTERS: Right. You know the drill …

WALTERS and ARTHUR apply artificial respiration.

ARTHUR: (*Slowly; working on TEMPLE*) One, two, three … One, two, three … One, two, three … Turn his head, Stan … That's it … One, two, three … One, two, three … One, two, three …

FADE SCENE.

FADE UP:

ARTHUR: One, two three … One, two, three …

WALTERS: He's coming round!

ARTHUR: Thank heavens for that, I'm just about all in …

WALTERS: All right, sit him up! That's it …

TEMPLE: (*Dazed; exhausted*) Steve! Where's my wife? Where's … my … wife? Steve …

ARTHUR: Now take it easy, chum! Take it easy!

WALTERS: Wait a minute, Arthur! Mr Temple, was your wife with you?

TEMPLE: Yes … Where is she? What's happened to her? …

WALTERS: Look, Mr Temple, what happened to you? Did you go out in the bay?

TEMPLE: Yes … there were three of us … we were in a dinghy – it … overturned …

ARTHUR: (*Softly*) Oh, my God …

WALTERS: Who were the other two?

196

TEMPLE: My wife, Steve, and … a … man … called Brian Dexter …

WALTERS: But what were you doin' out in the bay at this time o' the day?

TEMPLE: (*Still obviously exhausted*) We … were … going out to a yacht … for …

TEMPLE starts coughing.

ARTHUR: Steady, now! (*To WALTERS*) He's just about all in, Stan – the sooner we get him ashore the better.

WALTERS: Yes.

TEMPLE: (*With an effort*) You can't go back yet … You've got to help me find my wife, she …

WALTERS: Look, it was a slice of luck spotting you in this weather; how the devil can we hope to find your wife?

TEMPLE: Please don't go back … Not yet … You've got to help me find my wife …

ARTHUR: Now take it easy! We're only doing what's best for you. If we see your wife we'll pick her up, of course, but …

WALTERS: (*Interrupting ARTHUR*) Steady, Arthur! (*To TEMPLE; quietly*) This mist is pretty bad tonight, Mr Temple, but we'll drift around and keep our fingers crossed.

ARTHUR: Shall I take the oars, Stan?

WALTERS: No, I can manage. Just keep your eyes skinned. Give a short every now an' again, Arthur.

ARTHUR: (*Calling*) Mrs Temple! Hello, there!!! Mrs Temple!!

START FADE.

TEMPLE: (*Calling*) Steve! Steve!

FADE OUT.

FADE IN the sound of the boat and oars in the water.

WALTERS: (*Wearily*) We've been searching the best part of an hour, sir. We can't go on like this.

TEMPLE: Yes, all right. (*In despair*) We'll do as you suggest.

WALTERS: I think we'd better make for the harbour, sir. You can contact the coastguards later.

ARTHUR: She may have been picked up, sir. You never can tell.

WALTERS: How far were you from the yacht when it happened?

TEMPLE: Oh, quite a distance.

A moment's pause.

WALTERS: I suppose you didn't see the launch you were telling us about?

TEMPLE: I saw it, of course, but the whole thing happened so quickly. It suddenly got misty and we lost sight of it.

ARTHUR: Yes, that's what happens in these parts.

TEMPLE: It's pretty bad now, isn't it?

WALTERS: Yes; if you ask me we're going to have a job making the harbour.

ARTHUR: Have you lost your bearings, Stan?

WALTERS: Well – I'm not too sure of myself, Arthur.

ARTHUR: If you want my opinion we're drifting against the … (*He stops*)

TEMPLE: What is it?

ARTHUR: I thought I saw something …

TEMPLE: What do you mean? Someone in the water?

ARTHUR: No, I thought … (*Suddenly*) Yes, there it is – it's the yacht! Look!

WALTERS: My golly, you're right!

ARTHUR: Isn't that the yacht you were going out to?

198

TEMPLE: Yes, that's it! Get closer ... Get closer, they may have heard something ...

WALTERS: Keep your eye on it, Arthur. We can easily lose it ...

ARTHUR: (*Peering*) I've lost it already ...

TEMPLE: No, there she is ... Look! Keep going, you're all right ... That's it ... Keep going ...

WALTERS: Don't lose it, Arthur.

TEMPLE: (*Shouting*) Hello, there! Hello, there!!!

ARTHUR: It's no good shouting yet, Mr Temple. We're too far away!

FADE UP the sound of WALTERS manipulating the oars in the water.

FADE OUT.

FADE IN the sound of the oars.

TEMPLE: (*Shouting*) Hello, there! Can you hear me? Hello, there!!! (*A moment's pause*) There doesn't appear to be anybody on board ...

We hear WALTERS skipping the oars.

WALTERS: Phew – am I exhausted ...

TEMPLE: Yes, I expect you are. Thank you. I'm very grateful.

WALTERS: I don't see there's anything else we can do.

ARTHUR: There doesn't appear to be anybody on board the yacht, Mr Temple.

TEMPLE: But there must be. They were expecting us.

ARTHUR: Yes, but that's some time ago. They may have left the yacht by now.

WALTERS: Not in this mist, Arthur.

ARTHUR: Well, where is everybody then?

TEMPLE: (*Calling*) Hello, there! Anyone aboard? De Silva, can you hear me? Hello, there!

A pause.

WALTERS: It's no use. We'd better make for the harbour.

WALTERS is interrupted by DE SILVA.

DE SILVA: (*Calling down from the yacht*) Hello, there! Where are you?

TEMPLE: There's someone calling –

WALTERS: (*Calling back*) We're over here – on the starboard side.

TEMPLE: (*Calling*) Is that you, de Silva?

DE SILVA: (*Calling back*) Yes – who is that?

TEMPLE: (*Calling*) This is Temple – Paul Temple! Stan, get closer! Pull in closer! Get the boat closer!

We hear the sound of the oars.

The boat draws closer to the yacht.

DE SILVA: Temple, are you all right?

We hear the sound of water lapping against the side of the yacht and the boat.

The boat drifts nearer the yacht.

TEMPLE: (*Calling*) Yes, we had an accident, the dinghy overturned and …

DE SILVA: (*Calling; interrupting TEMPLE*) Yes, I know, we picked up your wife about an hour ago …

TEMPLE: You picked her up?

DE SILVA: (*Calling; closer*) Yes …

TEMPLE: Is she – ?

DE SILVA: She's all right. There's nothing to worry about.

TEMPLE: (*Softly; to himself*) Oh, thank God …

FADE SCENE.

FADE IN of STEVE.

STEVE: … (*Speaking with an effort*) Everything seemed to go dark, I couldn't see anything. I heard you shouting and I tried to shout back but I kept swallowing water.

TEMPLE: Go on, Steve.

STEVE: I caught a glimpse of Dexter; he seemed to be holding on to something; I tried to get across to him because I thought he might be able to tell me where you were. Suddenly, while I was swimming towards him, he disappeared …

TEMPLE: What do you mean, Steve – he disappeared? Did he go under?

STEVE: I just don't know.

TEMPLE: Did you see Dexter, de Silva?

DE SILVA: No, we never caught a glimpse of him.

TEMPLE: Go on, Steve.

STEVE: Well, I swam about for a bit, not knowing quite what to do. I got panicky and started to shout.

DE SILVA: That's when I first heard you, Mrs Temple. I was on deck waiting for the dinghy. Suddenly I heard your wife shouting for help.

TEMPLE: Thank heavens you did!

The door of the cabin opens.

JULIE: (*MRS DE SILVA is a sophisticated woman in her late forties; at the moment she is a shade on edge*) Here's the brandy, Ernest. Sorry to have been so long.

DE SILVA: Thank you, Julie. Here you are, Temple, drink this. You can do with it, I'm sure.

TEMPLE: Thank you.

TEMPLE drinks the brandy.

JULIE: I've just been giving your friends a whisky and soda, Mr Temple. I'm sure the poor souls would have preferred beer but I'm afraid we haven't any at the moment.

TEMPLE: (*Sipping the brandy*) I should imagine the poor devils were grateful for anything, they must be just about all in.

JULIE: They certainly look all in! That man Walters is quite exhausted.

DE SILVA: I wish to heaven there was something we could do about Dexter.

JULIE: What can we do? The mist doesn't seem to be clearing.

TEMPLE: Of course, he may have got to shore all right; if he's a good swimmer it's just possible …

JULIE: (*Interrupting TEMPLE*) But Brian couldn't swim …

DE SILVA: (*Surprised*) He couldn't swim?

JULIE: Well, hardly. You certainly wouldn't call him a swimmer.

DE SILVA: Oh dear, that doesn't sound very helpful.

STEVE: It certainly doesn't.

JULIE: Mr Temple, this boat – the one that caused the accident – did you see it?

TEMPLE: Yes, but it's very doubtful if I should recognise it again.

STEVE: The man wore goggles and a sort of windcheater thing.

DE SILVA: Do you think he knew what he was doing?

STEVE: He knew what he was doing all right!

DE SILVA: But it seems incredible!

JULIE: I can hardly imagine anyone doing a thing like that, quite deliberately, in cold blood.

TEMPLE: Well, he did, Mrs de Silva.

A pause.

DE SILVA: Would you like another brandy, Temple?

TEMPLE: No, thank you.

DE SILVA: Mrs Temple?

STEVE: No; I feel much better now, thank you very much.

A moment's pause.

202

DE SILVA: Temple, you remember, several days ago when you came to my consulting room you asked me questions about my chauffeur – a man called Barker?

TEMPLE: Yes.

DE SILVA: I suppose you heard what happened to Barker?

TEMPLE: Yes, I heard. I helped to identify his body.

DE SILVA: (*Surprised*) You did?

TEMPLE: Yes.

DE SILVA: Why was that?

TEMPLE: When the police searched Barker they found a wallet on him; in the wallet were several photographs of my wife.

DE SILVA: Of your wife! You mean – Mrs Temple?

TEMPLE: I've only got one wife.

DE SILVA: But that's extraordinary! Why should Barker carry photographs of your wife?

TEMPLE: Why, indeed?

JULIE: Was he a friend of yours, Mrs Temple?

STEVE: No; we'd never even met.

DE SILVA: Then why were you curious about Barker in the first place, Temple?

TEMPLE: I told you why. My wife was under the impression that she'd seen a friend of ours – well, an acquaintance – sitting in your car outside of the Stags Head at Maidenhead. I disagreed with her. I didn't think it was our friend. We had a little argument about it and I decided to find out whether she was right or wrong.

JULIE: And was she right?

TEMPLE: Yes, she was right, Mrs de Silva.

A moment's pause.

DE SILVA: Who was this friend of yours?

TEMPLE:	A man called West – Salty West.
JULIE:	(*With surprise*) Salty West?
TEMPLE:	Yes.
DE SILVA:	Do you know this man, Julie?
JULIE:	I don't know him, but I've heard of him. He's a native of these parts. Quite a character, I believe.
DE SILVA:	Was he a friend of Barker's?
JULIE:	(*Slightly irritated*) I wouldn't know, Ernest. I didn't make a habit of mixing with Barker's friends.
DE SILVA:	You know perfectly well what I mean, Julie. Did you ever see them together?
JULIE:	No.
TEMPLE:	Did Barker ever come to Downburgh?
DE SILVA:	Occasionally; he drove my wife down here once or twice.
TEMPLE:	I take it you're rather fond of Downburgh, Mrs de Silva?
JULIE:	I'm fond of yachting, Mr Temple; I find this a convenient centre.
TEMPLE:	I should have thought Cowes would have been much more convenient.
JULIE:	I don't happen to like Cowes; neither did – does Brian.
TEMPLE:	Was Dexter an experienced yachtsman?
DE SILVA:	Very. That's why my wife and he were such good friends. Apart from the fact that I can't afford this sort of thing I must confess I'm not really keen on it.
JULIE:	You loathe it, Ernest. You're the world's worst sailor.
TEMPLE:	Mrs de Silva, will you forgive me if I ask you one or two rather personal questions?

JULIE: (*Hesitantly*) What kind of personal questions?

TEMPLE: Is Sylvia Ross a friend of yours?

JULIE: Sylvia Ross?

TEMPLE: Yes – she's the daughter of Sir Carlton Ross.

JULIE: I've never heard of her.

TEMPLE: She's a friend of Mr Dexter.

JULIE: That may well be. I still haven't heard of her.

TEMPLE: Have you heard of a man called Teako – Johnny Teako?

JULIE: Why, yes. He's on the radio; isn't he something to do with a dance orchestra?

TEMPLE: He runs a dance orchestra. Is he a friend of yours?

JULIE: Why no, of course he isn't.

TEMPLE: You've never met him?

JULIE: No.

TEMPLE: Both Teako and his wife were in Downburgh this morning. They had lunch at the hotel.

JULIE: Well?

TEMPLE: Did they come out to the yacht?

JULIE: (*Angrily*) Of course they didn't! I've told you. I've never even met them.

DE SILVA: (*Quietly*) I know Mr and Mrs Teako. They're patients of mine.

TEMPLE: Did you know they were in Downburgh?

DE SILVA: No, I didn't, there's no reason why I should.

TEMPLE: Do you know many of the local people, Mrs de Silva?

JULIE: Not a great many; the shopkeepers, of course.

TEMPLE: Did you ever meet Bob Gardner?

A moment's pause.

JULIE: Yes.

TEMPLE: When was that?

JULIE: Oh – about a week before the accident.

DE SILVA: Who's Bob Gardner?

JULIE: (*Faintly irritated*) He's one of the local fishermen – or rather he was. He had an accident on Lighthouse Cliff and was killed.

DE SILVA: Oh, yes, I seem to remember reading something about it …

STEVE: He had a sister called Mary …

DE SILVA: That's right. Mary Gardner … (*Suddenly*) But you knew Mary Gardner, Julie. She was a friend of yours.

JULIE: Well – hardly a friend, Ernest. (*To TEMPLE*) She came out to the yacht once or twice. She was rather handy with the needle and she altered one or two dresses for me.

There is a knock on the door.

TEMPLE: I see.

DE SILVA: Come in!

The door opens.

WALTERS: Excuse me, sir …

DE SILVA: Come in, Walters!

TEMPLE: Do you feel better?

WALTERS: Yes, much better, thank you, sir.

JULIE: Would you like another whisky and soda?

WALTERS: No, no, thank you. You've been very kind, ma'am. (*To TEMPLE*) The mist seems to be lifting quite a bit, Mr Temple. I think it might be a good idea if we made a move.

TEMPLE: Yes, all right. (*To STEVE*) Do you feel up to it, darling?

STEVE: Yes, I'll be all right.

JULIE: You can stay the night if you like, Mrs Temple; we haven't a lot of room but I dare say …

STEVE: No; I'd like to get back to the hotel and change, if you don't mind.

206

JULIE: Yes, of course.

DE SILVA: Let us know if there's any news of Dexter.

WALTERS: We'll keep our eyes open on the way back, sir. Are you ready, Mrs Temple?

STEVE: Yes, I'm ready.

FADE IN incidental music.

FADE MUSIC.

FADE IN STEVE speaking.

STEVE: (*In bed; slowly waking up; she stretches and yawns. Suddenly, surprised*) Oh, hello, Paul!

TEMPLE: Good morning! I've brought you your breakfast!

STEVE: (*Stretching herself*) Oh, I've had a wonderful sleep, darling!

TEMPLE: Do you feel better?

STEVE: I feel wonderful!

TEMPLE: Would you care for a swim?

STEVE: (*Laughing in spite of herself*) Oh, darling, don't!

TEMPLE: Where shall I put this tray?

STEVE: I'll take it.

STEVE takes the tray.

STEVE: M'm – smells delicious. Lovely toast!

TEMPLE: I didn't know whether to bring you breakfast or lunch.

STEVE: Why, what time is it? (*Suddenly; shocked*) Paul, it's not –

TEMPLE: (*Laughing*) It is! Quarter past eleven!

STEVE: Why on earth didn't you wake me? I can't stay in bed all day!

TEMPLE: You stay where you are, and eat your breakfast!

STEVE: Have you had yours?

TEMPLE: Yes, hours ago. I had it with Sir Graham.

207

STEVE:	Is Sir Graham still here? I thought he'd have gone back to Town by now.
TEMPLE:	No, he went out to the yacht to interview the de Silvas.
STEVE:	I suppose there's no news of Dexter?
TEMPLE:	No, I'm afraid not.
STEVE:	Oh, Paul, I feel awfully bad about that.
TEMPLE:	Don't be silly, Steve, it wasn't your fault. What on earth could you do? What could either of us do, if it comes to that?
STEVE:	Paul, there's no doubt in your mind about last night, is there?
TEMPLE:	What do you mean?
STEVE:	It was done deliberately, it wasn't just my imagination?
TEMPLE:	It wasn't your imagination, Steve. Now come along, eat your breakfast.

STEVE pours herself a cup of coffee.

STEVE:	What are you going to do this morning?
TEMPLE:	I'm going to get the car and then I'm going down into the village. I want to see if I can find a girl called Jill Chepstow.
STEVE:	Jill Chepstow?
TEMPLE:	Yes. Remember, I mentioned her to you last night.
STEVE:	She was engaged to Andy Cross, the boy that committed suicide.
TEMPLE:	That's right.
STEVE:	Why do you want to see Jill Chepstow?
TEMPLE:	I really don't know why, but I've got a funny sort of feeling about Jill Chepstow; call it a hunch if you like …
STEVE:	Darling, you leave the hunches to me, they're my speciality.

TEMPLE: (*Laughing*) Yes, but you haven't had one for ages.

STEVE: As a matter of fact I had one last night.

TEMPLE: Last night?

STEVE: Yes. Well, I suppose it wasn't exactly a hunch, but – (*She hesitates*)

TEMPLE: Well?

STEVE: I overheard Mrs de Silva say something; she was talking to her husband. It was just after they'd picked me out of the water.

TEMPLE: Go on, darling.

STEVE: I was lying down in the cabin; de Silva was getting me a hot drink and Mrs de Silva was rushing around for blankets and hot water bottles. When they came back into the cabin I had my eyes closed; I was feeling pretty exhausted and it must have looked as if I'd fallen asleep. Suddenly I heard Mrs de Silva say, "Foley isn't going to like this, Ernest." Her husband gave a little laugh and said: "It's a matter of complete indifference to me what your friend Foley likes."

A moment's pause.

TEMPLE: Is that all?

STEVE: Yes.

TEMPLE: You don't know what they were referring to?

STEVE: No, I don't, but –

TEMPLE: Well?

STEVE: Well, it struck me that this man Foley – whoever he is – must be a pretty important person.

TEMPLE: Why should you think that? Simply because of what you overheard?

STEVE: No, it wasn't so much what Mrs de Silva said as the way she said it.

209

TEMPLE: (*Thoughtfully*) Foley? You're sure you've got the name right?

STEVE: (*Not very definite*) I think so. It was either Foley or … Morley …

There is a knock on the door.

TEMPLE: I'll have a word with Sir Graham about it and see if he knows …

STEVE: There's someone at the door.

TEMPLE opens the door.

TEMPLE: Oh, good morning, Inspector!

IVOR: Good morning, sir.

TEMPLE: It's Inspector Ivor, Steve.

STEVE: Oh, come in, Inspector!

IVOR: Good morning, Mrs Temple.

STEVE: I don't usually have breakfast in bed at this hour of the day, Inspector.

IVOR: If I'd been through what you went through, Mrs Temple, I should spend the rest of the week in bed!

TEMPLE laughs.

IVOR: Sir Graham asked me to drop in on you, sir. He told me to tell you that he'd see you here for lunch.

TEMPLE: Oh, I see. Thank you, Inspector. Did Sir Graham go out to the launch?

IVOR: Yes; we both did. Oh – you'll be pleased to hear Mr Dexter's quite safe, sir.

STEVE: (*Quickly*) Quite safe? You mean – ?

IVOR: One of the fishing fleet picked him up late last night and took him to Melstone Cove.

TEMPLE: Have you seen him?

IVOR: Yes, I saw him this morning. He came out to the yacht while Sir Graham and I were there. He was

	relieved to hear that you and Mrs Temple were all right, sir.
TEMPLE:	How did he look?
IVOR:	Not too good; from what he told us I gather it was pretty nearly touch and go. We're making inquiries about the motor launch that was responsible for the accident. As soon as I hear anything I'll let you know.
TEMPLE:	Thank you, Inspector.
IVOR:	Well, I'll be making a move.
TEMPLE:	Yes, all right, Inspector. Oh, by the way, does the name Foley mean anything to you?
IVOR:	Foley?
TEMPLE:	Yes.
IVOR:	Why, no. Why do you ask?
TEMPLE:	My wife overheard someone mention the name and she thought …
IVOR:	(*Suddenly*) You don't mean Townley, sir?
STEVE:	That's it! Oh, Paul, I'm terribly sorry – I got it wrong!
TEMPLE:	Townley?
IVOR:	Yes. We had a memo through from Sir Graham about eighteen months ago. He asked us to be on the lookout for a man called Townley – Roger Townley. Apparently the Dutch authorities wanted him on some charge or other.
TEMPLE:	Why contact you?
IVOR:	There was a rumour he'd landed here. Don't forget we're opposite the Dutch coast, sir.
TEMPLE:	I see.
IVOR:	Who mentioned this name, Mrs Temple?
TEMPLE:	Mrs de Silva.
IVOR:	When?

TEMPLE: Last night; but I don't want you to say anything about it, Inspector.

IVOR: Yes, all right, Mr Temple.

TEMPLE: Is that a promise?

IVOR: Yes, it's a promise, sir.

TEMPLE: Inspector, you remember about twelve months ago a young man called Andy Cross committed suicide?

IVOR: Yes.

TEMPLE: I believe he was friendly with a girl called Jill Chepstow.

IVOR: That's right.

TEMPLE: Have you any idea where I could find Miss Chepstow?

IVOR: She works for her father. He has an ironmonger's. It's on the corner near Mrs Purdie's. They call the shop Handywork or something like that.

TEMPLE: Thank you, Inspector.

IVOR: (*Curious*) Why are you interested in Miss Chepstow?

TEMPLE: (*Vaguely*) Someone told me about Andy Cross and I thought I'd like to have a word with her.

IVOR: But it's over a year since the boy committed suicide, and incidentally it was suicide, there was no doubt about it.

TEMPLE: I don't doubt it, Inspector.

IVOR: Then what do you doubt?

TEMPLE: (*Smiling*) I don't know that I doubt anything. I just want to have a chat with Jill Chepstow.

IVOR: (*Almost a sigh*) All right, sir. Well – let me know if I can be of any help.

TEMPLE: I will indeed, Inspector.

IVOR: Goodbye, Mrs Temple. Take care of yourself.

212

STEVE: Goodbye, Inspector.

The door opens and closes.

STEVE: Paul, why do you really want to see this girl?

TEMPLE: I told you, Steve. It's just a hunch.

FADE IN of incidental music.

FADE DOWN of music.

FADE IN a shop door opening.

We hear the shop spring-bell ringing.

TOM CHEPSTOW: (*Behind the counter; a North Country man; about fifty-five*) Good morning, sir.

TEMPLE: Good morning. Mr Chepstow?

CHEPSTOW: Yes?

TEMPLE: My name is Temple, Mr Chepstow. Paul Temple. Perhaps you've heard of me, I'm a friend of Inspector Ivor's.

CHEPSTOW: Yes, of course I've heard of you, Mr Temple. What can I do for you, sir?

TEMPLE: I'd like to have a word with your daughter, Mr Chepstow. I understand …

CHEPSTOW: (*Interrupting TEMPLE*) I'm afraid that isn't possible, sir.

TEMPLE: Oh? Why not?

CHEPSTOW: She's gone up to London, Mr Temple. She left Downburgh last night on the six-fifteen.

TEMPLE: Oh, I see. Is she staying in London?

CHEPSTOW: Yes – so far as I know.

TEMPLE: (*Pleasantly*) Well, I'm returning to London myself today, perhaps you could give me her address?

CHEPSTOW: (*Hesitantly*) I could, but – what is it you want exactly? Perhaps I could help you?

TEMPLE: I rather doubt it, Mr Chepstow.

213

CHEPSTOW: (*Faintly aggressive*) If it concerns my daughter, it concerns me. Out with it.

TEMPLE: Your daughter was engaged to a boy called Andy Cross.

CHEPSTOW: That's right.

TEMPLE: He committed suicide.

CHEPSTOW: He did.

TEMPLE: (*Bluntly*) Why?

CHEPSTOW: (*With a note of sarcasm*) Don't you know why, Mr Temple?

TEMPLE: (*Quite pleasantly*) If I knew, I shouldn't ask you.

CHEPSTOW: It all came out at the inquest. It's been common enough gossip ever since. He had a tiff with Jill and got despondent.

TEMPLE: I see.

CHEPSTOW: But this is old stuff; why are you interested in what happened to Andy?

TEMPLE: I'm interested in the motive.

CHEPSTOW: What motive?

TEMPLE: Andy's motive; the reason why he committed suicide.

CHEPSTOW: (*Irritated*) I've told you the reason.

TEMPLE: You told me that he had a row with your daughter and he got despondent. That doesn't sound a very good motive to me.

CHEPSTOW: It was good enough for the Coroner.

TEMPLE: Was it good enough for you, Mr Chepstow?

CHEPSTOW: (*Suddenly; faintly aggressive*) No, it wasn't, and it wasn't good enough for Jill either.

TEMPLE: I see. Will you have a cigarette?

CHEPSTOW: I don't smoke.

TEMPLE: Do you mind if I –

CHEPSTOW: No, no, makes no difference to me. If people want to turn themselves into chimneys let 'em get on with it.

TEMPLE: (*Lighting his cigarette*) What sort of a boy was Andy Cross?

CHEPSTOW: Good looking chap; clever with his hands.

TEMPLE: Was he moody – highly strung?

CHEPSTOW: I shouldn't have said so.

TEMPLE: I understand he worked at a garage?

CHEPSTOW: Part o' the time.

TEMPLE: Part of the time?

CHEPSTOW: Look, Mr Temple, don't think me rude, but take my advice and let sleeping dogs lie. Jill was very upset when Andy died, very upset – as a matter of fact she's never properly got over it.

TEMPLE: I've no wish to upset your daughter, Mr Chepstow, on the other …

CHEPSTOW: Well, you will upset her if you ask her a lot of questions about Andy. Now just let the poor kid forget all about it, she had a bad enough time when it happened. My goodness, if it hadn't been for that hobby of hers she'd have had a nervous breakdown an' no mistake. I don't mind telling you her mother and I used to skit at that singing of hers but it's been a godsend during the past twelve months – an absolutely godsend.

TEMPLE: Singing, Mr Chepstow? You mean she's a singer?

CHEPSTOW: She sings with one of the local bands. Just an amateur outfit, o' course, but she's mad on it. Her mother and I never take her seriously, but

215

	this chap from London seems to think she's very good.

TEMPLE: Which chap from London?

CHEPSTOW: Why, the one that came down yesterday. Most impressed, he was – he's offered her a job.

TEMPLE: What was the man's name, Mr Chepstow? Was it Teako?

CHEPSTOW: (*Surprised*) Why, yes! That's right – Johnny Teako!

FADE IN incidental music.

FADE DOWN music.
FADE IN the sound of coffee cups.
There are background noises of a hotel lounge.

STEVE: Would you like another cup of coffee, Sir Graham?

FORBES: No, thank you, Steve.

STEVE: Paul?

TEMPLE: No, thank you, darling. Go on, Sir Graham, you were telling us about this man Roger Townley.

FORBES: Well, we first heard of Townley about two years ago. The Recherche – that's the Dutch police – warned us to be on the lookout for him. Apparently Townley had been running a diamond smuggling operation in Amsterdam; things got too hot for him and he decided to try his luck in this country.

TEMPLE: And did he?

FORBES: Well, there's certainly been a great deal more smuggling just recently and there's no doubt it's been carefully organised; on the other

	hand, we've no real proof that Townley's behind it.
TEMPLE:	Have you ever seen Townley?
FORBES:	No, but we've a pretty good description of him.
STEVE:	You say there's more smuggling just recently, Sir Graham?
FORBES:	Yes.
STEVE:	Of diamonds?
FORBES:	Diamonds, and drugs. Particularly drugs, Steve.
TEMPLE:	Is that why you came to Downburgh, Sir Graham?
FORBES:	(*Smiling*) I came to see you, Temple – to tell you about Sylvia Ross …
TEMPLE:	Was that your only reason?
FORBES:	(*Hesitating*) Well –
TEMPLE:	Look, Sir Graham, shall we put our cards on the table?
FORBES:	What do you mean?
TEMPLE:	Didn't you come down here to make inquiries about Mary Gardner?
FORBES:	Why should I do that?
TEMPLE:	Because at the back of your mind you've a shrewd suspicion that Mary Gardner was mixed up in this smuggling business. Am I right?

A moment's pause.

FORBES:	Yes, I think she must have been, Temple, and probably Salty West too. But that still doesn't explain how Sylvia Ross fits into the picture.
TEMPLE:	(*Significantly*) Perhaps she doesn't.
FORBES:	Well, if she doesn't, is it just a coincidence that she's a friend of Brian Dexter's? Is it a

217

	coincidence that the note she sent to Johnny Teako contained a reference to a Mr Lawrence? Don't forget the name Lawrence was in the letter that Bob Gardner – Mary Gardner's brother – sent to you.
TEMPLE:	Yes …
FORBES:	Temple, tell me: why did you want to see this other girl – Jill Chepstow?
TEMPLE:	Jill Chepstow doesn't believe Andy Cross committed suicide simply because they had a row. I don't believe it either. I think there was another reason for Andy putting his head in that gas oven; I want to find out what that reason was.
FORBES:	You think Jill Chepstow knows the reason?
TEMPLE:	I think she suspects it; in my opinion that's why Teako came down here and arranged for her to go to Town.
STEVE:	You mean he's whisked her off to London simply to stop her from talking?
TEMPLE:	That's my opinion, Steve – of course, I may be wrong.
FORBES:	But the fact that she's in London won't stop her from talking.
TEMPLE:	Miss Chepstow fancies her chances as a dance band vocalist. Teako's going to play that up for all he's worth. Isn't it obvious therefore that …

TEMPLE stops talking; he notices INSPECTOR IVOR coming towards the table.

TEMPLE:	Hello, here's Inspector Ivor!
FORBES:	(*Surprised*) Hello, Inspector!
IVOR:	Good afternoon, Sir Graham. I'm sorry to disturb you, sir.

FORBES: That's all right.

STEVE: Would you like some coffee, Inspector?

IVOR: No, thank you, Mrs Temple.

FORBES: Sit down, Inspector.

IVOR: Thank you, sir.

TEMPLE pulls up another chair.

TEMPLE: Here's a chair.

IVOR: Oh, thank you. I – er – I wanted to have a word with you, Sir Graham, because, well –

FORBES: Yes, Inspector?

IVOR: (*Quietly*) Well – it rather looks as if there's been a new development, sir.

FORBES: A new development?

TEMPLE: What do you mean?

IVOR: You know the seawall, Sir Graham, that runs between here and Felixstowe?

FORBES: I've seen it, of course.

IVOR: It's a large, wide, concrete wall above sea level; punctuated by boulders.

STEVE: Yes, my husband and I often walk along it.

IVOR: It's a very pleasant walk on a fine day.

TEMPLE: (*Interested*) Go on, Inspector.

IVOR: Well, you may have noticed, Mr Temple, about every half mile or so there's a bend in the wall and this usually produces a sort of cavity, a kind of …

TEMPLE: Artificial cave.

IVOR: Exactly. Well, early this morning a local tradesman found the body of a man in one of those caves. The man had been murdered and the body had obviously been dumped there.

FORBES: Are you sure it wasn't washed up by the tide?

IVOR: Yes, we're quite sure, sir.

FORBES: Go on, Inspector.

IVOR: Well, I went out to examine the body with Sergeant Moore and the local police doctor.

TEMPLE: What was the cause of death?

IVOR: According to the doctor death was caused by strangulation. Anyway, I followed the usual routine and searched both the cavity and the surrounding area. About a hundred yards from the body, actually on the seawall itself, I found this, sir.

STEVE: What is it?

FORBES: It looks like a watchchain.

TEMPLE: Yes, but it isn't. It's a bracelet.

IVOR: How do you know it's a bracelet, Mr Temple? Have you seen it before?

A moment's pause.

TEMPLE: Yes.

IVOR: Where?

STEVE: (*Suddenly*) I've seen it before too! Mr de Silva wears a bracelet like that – exactly like it.

FORBES: Mr de Silva?

STEVE: Yes.

FORB ES: But surely –

TEMPLE: Steve's right, Sir Graham. De Silva does wear a bracelet like that. I always thought there was an identity tab on it.

IVOR: (*Examining the bracelet*) There isn't at the moment, Mr Temple – but there may have been one.

FORBES: Inspector, did anyone identity this man?

IVOR: Yes, I did.

FORBES: (*Surprised*) You did?

IVOR: Yes, sir. I identified him from your description. His name's Roger Townley.

FADE IN closing music.

END OF EPISODE SEVEN

EPISODE EIGHT

RETURN TO LONDON

OPEN TO:

FADE IN the voice of DETECTIVE INSPECTOR IVOR.

IVOR: Well, I went out to examine the body with
           Sergeant Moore and the local police doctor.

TEMPLE: What was the cause of death?

IVOR: According to the doctor death was caused by
           strangulation. Anyway, I followed the usual
           routine and searched both the cavity and the
           surrounding area. About a hundred yards from
           the body, actually on the seawall itself, I found
           this, sir.

STEVE: What is it?

FORBES: It looks like a watchchain.

TEMPLE: Yes, but it isn't. It's a bracelet.

IVOR: How do you know it's a bracelet, Mr Temple?
           Have you seen it before?

A moment's pause.

TEMPLE: Yes.

IVOR: Where?

STEVE: (*Suddenly*) I've seen it before too! Mr de Silva
           wears a bracelet like that – exactly like it.

FORBES: Mr de Silva?

STEVE: Yes.

FORB ES: But surely –

TEMPLE: Steve's right, Sir Graham. De Silva does wear a
           bracelet like that. I always thought there was an
           identity tab on it.

IVOR: (*Examining the bracelet*) There isn't at the
           moment, Mr Temple – but there may have been
           one.

FORBES: Inspector, did anyone identity this man?

IVOR: Yes, I did.

FORBES: (*Surprised*) You did?

225

IVOR: Yes, sir. I identified him from your description. His name's Roger Townley.

FORBES: Townley?

IVOR: Yes, sir.

FORBES: Are you sure it's Townley?

IVOR: I'm absolutely positive, sir. There's no doubt about it. By a curious coincidence I was telling Mr Temple about Townley only this morning, sir.

FORBES: (*Curious*) Oh – why?

IVOR: (*Embarrassed*) Well –

TEMPLE: Steve thought she heard Mrs de Silva mention the name Townley.

FORBES: When was that?

STEVE: Last night, Sir Graham.

FORBES: Tell me about it. (*Pause*) Go on, Steve. What happened?

STEVE: It was just after de Silva rescued me. I was in the cabin – feeling pretty exhausted. Mrs de Silva turned to her husband and said: "Townley isn't going to like this, Ernest."

FORBES: And what did her husband say?

STEVE: He said, "It's a matter of complete indifference to me what your friend Townley likes."

FORBES: I see.

TEMPLE: Steve, do you think that Julie de Silva was referring to the fact that her husband had rescued you?

STEVE: That's what struck me at the time but it seems such an odd thing to say.

TEMPLE: Not so very odd.

STEVE: What do you mean?

TEMPLE: That was no accident last night, it was a deliberate attempt to get rid of me.

226

FORBES: And you think that Mrs de Silva knew that?

TEMPLE: Not only that, but I think she was extremely angry with her husband for interfering.

FORBES: Well, if you're right, Temple, it's a lucky thing for Steve that de Silva happened to be down here.

TEMPLE: Yes.

STEVE: But it certainly couldn't have been Mrs de Silva in the speedboat because …

TEMPLE: I'm not suggesting that Mrs de Silva attempted to murder us, I simply said that she knew that an attempt was being made. If you want my frank opinion it was Townley who drove the speedboat and Townley who tried to murder us.

STEVE: But why?

TEMPLE: Because the poor fool was under a misapprehension, that's why.

STEVE: I don't follow you.

TEMPLE: Why did we come to Downburgh, Steve – in the first place, I mean?

STEVE: You wanted somewhere quiet to finish your book.

TEMPLE: Yes, but that's not what Townley thought. He thought I came here for a purpose. A particular purpose.

FORBES: I see what you're getting at. He thought you came here to make certain investigations.

TEMPLE: Exactly.

A pause.

IVOR: Mr Temple …

TEMPLE: Yes, Inspector?

FORBES: What did Salty West mean when he said, "Tell Paul Temple there isn't a Mr Lawrence"?

227

TEMPLE: He meant precisely that, Inspector. (*His thoughts elsewhere*) Precisely that.

FADE IN incidental music.

FADE DOWN music.
TEMPLE and STEVE are in front of their front door.
TEMPLE's hand is on the bellpush.
We hear the sound of the door bell ringing in the background.

TEMPLE: (*Impatiently*) Come along, Charlie! Come along!

STEVE: Be patient, darling!

TEMPLE: Yes, but he always seems to take such a time to answer the bell.

STEVE: Well, we're in no desperate hurry.

TEMPLE: I am. It's half-past seven. I want to see that fellow Teako as soon as I possibly can.

STEVE: Why do you want to see Teako?

TEMPLE: Because he's got that girl Jill Chepstow under his wing and after what's happened I don't want to take any chances.

TEMPLE presses the bellpush again.
The door opens.

CHARLIE: Sorry, Mr Temple, I was in the bath. Good evening, Mrs T.

STEVE: Hello, Charlie.

TEMPLE: (*Irritated*) Don't say Mrs T.

CHARLIE: No, sir – I mean, yes, sir.

TEMPLE: And take this suitcase.

CHARLIE: Yes, sir.

TEMPLE: The <u>heavy</u> one, Charlie!

CHARLIE: Oh, sorry, sir.

The door closes.

TEMPLE: Any messages – letters?

CHARLIE: No, sir.

TEMPLE: Nothing?

228

CHARLIE: Well, several bills, sir.

TEMPLE: Yes, I know that, but –

CHARLIE: Oh, a Mr Hailey rang up, sir.

TEMPLE: (*Interested*) Oh, yes – what did he say?

CHARLIE: He said he'd received your telegram, sir, and – (*He hesitates*)

TEMPLE: Yes?

CHARLIE: And the answer was – "Like a fish".

TEMPLE: Like a fish!

CHARLIE: (*Puzzled*) Yes, sir.

TEMPLE: (*Pleased*) Thank you, Charlie.

STEVE: Who's this Mr Hailey?

TEMPLE: (*Vaguely*) Oh, just someone I know.

STEVE: It wouldn't be Reg Hailey, the artist?

TEMPLE: That's right.

STEVE: Why on earth did you send him a telegram; you hardly know him?

TEMPLE: (*Smiling*) He was born thirty years ago and he went to Eton.

STEVE: Paul, be serious! Why did you send him a telegram?

TEMPLE: (*Amused by STEVE's bewilderment*) I've told you: he was born thirty years ago and went to Eton. (*Laughing*) Come along, Steve! Let's go upstairs and change.

FADE DOWN.

FADE UP JOHNNY TEAKO's dance orchestra at the dancing hall.

People are dancing to the music.

The music stops.

Applause.

TEAKO: Thank you – thank you. You have been dancing to the Johnny Teako orchestra conducted by the

229

Maestro himself. This is Johnny Teako saying au revoir but not goodbye. Hit the keys, Harry!

HARRY starts playing a gay number on the piano.

The dancers leave the floor.

STEVE: I don't see any sign of your friend Miss Chepstow.

TEMPLE: No, unless that's her over there, sitting with Linda Teako.

STEVE: No, she's one of the regular singers, I remember she was here before.

TEMPLE: I'm going to have a word with Teako. Stay here, darling.

STEVE: Don't be long.

TEMPLE: Don't worry; I can say what I want to say in two minutes.

FADE UP the sound of the piano.

The boys in the orchestra are chatting.

TEMPLE: Mr Teako, can I make a request?

TEAKO: (*His back to TEMPLE*) Why, sure, that's what we're here for! (*He turns*) You don't have to … (*He recognises TEMPLE; a slight pause*) Temple, what do you want?

TEMPLE: I want to talk to you, Teako. Have you got a dressing room?

TEAKO: (*Faintly aggressive*) Sure I've got a dressing room.

TEMPLE: Let's use it.

TEAKO: Look, I'm working. This is business hours. I'm on again in ten minutes.

TEMPLE: What I've got to say won't take more than two.

A pause.

TEAKO: Okay. Follow me.

FADE the piano to the background.

A door opens.

TEAKO: Here we are. In here.

TEMPLE: (*Entering the dressing room*) Thank you.

The door closes, completely cutting off the sound of the piano.

TEAKO: (*Abruptly; tough*) Well – what is it, Mr Snooper?

TEMPLE: Teako, when you were in Downburgh you met a girl called Jill Chepstow. You brought her back to Town with you.

TEAKO: Well?

TEMPLE: Why?

TEAKO: Why, what?

TEMPLE: Why did you bring her back to Town with you?

TEAKO: What business is it of yours?

TEMPLE: I'm asking you a question, Teako. I want the answer.

TEAKO: Miss Chepstow sings; she's got a good voice. I'm always on the lookout for girls with – good voices.

TEMPLE: Is she here tonight?

TEAKO: She will be later.

TEMPLE: How much later?

TEAKO: I told her to be here at ten o'clock.

TEMPLE: Where is she now?

TEAKO: (*A shrug*) How should I know? I'm not her guardian.

TEMPLE: You're responsible for her.

TEAKO: What do you mean?

TEMPLE: Teako, listen. Miss Chepstow was engaged to a boy called Andy Cross who committed suicide. The general impression was that he did so because he'd had a row with his fiancée. That's not what I think. It's not what Miss Chepstow thinks either.

TEAKO: So what?

231

TEMPLE: You brought Miss Chepstow to London because you wanted to keep an eye on her; you wanted to make sure she wouldn't talk.

TEAKO: That's not true! She's a singer! A first-class singer!

TEMPLE: I hope so.

TEAKO: (*Blustering*) What do you mean – you hope so?

TEMPLE: I'm holding you responsible for that girl. Scotland Yard know that she's in London, they know that you brought her here. If anything happens to that girl, Teako, I shouldn't like to be in your shoes.

A pause.

TEAKO: (*Nervously*) Nothing's going to happen to her!

A slight pause.

TEMPLE: I'm delighted to hear it.

START FADE.

TEAKO: Now, if you've no objection, I'd like to get back to the ballroom.

TEMPLE: I've no objection.

COMPLETE FADE.

FADE UP the piano and ballroom noises.

FADE the piano down to the background.

A pause.

STEVE: Did you see him?

TEMPLE: Yes. Come on, Steve, we'll go!

STEVE: But what about Jill Chepstow?

TEMPLE: I don't think we need worry about Jill Chepstow. She'll be all right. (*Pause; quietly, his thoughts elsewhere*) Are you ready, Steve?

STEVE: Yes, I'm ready. You look very thoughtful.

TEMPLE: M'm?

STEVE: I said you look very thoughtful.

TEMPLE: I was just thinking.

STEVE: About what?

TEMPLE: I was just thinking it's about time we gave
            another cocktail party.

FADE IN incidental music.

*CROSS FADE to the sound of a sophisticated West End dance
orchestra.*

FADE DOWN the dance orchestra to the background.

DEXTER: (*Faintly annoyed*) Excuse me – has someone
            left a message for me? My name is Dexter –
            Brian Dexter.

CLERK: Are you staying in the hotel, Mr Dexter?

DEXTER: No. I was asked to meet a friend here at eight
            o'clock but she hasn't turned up.

CLERK: Well, I'm afraid there's no message for you,
            sir.

STEVE: (*Approaching from the background; very gay*)
            Oh, hello, Mr Dexter!

DEXTER: (*Surprised*) Why, hello, Mrs Temple!

STEVE: You look very serious …

DEXTER: I'm rather annoyed; I was supposed to meet
            someone at eight o'clock and they just haven't
            shown up.

STEVE: (*Smiling*) It wouldn't be Mrs de Silva, by any
            chance?

DEXTER: (*Surprised*) Why, yes!

STEVE: (*Very gay*) She's upstairs with my husband;
            we're giving a cocktail party. (*Laughing;
            taking hold of DEXTER's arm*) Come along,
            Mr Dexter! Come along!

FADE UP the dance orchestra from the background.

FADE the orchestra to the background.

BURFORD: (*Quietly*) Good evening …

CLERK: Good evening, sir.
BURFORD: My name is Burford. Mr Paul Temple asked me to call and …
CLERK: (*Interrupting BURFORD*) Why, certainly, Mr Burford; Mr Temple's expecting you, sir. Room 13, on the first floor.
BURFORD: Oh. Oh, thank you. Thank you very much.
CLERK: Thank you, sir.
FADE UP of the dance orchestra.

FADE DOWN the dance orchestra to the background.
CLERK: (*Pleasantly*) Good evening, sir. Can I help you?
DE SILVA: Yes; I understand a Mr Temple is giving a cocktail party and …
CLERK: That's right, sir. Room 13. Is Mr Temple expecting you?
DE SILVA: Er – yes.
CLERK: May I have your name, sir?
A pause.
DE SILVA: De Silva …
CLERK: (*Consulting his list*) Ah, yes, of course! Mr de Silva. (*Pointing*) Will you take the lift, sir? Room 13, on the first floor.
DE SILVA: Thank you.
FADE UP of the dance orchestra from the background.

FADE DOWN to the background gradually.
TEAKO: (*Angrily*) Is she in the cocktail bar?
LINDA: No.
TEAKO: Have you looked in the dining room?
LINDA: Yes.
TEAKO: Have you looked in –
LINDA: (*Irritated*) Yes, she's not in there either.
TEAKO: Well, what the devil is she playing at?

LINDA: The telegram said eight o'clock.

TEAKO: So what? It's only twenty to nine, surely to goodness … (*He stops dead*)

LINDA: What is it, Johnny?

TEAKO: (*Almost a whisper*) Just look who's here!

STEVE: (*Very bright; gay*) Hello, Mrs Teako! This is a pleasant surprise!

TEAKO: (*Suspiciously*) What are you doing here?

STEVE: (*Pleasantly*) What are you doing here, Mr Teako?

LINDA: We arranged to have dinner with a friend of ours, but unfortunately …

STEVE: Not Mrs de Silva! Don't tell me it's Mrs de Silva!

LINDA: (*Taken aback*) Well –

STEVE: But she's upstairs with my husband! She's been here hours!

LINDA: Upstairs with your husband?

STEVE: (*Laughing*) Yes, we're giving a cocktail party. A lovely party, Mr Teako! (*Gaily, taking hold of DE SILVA's arm*) Come along, we'll be delighted to have you join us.

TEAKO: Now wait a minute! We didn't come here to go to any cocktail party!

STEVE: (*Innocently*) You didn't?

TEAKO: No!

STEVE: Well – what did you come here for?

TEAKO: I've told you, to see …

STEVE: To see Mrs de Silva! But I've told you, Mr Teako, she's upstairs – with my husband. (*Laughing; very gay*) Oh, come along, Mrs Teako, don't spoil the party. (*A sudden thought*) Oh dear, I've just thought – I do hope you're not superstitious!

LINDA: Why?
STEVE: (*Laughing*) The party's in Room 13!
FADE UP of the dance orchestra.

FADE DOWN the dance orchestra completely.
FADE UP a background noise of a fairly crowded room.
A door opens.
TEMPLE: (*Pleasantly*) So here you are, Steve! I wondered
            where on earth you'd got to!
STEVE: Paul, look who I bumped into downstairs!
TEMPLE: (*Greeting the TEAKOs*) Why, Mr and Mrs
            Teako! Come along! Come along in!
TEAKO: Look, Temple, your wife's persuaded us to come
            up here against ... (*He stops*) Julie, why didn't
            you wait for us in the lounge?
JULIE: What are you talking about? (*To TEMPLE*) Who
            is this person?
TEMPLE: This is Johnny Teako, Mrs de Silva. The Johnny
            Teako – in person. (*Very pleasantly; yet in
            complete command*) Now let me introduce you to
            everyone. First of all: Mr Brian Dexter.
DEXTER: How do you do?
TEMPLE: Max Burford ...
BURFORD: How do you do?
TEMPLE: Mr de Silva – you probably know Mr de Silva.
            Oh, and Detective Inspector Ivor.
IVOR: Good evening.
TEAKO: Look, Temple, I don't know what the ...
TEMPLE: (*Quietly*) Now what can I offer you? Sherry? Dry
            Martini? Gin and tonic? Mrs Teako?
LINDA: I think I'd like ...
TEAKO: (*Interrupting LINDA*) Now wait a minute! Wait a
            minute! What is all this? What's this all about?

236

TEMPLE: It's a cocktail party. That's all. Just a little cocktail party.

TEAKO: (*Distinctly ugly*) Now don't give me that!

TEMPLE: (*Innocently*) Oh, sorry! Perhaps you'd prefer a Gin and French!

TEAKO: (*Angry; yet faintly nervous*) Look, I'm leaving! I'm getting the hell out of here! No one's making a monkey out of me!

TEMPLE: No one's trying to make a monkey out of you, Teako.

STEVE: Who are we, to improve on nature?

TEAKO: (*Really angry*) Don't get fresh with me, lady, because …

TEMPLE: Because what, Teako? (*A pause; seriously*) You came here tonight, to this hotel, because you had a telegram from Mrs de Silva asking you to meet her here. Correct?

A pause.

TEAKO: Yes.

JULIE: (*Astonished*) What?

TEMPLE: I sent that telegram.

TEAKO: You did?

TEMPLE: Yes.

TEAKO: Why?

TEMPLE: (*Smiling*) Because I wanted you to come here, Teako - that's why.

DEXTER: (*Quietly*) I also had a telegram ostensibly from Mrs de Silva. Did you send that one too, Temple?

TEMPLE: I did.

DEXTER: Why?

TEMPLE: For the same reason that I sent one to Teako.

DEXTER: Wouldn't it have been simpler just to have invited me here?

TEMPLE: (*Smiling*) You might not have come.

BURFORD: Look, Temple, it's quite obvious you've got us all here for a particular purpose; don't you think it might be a good idea if you told us what that purpose was?

DE SILVA: I agree. If you've got anything to say, Temple, please say it.

A pause.

TEMPLE looks round the room.

TEMPLE: Very well, Burford – de Silva – I'll come to the point. The point is this; someone in this room murdered Mary Gardner …

There is a general stir amongst the guests.

TEMPLE: …Someone in the room was responsible for the death of Salty West … Someone in this room attempted to murder my wife …

A tense pause.

TEAKO: (*Tensely*) Well, don't look at me, for God's sake!

TEMPLE: I'm not looking at you, Teako. Why should I?

TEAKO: If you think I had anything to do with …

LINDA: Johnny, for heaven's sake shut up!

TEAKO: (*Blustering; getting tough*) Now listen to me, Linda, if you think I'm the sort of character that's going to be pushed around by …

DE SILVA: (*Acidly*) Mr Teako, if you've even a modicum of common sense – which I'm beginning to doubt – you'll take your wife's advice and remain silent. Now, Temple, at the risk of repeating myself, if you've got anything to say, please say it.

JULIE: Don't you think he's said enough? He's already accused one of us of being a murderer.

BURFORD: I agree, Mrs de Silva!

TEAKO: (*Tensely; unable to control himself*) Yes, but which one? That's the point, which one?

238

DEXTER: Yes, Temple, which one?

TEMPLE: Before I answer that question, Dexter, I'd like you to listen to Inspector Ivor. Go ahead, Inspector.

IVOR: Some time ago a man called Roger Townley formed a diamond smuggling ring which had its headquarters in Downburgh. We, at Scotland Yard, suspected the existence of the ring but were under the impression that it operated from London. Then one day, by pure coincidence, Mr Temple decided to go to Downburgh.

TEMPLE: My reason was quite simple; I was writing a novel and I wanted to be quiet. I knew nothing about the Townley ring. Townley, however, became suspicious. He felt that the novel was simply an excuse for making an investigation on behalf of Scotland Yard. I can assure you this wasn't the case. If I'd been left alone – or rather, if my wife had been left alone – I shouldn't have become involved in this affair. Now Townley had certain of the local people working for him and he believed …

JULIE: Local people? Who are you referring to – Mary Gardner?

TEMPLE: Mary Gardner, her brother Bob, Salty West … However, let me continue. When I left Downburgh Townley consulted his right-hand man; this gentleman – who for the moment we will call X – told Townley that he could take care of the Temple problem. Indeed he guaranteed that I would very quickly lose interest in the ring.

IVOR: In short, he presented Mr Temple – and Scotland Yard – with a much more intriguing problem.

DEXTER: (*With a smile*) The disappearance of Sylvia Ross.

239

TEMPLE: Exactly. The disappearance of Sylvia Ross. Would you care to continue the story, Dexter?

DEXTER: No, no, you seem to be doing very well. Carry on, Temple.

TEMPLE: Miss Ross was infatuated by X and she agreed to do what he wanted; so she disappeared for a few days. Sir Graham was perturbed and consulted me. Now here is the interesting point and I give our friend X full marks for it. As soon as he knew that I had been pulled into the Ross case he gave the whole affair a typical Paul Temple twist.

DE SILVA: What do you mean by that?

TEMPLE: He knew exactly the sort of thing that always intrigues me; he's obviously studied my previous cases. In short, he invented a mysterious name and a mysterious address.

STEVE: Mr Clive Lawrence, Hotel Schweizerhof, Zermatt.

LINDA: But that was on the note that Miss Ross gave to my husband!

TEMPLE: No, Mrs Teako. The note was simply a request for a dance tune; you were following your instructions from X when you told me about the name Lawrence. You see, X was determined that I should become more interested in the mysterious Mr Lawrence than in the activities of the Townley ring.

IVOR: He was probably hoping you'd take a trip to Switzerland.

TEMPLE: Exactly, Inspector. But he overlooked one important point, that there was a member of the ring who hated his guts. I'm referring, of course, to Mary Gardner. Why she hated X so vehemently it's difficult to say; probably …

IVOR: My guess is she blamed him for the death of her brother.

TEMPLE: That's possible, Inspector. Anyhow, Mary Gardner knew that X was throwing me off the sent by introducing a fictitious Mr Lawrence, so out of spite she produced a letter which was supposed to have been written by her brother Bob. The letter also mentioned Lawrence and apparently tied him up with the Downburgh affair.

IVOR: So naturally, you became interested in the Downburgh affair.

TEMPLE: Exactly; which was precisely what Mary Gardner intended.

DEXTER: But look here, if Mary Gardner was a member of the ring why should she throw suspicion …

TEMPLE: Mary was upset because of what happened to her brother; also she was afraid that sooner or later X would take over from Townley.

DEXTER: (*Thoughtfully*) I see.

DE SILVA: Temple, a few moments ago you said that the person who murdered Mary Gardner was here, in this room.

TEMPLE: That's true.

DE SILVA: In other words, you mean – X?

TEMPLE: In other words, I mean X, de Silva.

DE SILVA: (*Irritated*) Well, why the devil don't you come out into the open and tell us who this person really is?

STEVE: Paul, look out!!!

DEXTER: (*Desperately*) Stand back! Get away from that door!!!!

241

TEMPLE: Dexter, don't be a fool – put that revolver down!

DEXTER: I'm warning you, get away from that door!

IVOR: Dexter, listen! You'll never get out of here even if you get through the door. There's three men in the corridor and I've a man on every entrance.

DEXTER: You heard what I said – stand away from that door!!!

IVOR: Dexter, I'm warning you …

TEMPLE: Dexter, you know perfectly well that you haven't the remotest chance of …

STEVE shouts.

DEXTER fires the revolver.

There is general consternation.

BURFORD: (*Shouting*) He's going for the window!

IVOR: Stop him, Burford!

TEMPLE and DEXTER struggle.

TEMPLE: (*Tensely; trying to hold DEXTER*) Dexter, don't be … a … fool … you …

DEXTER forces TEMPLE to one side and dashes towards the window.

LINDA: (*A scream*) He's going to jump!!!!

As LINDA screams DEXTER throws himself through the window.

There is a tremendous smashing of glass followed by confused and excited voices.

STEVE: Paul, are you all right?

DE SILVA: My God, he deliberately threw himself through the window!

TEMPLE: Downstairs, Inspector! Quickly!

FADE UP of voices.

FADE IN of incidental music.

The music continues for a moment, then FADE DOWN.

FADE UP a background of street noises, traffic and excited voices.

VOICE 1: I was walking by and suddenly the whole window fell on top of me …

VOICE 2: You might have been killed …

VOICE 3: (*Excited*) I couldn't believe my eyes – he came straight through the window …

VOICE 4: He was covered in blood but he rushed across the road …

VOICE 5: I don't know what happened … I saw the glass … and then the man running across the road …

INSPECTOR IVOR, INSPECTOR VOSPER, and TEMPLE arrive on the scene.

TEMPLE: (*Breathlessly*) Did you see him, Vosper?

VOSPER: Yes. I was on the side entrance. I heard the glass crash and rushed outside.

TEMPLE: Well, where the devil is he?

VOSPER: He dashed across the road towards the car park …

IVOR: (*Breathless, astonished*) Well, why in heaven's name didn't you stop him?

VOSPER: (*Irritated*) Because I didn't realise who he was! I never imagined you'd let him jump through the confounded window!

TEMPLE: (*Suddenly*) There he is!

IVOR: Where?

TEMPLE: In that car! Come on!

VOSPER: Careful, Temple! Don't cross the road!!!! He's coming over here …

We hear the sound of an approaching car in the background.

IVOR: Look at him … Just look at his arm!

TEMPLE: He'll never drive like that!

IVOR: Look out, Temple! Look out, he's driving the car over here!

DEXTER's car races past at a tremendous speed.

TEMPLE: My car's on the corner, Vosper! Come on!

VOSPER: (*Stopping TEMPLE*) Wait a minute – there's another car coming!

We hear a second car approaching at great speed.

The car races past TEMPLE and VOSPER.

TEMPLE: It's a police car!

VOSPER: It's Sergeant Drake … (*Excitedly*) Good man, Drake! Good man!!!!

In the background we hear police whistles and excited voices.

FADE IN incidental music.

FADE DOWN music.

Continue the music in the background for the following effects:

The sound of DEXTER's car cornering at a tremendous speed.

FADE UP of the police car following: cornering at speed.

After a tiny pause:

FADE UP the sound of TEMPLE's car.

Continue the sound of TEMPLE's car.

FADE music completely.

Continue the noise of TEMPLE's car. It is travelling very fast.

TEMPLE: (*In the car; driving*) It looks as if he's heading for the Embankment. If we turn down Belton Street we may cut him off.

IVOR: (*Grimly*) … Or lose him.

TEMPLE: We'll have to take that chance …

VOSPER: Drake's still on his tail …

TEMPLE: Yes, but if he loses him we'll never cut him off!

IVOR: If he gets the other side of the river we've had it!

TEMPLE: Hold tight, I'm going round here!

TEMPLE accelerates and the car turns into a side street.

FADE UP the car travelling down the street.

VOSPER: Left at the bottom, Temple! No, left!

TEMPLE: I know what I'm doing, Inspector!

The car turns out of the street.

VOSPER: (*Surprised*) You're right, we're on the Embankment! I'm sorry, I thought …

IVOR: You've done it! There he is! You've cut him off!

TEMPLE: (*Quickly; tensely*) Brake, Temple! Brake!!!!

TEMPLE applies the brakes and his car skids to a standstill.

FADE UP in the distance the sound of DEXTER's car approaching.

IVOR: He hasn't seen us yet!

TEMPLE: Get out, Vosper, quick!

VOSPER, TEMPLE and INSPECTOR IVOR climb out of the car slamming the car doors.

TEMPLE: (*Suddenly*) He's spotted us!

VOSPER: He's coming towards us!

IVOR: What the devil is he going to do?

TEMPLE: (*Surprised*) By Timothy, he's trying to turn round!

VOSPER: He's lost control!

IVOR: (*Shouting*) He's going for the parapet!

There is a tremendous crash as the car hits the parapet, breaks through the wall, and finally crashes down into the river.

FADE IN incidental music.

FADE DOWN music.

FADE IN the sound of STEVE pouring coffee.

STEVE: Here you are, darling.

TEMPLE: Thank you.

STEVE: Are you sure you wouldn't like another cup, Sir Graham?

FORBES: No, thank you, Steve.

TEMPLE: Have another brandy, Sir Graham?

FORBES: (*Emphatically*) No, thank you, Temple!

TEMPLE: Just a spot.

FORBES: No, no, really, I … Er …

TEMPLE is pouring the brandy.

FORBES: Whoa! Steady, Temple!

STEVE: Paul, I think we need another log on the fire.

TEMPLE: Yes, all right, dear.

TEMPLE puts a log on the fire.

STEVE: You know, Sir Graham, there are still one or two things I don't understand about this business.

TEMPLE: (*Laughing*) By Timothy, here we go! I warned you, Sir Graham!

FORBES: Steve, you said if I came to dinner you wouldn't even mention the Lawrence affair!

STEVE: Well, we've finished dinner and there's lots of things I want to know!

TEMPLE: There's lots of things I want to know! What happened to that five pounds I lent you for …

STEVE: Keep to the point, darling!

FORBES: (*Laughing*) Go ahead, Steve! Fire away!

STEVE: Well, what about Salty West?

TEMPLE: What about him?

STEVE: Was he really a member of the ring?

TEMPLE: Of course he was. Townley realised that he couldn't form the ring without the help of some local people. So, after making discreet inquiries, he enlisted the help of the Gardners, Salty West, and young Andy Cross. Cross, poor devil, became conscience-stricken, and finished up by committing suicide.

FORBES: Incidentally, Temple, Miss Chepstow's gone back to Downburgh. Ivor took her back this morning.

TEMPLE: Oh, good. However, to return to Salty West. Salty didn't become conscience-stricken. On the contrary, he became rather full of himself. He

246

refused to take orders, refused to do any work, and simply pursued a gentle form of blackmail.

FORBES: (*Amused*) Townley couldn't do anything with him; he tried bullying him, cajoling him, and finally he dressed him up and sent him up to London to see Dexter. It's obvious he told Dexter to get rid of him. Dexter, however, realised that Salty didn't like Townley and that if, at a later date, he – Dexter – superseded Townley, Salty might prove a valuable ally. So, instead of doing what Townley wanted he made excuses and sent Salty back to Downburgh.

STEVE: But what was Salty doing in the car at Maidenhead?

TEMPLE: Barker, who was a member of the ring, took him out there to meet Dexter. If we'd turned up ten minutes earlier we should probably have seen the three of them together.

STEVE: You say Barker was a member of the ring?

TEMPLE: Yes.

STEVE: Did de Silva know that?

FORBES: He suspected it; but in actual fact it was Mrs de Silva who was in league with Townley. De Silva, poor devil, was under her thumb.

STEVE: Were she and Dexter - ?

FORBES: Yes, I'm afraid so; although he was also carrying on with Sylvia Ross. It was Dexter, of course, that hid Sylvia. I'm afraid Sir Carlton's got quite a problem with that girl, Temple – she really was infatuated with Dexter.

STEVE: But who murdered Barker?

TEMPLE: Dexter did; he thought that by doing that immediately after my visit to Harley Street it would throw suspicion on to de Silva; he

	continued to throw suspicion on to de Silva when he disposed of Townley.
STEVE:	I see.
FORBES:	Barker, of course, was responsible for the dummy handbag. That's why he had the photographs. They were purely a means of identification.
STEVE:	But tell me: did Salty West lie about Bob Gardner? He said he was with him when the accident happened.
FORBES:	It wasn't an accident. Townley murdered Gardner, although Salty was there when it happened. I think Townley was under the impression that Gardner had been passing information to your husband. Don't forget he saw the three of you together that afternoon out in the bay. It was Townley, in fact, who fired the shots.
STEVE:	And what about Freeman, Paul – how does he fit into all this?
FORBES:	Freeman was the fence, the go-between, but oddly enough it was Freeman who first spotted you, Steve, and drew Townley's attention to the fact that you were both staying in Downburgh.
TEMPLE:	Have you got Freeman?
FORBES:	Yes; Vosper picked him up this morning at Dover.
TEMPLE:	You seem to have quite a bag, Sir Graham.
FORBES:	Quite a bag.
STEVE:	But, Paul, Burford told us that when he went to see Freeman …
TEMPLE:	Freeman already knew that I had been in touch with Burford. He contacted Dexter and was told to put on a little show purely for my benefit.

STEVE: You mean all that business about Lawrence and the Isle of Skye?

TEMPLE: Exactly. Freeman knew that Burford would report straight back to me.

FORBES: Don't you see, Dexter was still trying to confuse the issue, trying to make us concentrate on the mysterious Mr Lawrence and the disappearance of Sylvia Ross.

STEVE: Then the telegram we found …

TEMPLE: Was carefully planted. But fortunately I didn't fall for it. I went to Downburgh, not to the Isle of Skye.

FORBES: (*Amused*) No, it was poor old Vosper who went to the Isle of Skye.

STEVE: You know, I think Dexter must have been one of the most callous individuals I've ever met!

TEMPLE: Dexter was quite a boy! And incidentally, quite a swimmer! I checked on that, Steve. Reg Hailey, who was at Eton with him, said he swam "like a fish".

FORBES: Well, there you are, Steve. That's the end of the Lawrence affair.

STEVE: Yes, but if you ask me it should have been called the Downburgh Case.

FORBES: I'm inclined to agree, Steve.

TEMPLE: I'll get your coat, Sir Graham.

FORBES: What are you going to do now, Temple – write another novel?

STEVE: No, we're going away for a few weeks, Sir Graham.

TEMPLE: (*Surprised*) Really, Steve? This is news to me.

STEVE: You need a holiday, Paul, after all this. We both do.

FORBES: (*Smiling*) Where are you going – Downburgh?

249

STEVE: Not Pygmalion likely!

TEMPLE: Well – where are we going?

STEVE: I'm going to pick a nice little place, somewhere in the country, miles from anywhere. We're not going to tell anyone where we're going, we're not going to leave a forwarding address, and we're going to call ourselves Mr and Mrs Smith.

TEMPLE: You wouldn't like me to wear a large black moustache?

STEVE: That's quite an idea!

FORBES: (*Apparently serious, but pulling STEVE's leg*) You'd better let me have your address, Steve, just in case I want to get in touch with …

STEVE: (*Horrified*) What! You're the last person, Sir Graham!

They all laugh.

FORBES: Well, I must be off! I've got a busy time ahead of me! Good night, Steve! Take care of yourself.

STEVE: Goodnight, Sir Graham!

FADE IN incidental music.

Slow FADE DOWN of music.

FADE IN background noises of a quiet country scene: birds whistling, etc.

A pause.

FADE the music completely.

STEVE: (*A deep breath; contented*) Isn't this heavenly?

TEMPLE: (*Bored*) Heavenly.

STEVE: Oh, Paul, it's so peaceful!

TEMPLE: Yes.

STEVE: (*Contented*) I'll bet those birds whistle all night.

TEMPLE: I'll bet they do!

STEVE: Aren't you glad we came here, darling?

TEMPLE: Steve, who recommended this place – the Curator at the British Museum?

STEVE: (*Innocently*) No, I was terribly lucky. I just picked it out of a book.

TEMPLE: Old Moore's Almanac?

STEVE: (*Laughing*) This used to be a very famous Spa.

TEMPLE: I can well imagine it.

STEVE: Even today people come just to take the water.

TEMPLE: I'll take a dry Martini.

STEVE: (*Taking TEMPLE's arm*) Well – what would you like to do now, darling? Shall we go back to the hotel?

TEMPLE: Yes, I think so. Steve, er – how long are we staying down here?

STEVE: I booked for three weeks.

TEMPLE: Three – weeks?

STEVE: Yes, but I dare say we can stay longer if we want to.

TEMPLE: I think three weeks should be quite long enough!

STEVE: Come on. I'll race you back to the hotel!

TEMPLE: What! And whip up an appetite? Don't be silly, dear!

STEVE laughs.

FADE UP of the birds whistling.

FADE SCENE.

FADE IN a background of noisy conversation.

The main hall of the hotel is thronged with male visitors.

STEVE: (*Amazed*) What's happened? Where have all these men come from?

TEMPLE: By Timothy, what's hit this place!?

STEVE: (*Alarmed*) Paul, look!

TEMPLE: It's Sir Graham!

FORBES: (*Very surprised; quite genuine*) Why, hello! What on earth are you two doing here?

STEVE: (*Weakly*) What's more to the point – what are you doing here?

FORBES: We're staying here! It's the International Police Convention.

STEVE: What!!!!

FORBES: Yes – we're here for three weeks.

TEMPLE: (*Much brighter*) Really, Sir Graham? How <u>very</u> interesting.

FORBES: (*Quite enthralled*) Yes. Meetings, conferences, lectures; practically the whole of Scotland Yard should be down here by tomorrow morning.

WAITER: (*Arriving; very bright*) Can I get you anything, sir?

FORBES: Yes, rather. Temple?

TEMPLE: (*Very pleased with life*) I'll have a dry Martini.

FORBES: A dry Martini and a Scotch and soda. Oh, I beg your pardon, Steve!

TEMPLE: What would you like, darling?

STEVE: (*Weakly; yet with almost a touch of hysteria*) Brandy … Brandy … Brandy …!!!!

TEMPLE and FORBES start to laugh.

FADE IN closing music.

THE END

Press Pack

... press cuttings about Paul Temple and the Lawrence Affair

Paul Temple Comes Back With A New Adventure
by **June Birson**

As each episode of Francis Durbridge's current television serial thriller *My Friend Charles* gets more and more mysterious, his latest Paul Temple serial starts on radio.

Paul Temple and the Lawrence Affair begins in the Light Programme next Wednesday, with the first of eight weekly episodes.

Since the first Paul Temple serial was broadcast in 1938, the suave detective has remained one of radio's most popular characters and has appeared in countless books, films, magazine stories and strip cartoons.

Peter Coke again plays the detective and Marjorie Westbury his wife, Steve. The producer is Martyn C. Webster, who first encouraged Francis Durbridge to become a radio writer during his undergraduate days.

Newcastle-upon-Tyne Evening Chronicle

Cloaks of Mystery and Smoke by **J.W.B.** (contains spoilers)
The new Paul Temple series is off to a good start. Eight episodes are promised, and Wednesday by Wednesday that takes us up to May 30, so obviously the start had to hit out at once challenging attention for something to last through evenings of spring.

Francis Durbridge shows no slackening of invention. His pleasant voiced and now almost legendary detective, played by Peter Coke, with Marjorie Westbury as his alert and perceptive wife, faced a positive bombardment of possible clues to the new mystery.

First we have an unknown man betraying interest in the Temples' movements during an off-season seaside holiday.

Then mysterious shots from a cliff top while they are out in a motor boat. Then the sudden death of their friend the boat owner, falling from that same cliff. Next, after a move to London, comes news of the sudden disappearance of a girl whose father (would you believe it!) happens to be the head of M.I.5.

Also thrown in: a rather shifty story from a man who spent the evening with the girl, a questionable contribution from a sneering band leader with a different version to the band leader's wife.

Yorkshire Evening Post

Sound Spot by **R.E.H.**
The first episode of Paul Temple's return to the air after an eight months absence shows that Francis Durbridge has no peer in the realm of crime thrillers.

Within half an hour he plunged us into the thick of a new mystery complete with a missing girl, flying bullets and what suspiciously looks like a case of murder.

What if the mixture is the same? Mr Durbridge keeps us on chairs-edge and leaves us waiting impatiently for the next instalment – and that is the real test.

Peter Coke and Marjorie Westbury, back again in their old parts of Mr and Mrs Temple, helped to provide a sense of cosy familiarity.

The Star

Radio Review by **Joan Newton**

I should think that Paul Temple and his wife, Steve, by now would be quite blasé about such little matters as being machine-gunned while out in a simple fishing boat.

This new serial promises to be as exciting as all the earlier ones. I must say, however, that we are always amused by the enormous amount of drink every one manages to tuck away.

Catholic Herald

www.ingramcontent.com/pod-product-compliance
Lightning Source LLC
Chambersburg PA
CBHW030751260626
47169CB00016B/758